primal
picnics

with Recipes

WRITERS
INVENT CREATION
MYTHS FOR THEIR
FAVORITE FOODS

Edited by Jennifer Heath

WHOLE WORLD PRESS

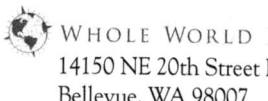
WHOLE WORLD PRESS
14150 NE 20th Street F1, #305
Bellevue, WA 98007
www.wholeworldpress.com

Special discounts for bulk purchases are available. Please contact Whole
World Press at bulksales@wholeworldpress.com for more information.

Graphic Design by Barbara Hodge

Primal Picnics: Writers Invent Creation Myths for their Favorite Foods
(With Recipes) / edited by Jennifer Heath
ISBN: 978-0-9845128-2-9
Library of Congress Control Number: 2010927351

Additional Note:
Whole World Press does not have any control over and does not assume any
responsibility for author or third-party Web sites or their content.

CONTENTS

INTRODUCTION

Jennifer Heath

"The universe is a series of stories."
—Thomas Berry

Once upon a time, humans were awed by the miracle of food and all that surrounds it. We treasured seeds and soil, celebrated harvests and hunts, ceremonially ate the first ripe fruits, or bread from the last sheaf of wheat, and gratitude was part of the ritual. Each morsel was a gift from the gods, infused, safeguarded, made sacred by their presence. In nearly every culture worldwide, food sources—individual plants and animals or the victuals and beverages concocted with them—were attached to myths that confirmed their divinity.

Thus, even the most basic modern American breakfast of Wheaties, milk and honey might tell the tale of the Greek Goddess of Grain, Demeter, with whom bees and the comforting colostrum of motherhood were also associated. Add a glass of pomegranate juice (all the rage these days as the latest, greatest antioxidant) and your meal now involves the goddess's beloved daughter Persephone, kidnapped to the underworld, torn between dark and light, summer and winter, life and death.[1] You have done more than merely shoved something (with added nutrients) into your mouth to fill your belly; you have consumed a tale that describes the birth of seasonal cycles, renewal and a vital mother-daughter archetype. All this before noon.

The gods were not only alive in our food sources, they hovered around the stove. I'm told that no self-respecting Chinese home would be without an image of Zao Jun, the Kitchen God, perhaps the most important of Chinese domestic deities. And everywhere, cooking was a sacred act and artform frequently involving community, veneration and storytelling. For many peoples—from Aztecs to Christians—certain foods especially embodied the gods. To consume them was to partake of divinity itself, a process called transubstantiation.[2]

(In the event hackles are raised by all this talk of the divine, please note that I am not advocating religion, but respect. In our era, we have manufactured a competition between science and spirituality, but none of that happens in this volume.)

Foods have functions far beyond satisfying hunger. Everyone knows, for instance, that apples are aphrodisiacs (as are mandrakes, mangoes, oranges, oysters, walnuts, etc.); ginseng and manna supply immortality; radishes, rice, cranberries, coconuts, lotus and lettuce are sources of fertility; amaranth, garlic and bear meat are among the comestibles craved by the dead; basil, cherries, lamb and salt are purificants, powerful as offerings to the gods; beer, wine, whiskey and a host of other intoxicants, along with hallucinogens, like morning glories, peyote and marijuana, can deify the one who ingests them, and bestow visions, as well as the ability to communicate with spirits and visit Otherworlds. And the list of medicinals is endless.[3] Nor should we forget the long, assorted inventory of foods that are taboo or fruits that are forbidden yet found in mythical gardens everywhere.[4]

Our ancestors' reverence for nourishment, which illustrated the connectedness of all life, is lost in today's so-called "developed" world[5] (is overeating at Thanksgiving, with a ballgame blaring on TV, actually sacred ritual? Maybe so…) and disappearing fast across the globe, sometimes by force, sometimes out of a misguided yearning for the comforts of consumerism. How can the gods hope to get a foothold through a hermetically sealed package of pork chops?[6] How can the muses manifest from a plastic box of attractively displayed herbs in a sterilized grocery store? With the decimation of small farms for housing developments and agri-biz in the United States since the end of World War II, and now with the "Monsanto-ization" of agriculture all over the world, our connection to the places and beings that furnish our provisions grows weaker and weaker.

Indian scientist / environmentalist / social activist Vandana Shiva was one of the first to raise the alarm: "Globalization has robbed people of their resources," she says. "Land has been enclosed, land has been taken over ....Today's industry is biotechnology; it's controlling all life on Earth...."[7]

Globalization also robs us of what's left of our relationship to Nature and ourselves as Nature, a process of disassociation that started even before the Industrial Revolution. To paraphrase Thomas Berry, we have moved from an ever-renewing agricultural economy to an extractive industrial economy, from understanding Earth as "a communion of subjects" to exploiting it as "a collection of objects."[8]

The seed for this book was planted years ago, when it was becoming evident that we are experiencing an inevitable food crisis. How could the center expect to hold? Thanks to unregulated capitalism, the rush to bio-fuels (our cars will run, but will we be able to drive them with empty stomachs?), environmental degradation, the destruction of wild lands for grazing (sometimes called "Burger Kinging"), the takeover by factory farms, corporate patents on plant and animal DNA (biotechnology), the privatization of water, food aid that has deprived communities of their autonomy (exchanging it for tyranny, dependency, war and famine) and on and on.

Anyone who does not yet know this drill isn't learning the hard way like the rest of us and/or lives in a cave in another universe. Deregulation, globalization (to the complete detriment of the local) and overpopulation[9] have led to deep imbalance, caused by greed, that all-too-human characteristic all too unrestrained (ref: the story of insatiable King Midas, who could turn everything he touched into gold and accidentally gilded his own darling child, a lesson learned too late).

Mulling this over as my grocery bill mounted, as we were bombarded by headline after horrifying headline about skyrocketing poverty and starvation, anger growing, heart bleeding, I had a whimsical-slash-activist notion to assemble an encyclopedia of food myths to remind myself (and perhaps others) of the sanctity of food and to reclaim the right of everyone on the planet, human and non-, to be fed. But there are numerous, magnificent dictionaries and encyclopedias of plant- and animal lore, mythographies, and a goodly number of histories, too, most notably Reay Tanahill's classic Food in History.[10] I reconsidered. Back to the cutting board.

Finally, it occurred to me that instead of regurgitating the work of others, it would be a clever bit of cookery to invite contemporary writers to invent origin myths for their favorite foods: to create foodlore. I was not asking for new "myths for the millennium"—too hubristic. And no chicken soup for [fill in the blank]. I asked them merely to choose a food, any food, so long as another contributor hadn't snagged it first, then describe how it might have become. There were no overlaps, except for two very different kinds of puddings set far from one another in time and geography. Anyway, let's face it, you can't have enough pudding.

Needless to say, since these are creative writers—some emerging, some renowned and all notably talented—they took the assignment where they wanted to go. They ventured into various realms in various styles. Our menu ranges broadly in tastes and traditions, with something for everyone.

These "just-ate stories" (as contributor Andrew Wille calls them) are charming, indeed, some are literally charms. They are at times wacky, always surprising, occasionally disturbing, lyrical, spicy, saucy, sweet, salty, peppery, fishy, fleshy, pungent, lip-smacking, gut-clutching…. Some writers chose to explore the fodder of our times: Twinkies, Steak-Umms, Oreos, peanut butter. Some wrote modern fairy tales and some wrote parodies. Some used memoir as their jumping off points and, for some, transubstantiation is the driving force. Tuck in and enjoy.

Most of the stories are followed by recipes, some more digestible than others. Most have been tested and are delicious, but here is a caveat: this is *not* a cookbook; do not, as my mother used to say, try these recipes out on the guests.

Food and Culture Encyclopedia lists a certain Grimod de la Rayonier (1758-1837), who enjoyed stuffing one bird into another like Russian nesting dolls—warbler into ortolan bunting into lark into thrush…until at last a duck was crammed into the cavity of a turkey and finally the turkey was shoved into a bustard.[11] Not that de la Rayonier was unique in this indulgence. Robber barons and royalty across time and space have enjoyed such culinary displays of power. We could top off earlier sagas of gluttony with the notorious excess of members of the G-8, the international forum for industrial nations, who, at the opening meeting of their 2008 summit in Japan, indulged in an eighteen-course banquet during one of the worst periods of hunger ever to take place worldwide. Let 'em eat cake.

In many places, people consume the hearts of lions, wolves or bears to become endowed with the animal's courage. It seems likely therefore that the G-8 banquet featured shark. The magnificent 19th-century actress, Sarah Bernhardt, loved to eat larks, maybe in order to ingest their free spirits, their dramatic and lilting songs. On foodreference.com, we discover Bernhardt's own recipe:

Pound in a mortar the flesh of two larks; add some butter, some chopped samphire, some breadcrumbs soaked in milk, some Malaga raisins, and some crushed juniper berries. Stuff a third lark with the mixture and roast it on a spit covered with samphire leaves and a strip of fat bacon. Serve on a crouton soaked in gin, then toasted and buttered.[12]

The gin would certainly help wash away any guilt. Happily, slaughtering larks is now illegal in France.

I tender my profoundest gratitude to the wonderful writers who gave of their ripe imaginations to make this book, for their enthusiasm, patience and talent, and for being such good sports. Thanks to Andrew Wille for his usual kind and brilliant editorial guidance; to Jack Collom, as always, for his dear, unflagging support (and for being such a tolerant eater!); to Marda Kirn and Nan de Grove for long friendship; to Rickie Solinger for inspiration; and to Jane Saltzman for her generosity. Thanks to Jack Zipes for early encouragement and to Laurieann Aladin. Thanks to Jill Foulston and others for passing the word and thus helping to bring on board fresh voices, writers I did not know but whose work I have come to love. And there are many more to whom I owe a grande bouffe of thanks. I hope one day we all can break bread together. Potluck, of course.

This book is dedicated to Sierra Collom.

NOTES

1. In Greek mythology, Demeter, Goddess of Grain (Barley), seeks high and low for her beloved daughter, Persephone, who has been abducted by Hades, God of the Underworld. After much journeying and many negotiations, Persephone is returned to her mother, but warned to eat nothing or she will be forced to stay with Hades. Nevertheless, the maiden swallows three seeds of a pomegranate and is thus shackled forever to the Underworld. (Some interpret this as a deliberate act of rebellion, the desire to separate from a strong mother, etc.) But Demeter strikes a bargain with Hades that Persephone will be permitted to return to the land of the living for part of each year. Like a seed, Persephone is temporarily entrusted to the dark of the Earth. With her arrival aboveground comes spring and the emergence of new sprouts. The ancient Greeks celebrated this annual event with the Eleusinian Mysteries.

    The dying and rising god, Osiris, plays the same mythic role in ancient Egyptian cosmology: he is murdered, dismembered and his body scattered like seeds by his brother Seth. But his wife and sister, Isis, finds his most essential part, which she causes to rise, as the Nile rises, and life returns. Worshippers in the cult of Osiris planted wooden funerary beds with sprouted barley to symbolize the resurrection and rebirth. There is a gorgeous example of such a bed at the Cairo Museum of Antiquities in Egypt.

Today in Afghanistan, a festival called Nazr-e Samanak takes place each year around the spring equinox, when the women of a community ceremonially sprout wheatgrass, mold it into a kind of bread (samanak) and eat it in celebration of the new year, called Nawruz. The ritual goes back to ancient Zoroastrian times.

2. For special occasions, some peoples, among them the ancient Celts, shape loaves of bread into human form before consuming them. The ancient Slavs apparently performed a healing ritual called "baking the child," putting the child into a warm bread oven so that she would be transformed by metaphorically returning to the mother's womb to be born again healthy. The child, like wet bread dough, goes from raw to cooked. The Slavic Baba-Yaga tales and the German folk tale, "Hansel and Gretel," are reflections of this ritual.

3. The healing properties of many foods have been extracted by pharmaceutical companies for use in allopathic medicine. Wild yam, native to North America, Mexico and Asia, is one of many examples. Traditionally, Native Americans used wild yam to relieve labor pains, morning sickness, colic, asthma, rheumatism, joint pain and gastritis. The Chinese used it to help the liver, aid digestion and relax the muscles. In India, Ayurvedic practitioners used yam against impotence and infertility. Today, the wild yam is employed as a source of progesterone.

4. See also: Tamara Andrews, *Nectar and Ambrosia: An Encyclopedia of Food in World Mythology*, Santa Barbara, CA.: ABC-CLIO, 2000, Appendix II, 259-264.

5. I quibble with the terms "developed" and "developing" world(s). Despite its technological advances, the "developed" world is frequently ignorant, retrograde and dangerous, whereas

countries referred to as "developing," are often rich, ancient civilizations, cultures that have been ground down or are on the brink of destruction thanks to "progress," introduced by those who consider themselves developed.

6. Pig flesh is widely despised and pigs are seen as unclean, particularly in Judaism and Islam. But in some societies, though it may have occasionally been associated with evil (as in ancient Egypt), the pig was nevertheless a sacred animal. In ancient Greece, the pig embodied vegetation gods—Adonis, Attis or Demeter—and could therefore not be eaten. In China and Oceania, the pig represents prosperity and abundance and is devoured with gusto.

7. Vandana Shiva is the author of many books, including *Earth Democracy: Justice, Sustainability and Peace* (South End Press, 2005), *Water Wars: Privatization, Pollution and Profit* (South End Press, 2002) and *Biopiracy: The Plunder of Nature and Knowledge* (South End Press, 1996). This quote was taken from "Vandana Shiva: On Gandhi," an interview with David Barsamian for Alternative Radio in New Delhi, India, on 31 December 2008, www.alternativeradio.org. The interview was excerpted in the Summer 2009 edition of *YES!* magazine.

8. Thomas Berry, who died on 01 June 2009, was a Roman Catholic priest of the Passionist order, a cultural historian and self-described ecotheologian, an advocate of deep ecology and ecospirituality. Among his many books is *The Great Work: Our Way into the Future* (Bell Tower/Random House, New York, 1999). I recorded his words from a documentary, *Thomas Berry: The Great Story*, directed and produced by Nancy Stetson and Penny Morell (Bullfrog Films, Boulder, CO., 2002).

9. According to Tony Pereira, in his paper, "Sustainability: An integral engineering design approach," just five percent of the world's population consumes twenty-three percent of its energy. With less than five percent of the world's population, the United States alone consumes about one-third of the world's resources (*Renewable and Sustainable Energy Reviews*, Volume 13, Issue 5, June 2009).

10. Our dog-eared family copy of Reay Tanahill's *Food in History* was published by Stein and Day (New York), in 1973.

11. I have lost my exact source, although I'm sure I got it online. Readers can look it up themselves. This is why the goddess invented Google.

12. Sarah Bernhardt's recipe for lark can be found on http://www.foodreference.com/html/larkssarahb2.html.

I

$\mathcal{B}$ *In the* EGINNING

"Eve and the Serpent," Biblia Pauperum, 1440

THE SOUP COURSE
Jane Wodening

he Grandfather Stone People were born out of Grandmother Earth and the first thing they did was to fly up very nearly to the heavens and it wasn't until after they came down again to the surface of Grandmother Earth that they solidified into stone. And for a long time the Grandfather Stone People waited until Grandmother Earth calmed down enough so that life could begin.

Soup goes way back. To truly understand soup, we must go in our minds to the beginning of life on earth and that life was called The Primordial Soup.

Before The Primordial Soup, the earth was an inhospitable place with thunder and lightning and volcanoes and rocks with no lichens on them. And no dirt, no dirt at all. But among all those harsh things was water. Water came very early on. To Grandmother Earth, water can be soothing. It was in quiet watery places that The Grandfather Stone People could feed the vibrant pulse of the earth's electric and volcanic dynamism quietly into making life out of organic compounds and unconnected proteins in those watery places on the surface of the earth. There are many other spirits working in the world, doing other things, but The Grandfather Stone People can bring all the Relatives, the things with spirits and living things, together into one place; The Grandfather Stone People work, among other things, with The Soup.

Life didn't begin like a light bulb turning on; it began as a sort of quivering glimmer in grottos and under glacier ice and alongside some of the lesser and more stable volcanic vents where the warmth comes gently out from Grandmother Earth into quiet waters. And this continues to happen even now.

And for millennia after millennia, The Primordial Soup simmered in these secret places like a broth or like vichyssoise or a smooth borscht or any soup that has been blended to the smoothest and finest texture. One day inexplicably it seemed only right for life to form itself into cells because then there would be individuality and with individuality would come diversification and variety. And these cells developed ways of changing where they were in the water, which is to say that they learned to swim.

Eventually these one-celled lives distinguished themselves as either plants or animals and then a recognition of unity and relatedness swathed every living thing into a recognition of The Symbiosis of all the varieties of life on Earth. The Symbiosis was the first dance; it is a dance in which every member is different from every other and as they move together, each moving differently from every other, they find that they help each other by their very differences. After the discovery of The Symbiosis, another great leap of the forms of life happened and the cells joined together in an amazing harmony with such teamwork that thousands and then millions of cells would make up one individual living thing and then some of these great composite lives crawled or splashed out of the water and commenced living on the ground. And at the time, this seemed like a minor occasion but later on, it became a very important step in the history of Grandmother Earth.

It wasn't then that the first dirt was formed. It had been forming in the waters as life would excrete or die and that compost and dead matter in fact stirred around in the waters and fed the living, and that was a cycle of life.

But when some living things crawled or splashed up out of the water, out of The Primordial Soup onto the land, and it was the lichens still beloved by caribou (and I believe there is a Finnish lichen soup but I can't imagine the recipe) that splashed up first and others followed to eat the lichens, then it took many millennia to create enough good loam dirt to make an ecology of luxurious life. As life grew sumptuous on the land, dotted all over the world were swamps that enlarged upon the image of soup, thick with life, steaming with will-o-the-wisps and often through the ages feasted upon with gusto by Diplodocus, Hippopotamus, Moose, Muskrat and many others.

There was much food for myth and wondrous tales in the Paleozoic, Triassic, Jurassic, Cretaceous and Cenozoic Periods or Eras but very few of them deal with soup until the Holocene Epoch, which is The Now. And so, clinging to the essential thread of dirt, we may walk wistfully past those wondrous and very probably delicious ecologies, past even the emergence of humanity and its several mysterious false starts, past the great days of Cave Art followed closely by the beginning of agriculture very like Rembrandt was followed closely in the history of Holland by the tulip industry, and here in the beginning of agriculture we find some reference to soup.

I have faith that there was soup much earlier in the history of humanity but sadly even in the most carefully preserved cave art or in the wonderful petroglyphs that can be found all 'round the globe, I have found no reference to soup, no image that could be taken to be a soup kettle, and the problem may have been just that, the difficulty of the kettle really needing to be made of metal.

A case could be made that the invention of the kettle was a tremendously important step in the development and certainly the population growth of humanity, since it made possible the consumption of foods that were otherwise much harder to consume or assimilate and thus the soup kettle could feed more people with less food, also making some otherwise unassimilable leaves and roots and bone marrow more available and palatable.

There would have been containers like large gourds in which with the help of hot rocks, some soup could be made. Pottery must have made all possible, and even before pottery, it might have been that a concave rock could have been used, a fire built in the concavity until the rock was very hot, then the fire removed and replaced with water and whatever foods needed to be boiled. A rock can hold a lot of heat for a long time. This technique is used by some Native Americans for baking bread, although now they make the ovens of adobe but the principle is the same.

The Native Americans of the Sioux tribes have an old tradition of making soup in the stomach of a recently killed buffalo cleaned and stretched; the thick upper muscle made a working kettle lip. Stones were put in and water and on top of those stones were placed The Grandfather Stone People, stones that had been heated to red-hot in a fire that made the water boil, then the buffalo meat and bones and whatever vegetables and herbs might be available. And when they'd eaten the soup, they'd eat the kettle, too.

Hot rocks go way back in some Native American traditions–The Grandfather Stone People are much loved by the Native American peoples and are known by them to have helped them since the beginning, not only to cook their food but also to help them to get in touch with the Spirits.

In Ecuador even now, the main dish is usually soup.

As soon as the use of metal was well-established, the Cauldron was born, and into that Cauldron went toads and snails and slimy things out of the swamp, puppy-dog tails, witches' brews, unwary explorers, dead soldiers and magical mixtures that could achieve impossible things and did so often in lore and in nightmare across centuries, usually to the accompaniment of thunder and lightning and sometimes also in the presence of the possibility of volcanoes. Leprechauns are known to bury their treasure always in cauldrons under trees.

As to the dead soldiers, the *Mabinogion* tells that there was a very magical cauldron that brought soldiers back to life and it was given to Bendigeid Vran by a very tall yellow-haired man and a woman and he passed it on to Matholwch, King of Ireland, as part of the dowry of Bendigeid Vran's sister Branwen. These were two of the children of King Lear whom William Shakespeare later put into a play but he left out the part about the cauldron. Matholwch took the cauldron home to Ireland with Branwen and when Bendigeid Vran invaded Ireland to rescue his sister from her husband, Matholwch used the cauldron on that occasion. All the Irish soldiers that died in a day's battle were put into the cauldron overnight and in the morning they were well and able to fight except that they had lost the ability to speak. And thus Bendigeid Vran was vanquished by his brother-in-law and by his own gift of the cauldron.

Another cauldron mentioned by the *Mabinogion* is the cauldron of Tyrnog; if meat were put in it to boil for a coward it would never be boiled, but if meat were put in it for a brave man, it would be boiled forthwith.

There was found in a peat bog in Denmark a great and beautiful Silver Cauldron that is now named Gundestrup. It resides now in a museum but nothing is known of what it could do. Some archeologists think it might have been used to catch heads in human sacrifice.

Usually, given encouragement, a good thing will get its day, and soup got staunch encouragement across all the ages.

Li Po dreamed of soup:

When I was very small
Sometimes I used to call
The moon in heaven a jade-white
Soup tureen;
Sometimes I thought it was
A sort of magic glass,
Flying across cloudbanks of pale
Blue-green.

Twice, Basho put cherry blossoms into soup:

From all these trees
Into salads, soups, everywhere,
Cherry blossoms fall.
Under the Cherry Tree
Blossom Soup,
Blossom Salad.

Early next spring I must try cherry blossoms in soup—perhaps a light miso, a few fine shavings of last year's leeks and carrots just pulled out of the ground, some dandelion, rosemary and mint and at least three cherry blossom petals in every spoonful, floating on top.

It was The Grandfather Stone People who originated the story of Stone Soup. It happened in Europe where The Grandfather Stone People are all but forgotten. This is the tale in which two travelers wander through the later years of The Dark Ages from one grim stark and starving village to another and they carry with them a magical stone that makes a very good soup and wherever they go, they make this soup, saying to the villagers, well, it would be better yet with a handful of barley and a bone, some vegetables, perhaps a dab of butter, herbs, salt and pepper, whatever they can glean from the various people of the village where they stop—and truly, the great thing about soup is that it doesn't take much of anything to make it. The Nail Broth story from Sweden is much the same, although the story is of one tramp who carries a nail and one reluctant woman and the story seems to have the possibility of a sexual connotation. But in the end in both cases, with the stone and with the nail, the people are filled with joy to know how to make such good soup with a stone or a nail.

It is said and it makes a lot of sense that the Great Depression brought people together making soup time and again. Someone would have an onion and someone else a ham hock and if they'd see someone with a potato, a parsnip, a handful of peas, they'd get them involved. Soup is definitely a case of the whole being far greater than the sum of its parts.

And so the amazing magic of soup bubbles on through the ages and is still going strong even now. Here with many vegetables in my backyard garden I strive to make many different soups out of the garden often.

During January, February and March I have used potatoes, carrots and onions for a good potato soup in a chicken-flavored broth or a simple borscht with beets replacing the potatoes and caraway replacing the chicken flavor. When there's still some winter squash left in the root cellar, wonderful soups or stews can be made with it. And fish soup can be most exquisite, so also can carrot soup.

In April this past year after two or three months of hard frost that kept me from digging up anything at all, the beginning of the Spring Thaw let last year's leeks leap up and present themselves just as I in haste hacked and bashed the Jerusalem artichokes up out of the icy ground, before they commenced sprouting, for an amazing springtime jet start of a soup made of the two of them with some creamed portobello behind it.

The asparagus soup didn't happen this year; I think the asparagus plants needed more water deep down at their roots but last year's was still a fond memory.

On through the year—spinach soup with scallions, gazpacho, tomato soup, cauliflower soup, a soup of green weedy things—purslane and rat-tailed radishes, beet greens, borage, nasturtiums, nutritious burdock, a grating of horseradish root. Then into autumn with broccoli and new carrots, cabbage stew and enter the winter with sweet potato soup or dhal.

I don't mention meat in any of these (except for the chicken flavor in the potato soup which in my case is a vegetarian fake), not being much of a fan of meat. But great honor must be given to grand soups like mulligatawny and clam chowder, chile con carne, duck soup, gumbo. Then there's matzo-ball, cornish game hen or chicken soup, three of the great healers. There's oyster soup, split pea with ham, won ton, bouillabaisse—all 'round the globe, great soups—and each very different from all the others. Each, in its way, a healer, for they all go back to times when the scant foods that were available were brought together and, by feeding and delighting the people, made everything better and made history.

Soup has a way to mysteriously fill and nourish, clarify and bring comfort. Perhaps this is because a good soup connects us again to The Symbiosis, the old but still-remembered dance from which we have never really escaped nor cared to escape, the basic mix of life, The Primordial Soup.

Jane's Potato Soup

About 5 medium red potatoes
About 3 pints stock

Cut the potatoes and boil in the stock.

3 or 4 big carrots
2 or 3 medium to smallish onions
2 or 3 Tbsp. diced garlic—to taste
a few Tbsp. olive oil & margarine

Sauté carrots, onions and garlic in oil and margarine rather slowly, stirring occasionally, till soft but not browned—not much, anyway.

When onions and carrots are al dente, combine in the potato pot along with perhaps some—to taste—

pepper
basil
paprika
spike

Blender. Many say to leave some lumps.

Keeps well in the freezer. Very presentable.

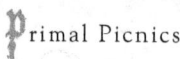

Zucchini Salad for Eight

1 gallon or so zucchini, cut up
1 small white onion, small strips
2 small leeks sliced thin
1 red pepper, sliced thin
20 pimento olives, halved
3 or 4 pickled eggs, cut up
1 pint zucchini relish
2 Tbsp. mayonnaise
3" cube sheep feta, crumbled
2 cups beet greens, sliced thin
1 cup red cabbage, sliced thin
Juice of a lime
Hot sauce like Cholula
1 Tbsp. fresh horseradish, grated
1 Tbsp. fresh ginger, grated
1 carrot, grated
2 or 3 Tbsp. ginger/garlic mix
black pepper
Spike
½ to 1 cup cooked mushrooms

BOULDER VALLEY SURPRISE

John Wright

oil igneous rock for millions of years
　　let stand until cool
　　when inland seas subside
uplift red sandstone, crimp edges
grind soil with glaciers
decorate with trees, evergreen and deciduous
then add large mammals, fish and birds
transfer humans with stone weapons
across the Bering Strait
convert large mammals
to food, clothing and shelter
now add other humans from the east
sprinkle liberally with iron and gunpowder

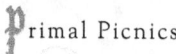

in a large well-wooded valley
sift for gold dust
construct wooden buildings, then add brick
steam railroads, a shot of whiskey
then, with a large spatula
smooth out even layers of concrete
on any possible surface
sauté in carbon monoxide
bake with electromagnetic waves until saturated
in a large sealed container
cook plutonium until doomsday
garnish with shopping malls, tanning salons
takeout chicken, video arcades and massage parlors
set blender on puree
bring to a boil
run from the kitchen

MRS. YAHWEH GIVES LILITH THE RECIPE FOR MANNA

Patricia Alford

Lilith appears at the door and invites herself in for tea. And while it's true Lilith is losing her edge, she hasn't softened to the extent of carrying a cell phone and calling to announce her arrival or to ask if it's convenient. She just shows up. Mrs. Yahweh doesn't mind. Not everything has gone to hell. For here is Lilith, looking more slept-in than demonic, yoo-hooing through the screen door.

"Oh, Lil, come on in, I'll put the kettle on. His Nibs is asleep."

Lilith is glad to hear this. Though they let bygones be bygones millennia ago, Lilith still avoids Him if she can. Lilith was Adam's first wife, but when she complained to

Yahweh about Adam's sexual, um, proclivities, Yahweh barred her from the garden and brought in Eve, who was supposed to be an improvement. Mrs. Yahweh gives Lilith a big warm hug. That's her way. Lilith gives Mrs. Yahweh a peck on the cheek. Mrs. Yahweh bustles around in her apron and feathered mules. She puts the kettle on and rummages in the pantry for a slice of something sweet.

"Sorry, Lil. All I've got's this day-old manna. If I knew you were coming I'd have baked a cake."

"Hired a band?"

"Best in the land."

And together they chime, "How'd ya do How'd ya do How'd ya do." Much of the music on Earth is composed in Heaven, but not this ditty which Lilith and Mrs. Yahweh picked up on an outing to New York in 1949. Lilith and Mrs. Yahweh form a chorus-line, do a few kicks and collapse onto the kitchen chairs laughing and shushing each other. Don't wake Yahweh!

"My stars, Lilith, I miss you when you're gone. Where've you been? Steal any good fat babies lately?"

"No, baby stealing isn't a viable racket any more. Babies are all under surveillance these days. Baby monitor, nanny cam. You can't get them from the hospital because they put this bracelet on them that sets off an alarm if they leave the building unauthorized." Lilith reaches for a slice of manna, spreads it with clotted cream and jam. "Mmmm this is good, Dora, nobody makes manna like you."

"Lil, nobody *but* me makes manna. I hate the sight of it. But Yahweh gets a hankering for his old Vengeful God days. He still likes to make up lists of rules, but he can't get anyone's attention. One day he turned on the burning bush, just to see if it would work. Next thing you know half of California is in flames and folks are blaming the Santa Ana winds. Airplane dumped a load of fire retardant right on him. We had to throw his robe out. You can't get that stuff out. I said, 'You look like Old Harry, all red like that.' But I shouldn't have. Doesn't like to be teased. Gets his dander up. You'd think I'd learn sometime. "

Lilith is on her third slice. She's got crumbs on her lap and a bit of jam on her upper lip which Mrs. Yahweh finds endearing. She imagines leaning over and wiping it gently away with her thumb, but Lilith doesn't like to be touched. There'd be a flap of black wings and she'd be gone. Instead, she hands Lilith a serviette. Lilith is trowelling more butter on a slice of manna and licking her fingers at the same time.

"What do you put in these things, Dora? I could eat these for forty years myself."

"Oh, you know—the usual. Flour, eggs, milk, honeydew."

"You know me. Can't bake to save myself. But you, you must have made a million of these. I don't know how you did it."

"It was the old days. We were all gung-ho. We were eager. But it's not what people think."

"Nothing is."

Mrs. Yahweh shuffles off into the pantry for more manna. She takes another packet out of the freezer to thaw for Yahweh's tea when he wakes up.

"So how'd you do it?" Lilith's mouth is full of her fifth slice, swallowing it whole, choking till her eyes tear up and Mrs. Yahweh has to bang on her back.

"Have some more tea. Manna's dry. We made it every day. It didn't have to keep, so we didn't worry about that. In fact, Yahweh had a thing about that. New manna every day. I mean, he was God, he could have made the desert bloom; there could have been wheat fields and orange groves. Forty years is a long time, crop-wise. But Yahweh wanted the food to not just *be* miraculous but *seem* miraculous. It had to fall from the sky. If it grew from the earth, people would just say it grew there naturally. That really infuriated Yahweh because he claimed that EVERYTHING was a miracle. So Yahweh was reduced to giving people wonders and signs, something they'd never seen before. It was inconvenient, but we just made it up here in Heaven every night and tipped it down on their heads in the morning. One omer per family."

"Riiiigght, what's an omer?" Lilith in her best Bill Cosby imitation.

"A tenth of an ephah."

"More or less than an ice cream pail?"

"Less. About a half. Six manna."

"A half an ice cream pail per family? That's not very much. I've eaten half that much already just now."

Actually, thinks Mrs. Yahweh, you've eaten exactly an omer—but who's counting? "Yahweh didn't want the chosen people too comfortable. So we had to make the manna filling. If I had it do over again, I'd put in more fiber. But we didn't know about fiber then. We were gods, not nutritionists. Yahweh always said the Israelites were a stiff-necked people, but if you ask me it was the opposite end of the digestive system that was stiff."

"No wonder they were so grouchy."

"Exactly. Not that you can blame them. Forty years to make a two-week trip."

"Two weeks for a man on a swift camel."

"Right, and they had women and children, sheep and goats, household slaves. But not as many as people think. The Bible says an army of 600,000. *Plus* family and slaves and animals. Maybe two or three million. 'A mixed multitude went up with them.'"

"That's ridiculous. The Sinai is only two hundred miles wide. Three hundred to Jericho, max."

"But they didn't go direct. They looped around."

"Even so, two million people on the march would make a mighty long line. Like from Egypt to China!"

"'Thousands' is a mistranslation. It means families. Six hundred families. Maybe twenty thousand in all."

"That's more like it. Still that's a lot of manna every day. You must have been busy."

"I was, but I had help, too. I had the whole heavenly host breaking eggs and mixing batter." Mrs. Yahweh chuckles at the memory. She has a mind like an abacus and she remembers exactly. Six manna a day for twenty-two thousand people is 132,000 manna a night. Eleven hundred pounds of flour, 22,000 eggs, 1,375 gallons of milk and 500 gallons of honeydew. Twelve griddles going all night long manned by twelve angels making 144 manna every five minutes.

Lilith snorts, spraying crumbs over the table, remembering the angel who banned her from the garden. "Heavenly host. Don't give me the heavenly host. That lot can't have been much help."

"Well, the flaming swords came in handy keeping the griddles hot. We didn't have gas back then."

"If you don't count Yahweh himself," chortles Lilith. "And the seraphim. I can just see that. Wore calico aprons, did they?"

No, thinks Mrs. Yahweh, snow-white linen, and smart bakers' caps. "Some of them were quite handy with a spatula, I'll have you know."

"And the cherubim. They love to help."

Mrs. God sighs, remembering the cherubim. Standing on stools to reach the counter. Splattering dough everywhere, making a colossal mess and then getting bored and flitting off somewhere to play. "They licked the bowls."

"I'll bet they did. Why they're so friggin' fat."

Lilith can be abrasive. Mrs. Yahweh remembers that now. She's glad to see Lilith come and relieved when she goes. Yahweh has a point about her, no denying it.

"Oh, look at that. Time for Yahweh to have his tea. He gets grumpy if it's late."

Dora watches Lilith gather up her hat and bag and scuttle out the door. "Not going already? Well, come again. Bye-bye," she calls after Lilith's back as the garden gate slams shut behind her. "And, by the way, you've got jam on your face."

Heavenly Jam

Good on day-old manna, as manna kept
overnight tends to be dry.

2 organic oranges
1 organic lemon
6 pears
6 peaches or an equal quantity of apricots. Apricots are tastier.
6 apples (yes, apples! They make the jam thicken.)
sugar

You want to use organic citrus fruit because the peel is
included in the recipe. Grind up the oranges and lemon
and put them in a big pot. Add the baking soda and cook
for 10 minutes. Peel the rest of the fruit and crush or grind
it. Add it to the citrus mixture with an amount of sugar
equal to the total amount of fruit. Boil about half an hour
until thick. Pour into sterile pint jars, leave ½ inch head
space, screw on lids and process 20 minutes in the canner.
Makes about 7 pints.

THE UNEXPECTED MARRIAGE OF VANILLA TO THE STARS

Elisabeth Russell Taylor

lanet Earth was dead. The blistering Sun had all but expired, taking with it the milky Moon. The Stars looked down in despair, for their view had been eclipsed. Falling through the Void, shooting from one to another and sparkling for themselves alone had lost its charm. In lively exchanges, they struggled to remember how long they had hung disconsolate in the great Void of Thead. They beamed in excess of twenty-digit numbers across the electric highways and as each made its calculation and, having agreed on a figure of time just short of infinity, they reckoned it might still just be possible to galvanize Planet Earth into life.

The regeneration of Planet Earth was urgent on two counts: first, the aesthetic—they'd had nothing to view for eons; secondly, the gastronomic—their populations were bored with their diet of thin air. Archaic wisdom had it that, unlike Stardom, Human Beings supported their existence by ingesting material from beneath their feet, from creatures that trod and from slimy, silver softnesses gathered from the oceans. The Great Chunks, star elders who ruled, and the Shards, their minions, had maintained stony acceptance of their lot until recently, when the Shards expressed some dissatisfaction that they had nothing to gaze at, nothing to savor. Jouissance was no longer a factor of their existence. Perhaps there was something to be learned from Planet Earth?

The Sun retained a few tepid embers among its clinkers. The Moon had a flickering memory of its days of contemplation and its nights of teasing itself into segments, lowering and raising the light of the night sky, drawing the tides back and forth. But both Sun and Moon were old and tired. Neither could muster the energy to support the other, but together they indulged in pitying complaint against their erstwhile collaborators, the Cardinal Winds, who had abandoned them.

The Stars harmonized in the Great Void of Thead. The Great Chunks spoke in the name of their population of Shards: regeneration, they said, could not be accomplished alone; the cooperation of the Winds was essential. But this would not be easy to arrange. The Winds had become unruly, with a tendency to continuous dissent. One could no longer appeal to the better nature of the Soft Breeze without the Raging Tempest gathering momentum. One could not, however courteously, demand a little cloud formation with a following shower, but a Hamsin would ensue. The Great Chunks agreed: the Cardinal Winds were vain. Perhaps they might be flattered into consent?

And so it was decided to lure them with the promise of an EVENT in their honor: a one-off light and music extravaganza such as had never before been seen, to which the Winds would be invited to lend their formidable energies. They should get their cast together! Thunderbolts, Tornados, Tsunamis and Typhoons. All would be welcome.

A circle of the Greatest Chunks approached the Cardinal Winds, dozing in the Void of Thead, but the Winds proved impossible to rouse. One or two forced open an eye and appeared to listen; one or two raised themselves on a little pillow of squall and listened, but inattentively. Most slept on, apparently in dream. The Great Chunks were affronted. Their plan, an excellent one, had undeniably failed.

At the time of their omnipotence, the Stars had controlled the Winds. They must do it again. Entreaties fell on deaf ears. Flattery had no force. It was useless to persist in cajoling such fickle, mutable energies. The Winds would have to be overtaken, captured, made prisoner, tied in knots according to the temperament of each, then unleashed as required.

The Great Chunks were the founding rocks, stolid, dense and impermeable. They had existed since the echo of creation and nourished their rock-hard selves on the elements of their conception. The Shards, on the other hand, were in the process of becoming: splinters cast off from the Chunks, their lean, pitted forms depended upon thin air passing through them. They had unfulfilled yearnings for jouissance, which left unmet, might create unrest. It was this that prompted the Great Chunks to suggest a contingent of Shards gather and form in the most efficient configuration for a launch to Planet Earth, there to see for themselves whether the merest, unbreathable ingestible had survived the unawakened death of the host.

The journey was hazardous, the view in eclipse. The Shards clung together in a stream of their own light as they shot through the Void.

The breathing world was dead, the surface of the Planet a dustbowl. No human being, no four-legged creatures, nothing emerging from the debris. Planet Earth, a midden, was shrouded in the dirty brown texture of indifference. The Shards dragged themselves over the unstable surface, the interstices in their tough-cast forms clogged with the fetid air of death and decay. Meanwhile, other Shards accompanied prisoner Winds to the Sun and Moon. One lot unleashed a Hamsin on the Sun and ordered it to work its monstrous bellows furiously to stoke the flickering cinders. The Sun was unresponsive. Another lot accompanied a Great Blizzard and unleashed it on the Moon, but their torrents of hail quickly melted. The Blizzard recoiled. All Shards reporting back to the Great Chunks confirmed that the Sun remained cold and colorless and the Moon tepid and unlit. Heavenly bodies no longer had influence.

A Hurricane unloosed to rage over Planet Earth dispersed the dust and a Thunderstorm's deluge laid the debris. The Shards, optimistic at first, waited expectantly, but all that confronted them was undulating, brown sludge, stretching in sullen uniformity into infinity. Weakened, their mental concentration slipping away, they remembered nostalgically the immaculate, silver domain they had left behind and were tempted to give up, to return to the Stars, but to admit failure was too dire to contemplate. With the terrain cleared, albeit corrugated, it was just possible to drag themselves across the surface of Planet Earth and while so doing to *think*. What, they wondered, lay *beneath* the surface?

They sent back to the Stars for Meteorites, to rip through the crust of Earth and penetrate to its interior. That done, Shards gathered at the rim of the crater and peered into the exposed bowels of Planet Earth.

The landscape was unlike anything they had seen or imagined. They had no names for what confronted them. For a long while they hesitated, frightened to probe the chasm; all they could make out within were hollows, caves and cells. They took measure of what lay ahead against their own size and that of the Great Chunks and found it awe-inspiring.

A few Shards moved toward the rim. Cautiously, little by little, they dropped into the great bottomless hollow, drawn by uncontrollable forces, prompted by something in the air.

Little flares beamed from individual Shards did nothing to light a pathway, and so they gathered together and moved in clusters, led on hypnotically, deeper and deeper toward the center. The air that had previously clogged their breath gave way to something permeable and alluring, something that excited them to explore.

More and more Shards plunged through the Void of Thead and into the chasm, sent by the Great Chunks to report back on the findings made by the expeditionary team. But the Shards returned no messages, for each successive group had fallen under the same spell. With each inhaled breath of the air, all thoughts of their domain in the Stars evaporated.

While the mercurial Shards gathered in pleasure, the Great Chunks agonized in stasis, their habitual stance in the acceptance world shattered. Had the Winds turned against their captors? Had the Shards found nourishment and vision and failed to return their bounty to the Stars? Were they injured, their lights permanently extinguished?

The Shards continued to lower themselves and sometimes, in their haste, fall toward the source of the spicy fragrance that aroused within them an unfamiliar gratification. With no thought of their safety in this alien world, no thought of how they might get out and return to the Stars, the Shards plunged on, ever deeper, their enjoyment intensifying.

At last, they found themselves in a warm, moist atmosphere. Their precipitous fall gave way to drifting and they came down gently to luxuriate on a bed of fleshy stems and leaves, dotted with small, greenish flowers. In the silence of the dark chasm they thought they could make out the repetitive buzz of bees and hum of birds.

At the center of Planet Earth, the Shards discovered the long lost echo of the Sacred Vanilla, a plant with a mission to delight, a mission of such unique significance that when the Sun, Moon and Planet Earth died, it alone was given a role in eternity.

Every Shard dispatched from the Stars to find and return their fellows to the Heavens became intoxicated with the sacred fragrance, and, in return, watered the Vanilla with their *sputum lunae* and lived on in eternal jouissance.

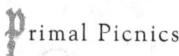

Vanilla Bean

It has been traditional to use a vanilla pod in the preparation of sweet sauces, soufflés and souses. More recently, in paste form, it has found its way with success into seafood dishes. Vanilla associates well with fruit: apples, plums, apricots and figs, any one of which, compotted individually in a light syrup to which a pod of a vanilla liquor is introduced, makes a refreshing end to a rich meal.

An excellent nightcap of dark, block chocolate dissolved in milk and cream may be subtly transformed by a few drops of vanilla essence. And cocktails, preferably with a vodka base and the addition of fruit liquor, may also be enhanced with a few drops of essence. This aromatic spice adds something barely discernible, yet essential, to the balance of a complex mix.

A friend of mine, addicted to the scent of this spice, wore dabs of essence behind her ears and in her décolletage.

BLACK TEARS (WITH A SIDE OF MELTED BUTTER)

Bruce Watson

In the beginning, when she was just a girl, Ocean would lounge across Earth, rolling over its surface and delighting in its tickly ridges and open plateaus. Earth was her world, and hers alone, and she explored every inch of it. She slid into its deep trenches, brushed over its mountains and felt herself tighten in the chill of its poles. She basked around its equator, reveling in the warmth, then explored the endless darkness at its depths. Every day was spent in the search for new experiences and the lazy enjoyment of old ones, and the world was both endless and new.

In time, Ocean grew older, and with age came loneliness. While the pleasures of the Earth were endless,

Ocean had no one to share her joy. As much as the trenches might hold shivery excitement and the mountains might hold rising exaltation, without a companion to share these joys, they no longer held the ability to rouse her. She tried talking to the Earth, for she often heard it speaking, but she grew to suspect that Earth was actually rumbling quietly to itself, utterly unaware that she existed. Her few conversations with the planet were terribly one-sided and made her feel only lonelier.

Ocean also tried talking to the fish that ran through her, but they didn't seem to realize that the currents they rode and the cold depths they probed had any feelings at all. As much as she might try to join in the delightful laughter of dolphins, the bloodthirsty biting of bluefish or the staccato snapping of crabs, all they heard was the sound of her waves and the splash of her waters. Even when she twisted her currents to speed them through her depths, the fish only complimented themselves on their amazing ability to navigate the tides.

Part of the problem was, admittedly, that of expectation. Hearing the birds screech their joy and the fish burble their fears, Ocean suspected that half the fun in life lay in discussing it with others. However, she didn't have any way to test her hypothesis, which only made the idea of a companion more desperately attractive, and this only made Ocean more desperately lonely. She found herself constantly dreaming of a friend, like her, but not of her, a being with whom she could bubble her joys and into whom she could pour her sorrows. But it was not to be, and so she made the best of her loneliness, swimming through her own depths, cataloguing her favorite peaks, and imagining the words that she would use to describe herself to a friend, if ever one happened to come along.

One day, rolling across a wide plateau, she noticed something that she had never seen before. Curled up at the edge of a trench, there was a piece of Earth poking above her surface. It was strange and brown, as empty as a child, yet already showing a few glints of mature green on its broad shoulders. The growth was all crouched energy and undiscovered potential, yet Ocean could already see the promise of its maturity. Coming a little closer, she noticed that the little pile of earth was watching her. His eyes followed her every movement, but he didn't say a word. This, she thought, was quite rude, and displayed incredibly poor manners (even though mothers didn't exist yet, manners were already around). Still, Ocean was an outgoing sort, and wasn't one to stand on ceremony, so she asked the stranger who he was.

Land (for that was his name) wasn't actually all that rude, but he was very young, very lonely and very shy, and was not at all sure that he enjoyed finding himself so suddenly forced into conversation with a beautiful, flowing stranger. He arranged his body into what he hoped was a cool, stylish pose, wished that he had a cigarette (cigarettes, like mothers, didn't exist yet), and pointedly looked away from Ocean. "I'm Land," he said, trying to seem a little mysterious, even without a cigarette.

Seeing Land's strange, uncomfortable position and hearing the quaver in his words, Ocean decided to look beyond his attitude. For all his posturing and rudeness, Land was clearly little more than a child. He was confused and nervous, as lonely as she was, and was clearly trying to find something that would make him feel larger and stronger. Being a compassionate sort, and tired of talking to the unresponsive Earth and the babbling fish, she decided to give the kid a shot. "I'm Ocean," she said brightly, and (because Land continued to stare at her in silence) she let the sun glisten off her back to show that she could be playful.

Land remained silent and pretended that he was caught deep in thought, contemplating unknowable, endless ideas that Ocean couldn't possibly comprehend. He pretended that he was immune to loneliness, and that he didn't notice the beautiful sheen of light dancing on Ocean's skin. After a while, Ocean realized that Rome wasn't built in a day, and that she would need to take her time if she truly hoped to make a friend of Land (Rome, of course, didn't exist yet, but Ocean had an ear for aphorisms and was sure that, when they got around to building it, Rome would take quite a while to erect. Besides, the saying just *sounded* good). Ocean waved goodbye to Land and swam away to do laps around the Equator before taking a nice cooling dip off the North Pole.

Ocean was patient and persistent, intrigued and excited. She came back, and came back again, and came back again. Over time, Land loosened up more and more, allowing himself to spread out and bask in the joy of Ocean's friendship. He found himself looking forward to Ocean's visits, dreaming about the way that she lapped at his shores and made him feel more defined. She complimented him on his pronounced Himalayan backbone, the rippling muscles of his Norwegian shore, and his large, well-developed Florida (of course, Ocean knew that it's not the size of one's Florida that matters, but rather how one uses it. Still, sensitive about Land's insecurity, she chose to keep that information to herself).

And Land loved Ocean, too, even if he showed it in ways that were strange and sometimes silly. He delighted in naming parts of her: her Pacific, where she was large and broad and calm; her Indian, where she was hot and spicy; and her Arctic, which he thought just sounded cool.

So Ocean defined Land and Land embraced Ocean, and they met in the sandy places and made love in the flow of tides. It was very, very good for a very, very long time, but even the best, most secure relationships don't always last forever. Over time, Ocean started to pull away and Land started to feel old. Ocean went to visit her favorite spots and see what was going on with her depths, while Land searched for something to make him feel strong again. In time, their words grew stiff and old, like a well-worn script that has almost lost its meaning. Every day, Ocean complimented Land and Land embraced Ocean, but Land started to worry that Ocean's words were more a matter of habit than love.

(And perhaps they were. There are only so many ways to compliment the burly ridges of a Scandinavia, the exotic heat of an Africa or the manly girth of a Florida. After eons together, Ocean had exhausted her store of compliments and Land's neediness had exhausted her patience. Besides, a girl needs to hear the occasional compliment from time to time, and Land never seemed confident enough to look past his own insecurity. Ocean would comb her hair on Land's reefs, slide her belly along his shelves and reach her fingers into his fjords. All she got for her trouble was endless complaints that she was flooding his banks and that erosion was making his rippling mountains shrink into the sea.

Regardless of the reasons, Ocean longed for the attention that Land couldn't (or wouldn't) give her and Land longed to hear his praises sung by other mouths. He slowly began to surround portions of Ocean, separating them from the whole. He would whisper to these areas, tickle them with his shores and delight in their playful giggles. Some of them he named in silly ways, like Lake Titicaca, which he made up when he was drunk on Southern heat and giddy with the wonder of his own creation. Then there were the Red Sea, the White Sea and the Black Sea, all of which he named during periods of stoic minimalism. There were the Great Lakes, which he named when he was feeling grandiose, and the Great Salt Lake, which is what he called his belly-button. In the flurry of embracing, naming and embracing again, Land forgot about Ocean.

Floating nearby, Ocean listened to Land seducing these small parts of herself, reveling in their newness and freshness, pretending that he didn't know that they were only tiny fragments of the whole, pale reflections of the watery mistress that he had always loved. One day, Ocean noticed him lounging around a small sea that he had almost completely set off from her, a beautiful glistening blue section of herself that she had always particularly admired. He called the new mistress "Mediterranean," for he saw her as the center of his world. Ocean heard the sea's girlish giggle as Land told Mediterranean about his rugged Scandinavia and offered to show her his impressive southern coastline.

It is, of course, galling to hear one's beloved courting another. This is only compounded when the new love is a part of oneself. Ocean heard her own compliments echoing out of Land's mouth as he pompously seduced what she had always seen as a particularly attractive limb, or maybe her kneecap. The sadness and absurdity of the situation made her want to laugh, but she was all out of giggles.

Enough was enough. If Land was going to deal with his insecurities by running to younger, sillier bodies of water, Ocean wasn't going to stop him. However, she also wasn't going to hang around to watch. She retreated to the edge of her beaches, shored up her coastline and turned her back on Land.

It would be nice to say that Land noticed immediately, that he felt some part of him empty out, that he missed his lover when she left. Failing that, it would be nice to say that he thought of her constantly when she was away, went off in search of her, and they found each other in a foamy embrace of earth and water.

It would be nice to say those things, but they would be untrue.

Land was too busy with his giggling harem to notice anything for a very, very long time. One day, however, he heard a hollowness in the laughs of his little seas and lakes. He tried to ignore it, delighting in the reflection of blue sky on deep water, but that only reminded him of the shimmering light that had reflected off Ocean's back when they first met. As much as he might try to ignore it, Land started to realize that the adoration of his little lakes and seas, which he had once found so energizing, was just an echo. He felt that something was missing, a deeper tone that called to him and touched his soul. He reached around himself and felt the cold ocean lapping at his edges. He called her name, but there was no answer.

Every night, Land looked out over the water and remembered his great love. In time, the gay chatter of his adoring seas grew more and more empty, until it caused him agony to hear it. He turned his back on his girlfriends and watched the endless expanse of the ocean. Day after day and night after night, he scanned the cold blue waves, hoping that Ocean might toss her hair for him or show him the arch of her back. He remembered his silence and neglect and tried to recall a time when he had told her of the joy that her beauty brought to him. To his shame, he couldn't.

Whenever he thought of looking away from the cold expanse that held his beloved, Land would remember how the girlish giggles of his seas had turned into shallow cackles, and he would gaze upon the ocean with renewed love and even more desperate desire. In time, his sadness welled up within him until it broke, flowing black tears of loneliness down into the cold silence of the waves.

There are those who say that Ocean died. However, the tides still flow and the fish still swim, which seems like strong evidence of life. Besides, we prefer happy endings.

There are those who say that she is still alive, but the warmth and sentiment and love that once filled her have burned away, leaving anger, hatred and envy. According to these people, she sits in her cold depths and snatches the warmth of life whenever a sailor becomes careless or a captain runs aground. We hope that this isn't true.

On the other hand, there are those who say that she cherishes those little tears of her lover and locks them away in black shells, holding them close to her heart. For this last group, the flavor of those tears will always be a reminder of love and loss and sorrow and forgiveness. And if Land decided to give these black tears a rough and ragged name to hide the tenderness they contain, perhaps we can forgive him his vanity. After all, who are we to hold a grudge when Ocean still seems so ready to open herself?

And "mussels" isn't really a bad name. At least he didn't name them "Floridas."

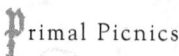

My Aunt Evie's Steamed Mussels

This is a somewhat traditional mussel recipe. However,
rather than use the traditional white wine, my aunt substitutes red,
which gives the mussels a more robust, richer flavor.

1 clove garlic, minced
¼ cup onion, minced
1 cup red wine
2 Tbsp. parsley flakes
2 pounds mussels, shells cleaned

When you get the mussels home, some of the shells may have
opened slightly. Before opening the bag, rap it lightly on a countertop
or table. Most of the mussels should close their shells;
discard the ones that don't. Clean the rest of the mussels.

Put the garlic, onion, red wine and parsley flakes in a large
heavy saucepan and bring just to a boil. Add the mussels,
put on a tight fitting lid and steam till the mussels open.

This takes several minutes, but be careful not to overcook them.

As soon as the mussels open, take them off the heat immediately
and serve with crusty bread to sop up the juices.

WE EAT MUD

Peter Marcus

We Eat Mud

One night us brothers, we got home from fishing fish out of the dirty river that runs its way through our dirty river town only to find our father there in the kitchen, our father standing where our mother so often always stood, in front of the stove, with his back looking back at us brothers, and his face facing away from us, and what it was he was doing, standing there like this, in front of the stove, was he was fixing us all up some supper: mud cakes is what he said he was almost done up cooking, when we asked what it was he was cooking up. And a mud pie, too, he said, and he opened up the oven's door, and when he did a muff of muddy smoke came coughing up and out. Out is all that our father said to us when we asked him where was our mother. Us brothers, we both of us, inside our heads, what we were wondering was out where?—though neither one of us wondered this out loud. Sit, sons, is what our father said to us next. Us, our father's sons, we did like our father told. We sat ourselves down, in the middle of the kitchen's floor, right where we were standing, us brothers, we plopped our boy bodies down, down on our hands and knees, and like this we waited for whatever our father was going to say or do to us brothers next. When our father turned back his face so to face his face at us boys, the look on his face told us that he was happy to see us, down like this, down on our hands and knees, us brothers—our father's sons—a couple of dirt-loving dogs who liked to get down and get dirty. It's hot is what our father said to us then, and he held out in his hands a pie that was made out of mud. Blow, our father told us. And we, us brothers, blew. The steam rising up and off of this baked to a crispy crusted mud, it curled up and around our boy faces—this steam became a pair of hands holding us in this place. This, this is where we belong is what these hands whispered to us. And it was like this, with us brothers down on our hands and knees, and with our mouths wide open, and with our father standing over us, watching over us brothers, with his boots skinned thick with mud: like this, we began to eat.

We Eat Mud: Revisited

Us brothers, we kept reaching down, with our hands, down into the mud.

We kept on with our hands reaching down, into the mud, and when we did, us brothers, we kept on pulling up mud. But then once, when we reached with our hands down into the mud, us brothers, we pulled up Girl. We pulled Girl up, out of the mud, until Girl became a tree. Us brothers, up this girl tree, up, us brothers, we climbed. We climbed up this girl tree that used to be Girl, this tree that used to be mud, until us brothers got up to this tree's top. Up here, at the top of this tree, us brothers, out of tree branches and tree leaves, all the color of mud, we made us a nest. In the sky above our heads, there was a cloud up there in the shape of a bird. This cloud, it was so shaped like how a bird is shaped that it became, it turned into, it was: a bird. This bird, it flew over to where, us brothers, we were standing up watching with our heads lifted up to see. When this bird that was once a cloud was close enough for us to touch it, us brothers, we reached out with our hands to touch it. We touched it. We touched this bird that was once a cloud once shaped in the shape of a bird, and when we did, this bird, it started singing. Then, this bird, this bird that, it was singing, then it and its singing, it flew away. When it came back, this bird, a little while later, like a good bird that always comes back, its bird mouth was filled with mud. This bird, with its bird mouth filled up with mud, this bird, it wasn't singing. What this bird did, even though it wasn't a bird singing to us brothers anymore, it flew back up close to us brothers above us our boy heads. Us brothers, looking up at this bird, we opened up our boy mouths. When we did this with our mouths, this bird, it opened up its mouth too, it started back up singing. And like this, with mud dripping down from this bird's singing mouth and down into ours, us brothers, we began to to eat.

Mud Soup

One night we see, down by the river, we see Girl. Girl is down by the river, down on her hands and knees, down in the river-made mud, and Girl is doing with mud what us brothers, we do not know what it is she is doing. I am making a pot, is what she tells us, when us brothers ask her what is she doing. When we ask her why after her telling us about her making a pot, she looks at us brothers like this, with this hungry sort of look looking out from her girl eyes, and then she tells us that she is making a pot for her to make soup in. Soup, we say to ourselves. What kind of soup? is what is next on our list of what we want from Girl to know. Climb in and take a look, is what Girl says to this. Us brothers, we do what Girl says. We climb up this pot's muddy sides and we dive down inside. Inside of this made-out-of-mud pot there is river water filled up to its top. This water is good and muddy, just the way us brothers we like it. There are some rusted jags of slag metal jutting up from the bottom of the pot, while up on top, afloat on the water's muddy skin, are the chopped-off heads and moon-shining eyes of dead fish glazing up. When we point all of this out to Girl, what Girl says to us is that this, the rusted metal, the fish heads, the fish eyes, this is all for the soup's flavor. Without this, Girl tells us brothers, this soup would be nothing but muddy water. I almost forgot, she then says, I need wood for the fire. Girl turns then and we watch her walk up away from the river, heading towards the woods that come between the river and the shipwrecked and silenced mill. When Girl comes back, she is holding in her girl arms an armful of ten-foot-tall trees, the dirt and the roots still dangling from that part of the tree that was closest to the earth. Us brothers, we poke our heads up over the rim of this pot to see Girl slide the trees up underneath this pot and we see her set them on fire. It doesn't take long for the water to heat up. Bath time, she says, when the bubbles start boiling up. Girl sticks a muddy finger into the water and tells us brothers that it's just about there. What, where, is there? is what the both of us brothers are mouthing to each other, but say this out loud so that Girl might hear it, this, we do not dare. When the skin of us brothers begins to pull away from the bone, it only hurts us just a little. It only hurts just a little the way sometimes it hurt just a little too when our mother used to hold our muddy hands under hot running water to get the caked mud off. When the skin slides off of the bone, and the muscles beneath the skin are tender and red, this is when Girl knows we are ready. She spoons us up, one brother per hand, and begins to eat.

Mud Soup: Revisited

There is mud, us brothers know, that it will not let you walk across it. When you try to walk across this mud, this mud, it swallows you up. It is like the river's water, but only thicker. Us brothers, we know boys who've gotten themselves sucked down to the neck in this kind of mud. Some boys, they call this mud quick mud. This mud, it makes soup out of boys not like us brothers—boys who don't know how to walk on water, boys who don't know how to walk across mud. Those boys are the kind of a boy who, when he sees this kind of mud, he does not see that this mud, it is the kind of mud that will not hold a boy up. One time, us brothers, we got it going on inside our boy heads to wonder: How deep into the earth did this kind of mud go? And so we dove down, head first, down into this mud. We dug and we dug and we mudded our way down, and downer, into the muddy earth—but after three days of us doing this, we did not get down to this mud's muddy bottom. So we dug back up, and we flapped with our arms back up, until we had mudded our way back up to the top of all this mud. When we got back up, us brothers, we were covered up with mud. Girl was up there waiting for us when we got back up. We told Girl our story, that there was no end to this mud that we could see: that we could not get down to this mud's muddy bottom. But Girl didn't believe us. Girl said we were making it up. Then Girl stepped with both of her girl feet into this bottomless mud. Us brothers, we watched Girl lift up the cottony hem of her girl dress. The mud reached up just barely to kiss Girl's knees. Girl's knees, they are the kind of knees that make us brothers want to stay forever kneeling. When Girl stepped into this mud, it was like dipping the oar of some rower's boat into a muddy puddle. It's true, Girl was that big. Girl was so big, us brothers, we climbed our way up the side of her mud-barked body as if she were a tree. This tree, we knew, we would never get up to the top. Something would stop us—the moon, the stars. Some passing by bird or airplane would get in our climbing way. The moon rising up rose, but it stopped rising up when it got all tangled up in Girl's hair. Girl didn't hardly notice the moon getting itself all tangled up in Girl's girl hair. Girl thought the moon was just a knot of hair that the wind had twisted up. Girl walked around for a month with this moon hat sitting on the top of her head. It wasn't until the thirty-first day of this did Girl reach up with her hand and Girl flicked the moon back up into its orbit. The moon rose like a balloon running away from the hand of a little girl who wanted to know what it would be like to see this balloon rise up and up until, in the sun's heat, it would get so close up, it would get so heated up, that it would break. It is true that the moon was rising up and away from the hand, from the head, of a girl, Girl, who did not realize that the moon could actually break.

When the moon in its rising up, when it got up too up close to the sun, it was too late for any of us to stop it from breaking. In the sun's molten light, in that blast-furnace fire, the moon, it shattered into a billion pieces. Each broken piece became a star.

How to Make Fish

Catch fish.
Take fish.
Clean fish.
Fry fish.

Take filet in hand.
Dip in egg.
Dip in breadcrumbs.
Fry in butter.

Cook till brown.
Flip.
Cook till brown again.
Eat.

How to Make Mud Pies

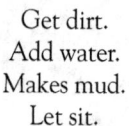

Get dirt.
Add water.
Makes mud.
Let sit.

Take mud-dirt mix.
Add water.
Makes more mud.
Eat.

Lick lips.
Wash down with water.
Mud in belly.
Add fish.

THE ORIGINS OF INDIAN PUDDING: A HISTORY

Tammy Donroe

It has long been assumed that Indian pudding is made from one hundred percent pure Indians. Not so. In fact, the residents of New Delhi recently filed a class-action lawsuit to clear their name from Yankee recipes everywhere (retroactive to the year 1620), since they have no idea how they ended up as the main ingredient in the first place.

The origins and proper edible components of this deliciously sloppy, corn-based dessert have been a source of contention between the British and any remaining Native Americans for centuries. Disagreements even occurred within their own ranks and can be traced back to before its invention:

Native 1: Well, we have corn, and we have water. What do you think about mixing corn and water together?

Native 2: No, that's dumb.

Cool-headed reasoning prevailed, as anthropological evidence shows the natives began supplementing their hunter/gatherer diet with some iteration of the mushy maize we call "Indian" pudding.

The British, however, having later colonized the area now known, coincidentally, as "New England," had staked their own claim on the dish, which they said bore a striking resemblance to their traditional hasty pudding. With one notable exception: the presence of corn.

Colonist 1: Have the ships with the flour come in, yet?

Colonist 2: (*sigh*) For the fifteenth time, no. They haven't. You'll know when they do because I'll be stowing away on the first Scurvy Train off this hellhole of a continent.

Colonist 1: But, I miss my Mum's pudding…

Colonist 2: Use dirt. Or those disgusting lobster things crawling around all over the place. I don't care.

Lobster it is. Colonist 1 tries stewing the lobster, pounding the lobster, even grinding the shells into a fine powder, but a delicious pudding it does not make (the bisque, however, is fantastic). Then, he tries pumpkins. Same disappointing pudding result (but, again, good soup). Finally, he cooks up some cranberries, but the resulting concoction ends up more like a sauce. One he suspects might pair well with game birds.

But, there's another tall, strange-looking plant that the Native Americans seem to be enjoying, and Colonist 1 is pretty sure it has the word pudding written all over it. The natives, sick and tired of finding their corn crop hacked to pieces in the night, decide to teach the colonists how to grow and grind their *own* corn.

Native 1: Like that, okay. Now, leave us alone.

Colonist 1: But, these plants take up so much space. We might need to cut down some trees.

Native 1: Keep the trees. Don't eat so much.

Colonist 1: But, I'm hungry.

Native 1: Eat other things. One can't live on corn alone.

Colonist 1: Not now, perhaps, but maybe some fine day...

Armed with the secrets to corn cultivation, Colonist 1 gets right to work on recipe development. His favorite rendition of Indian pudding catches on like wildfire among the other settlers, and he becomes the first celebrity chef in American history (catchphrase: "Jolly good!"). The natives, realizing their tactical error, get busy making some improvements of their own, and a vicious game of one-upmanship ensues.

Native 1: We'll be unveiling some innovative, new toppings today.

Colonist 1: We have toppings, too.

Native 1: Not like ours.

Colonist 1: Oh, yeah? Like what?

Native 1: Seeds and nuts. You?

Colonist 1: Cream. Maybe whipped, maybe frozen so that rivulets of sweet cream might melt and flow down the mounds of steamy pudding into shallow, milky pools.

Native 1: (*drooling*) That sounds awful.

The British colonists have other tricks up their sleeves, too. In addition to utilizing foreign spices, like cinnamon, ginger and nutmeg, they start importing molasses from the West Indies to sweeten things up a bit. But, when the troubled son of the Chief of the tribe sneaks out to the colony one night and steals a pot with the encrusted remnants of last night's pudding, the natives catch wind of these newfangled ingredients. Soon, they begin adding their own secret weapon: local, sustainably tapped maple syrup (for the kids, they insist).

When the colonists find out, they cry foul play (because, I mean, how delicious is maple syrup, and if the settlers had known American trees oozed sweet, sticky goo, they wouldn't have cut them all down to plant the corn in the first place). The natives retaliate with harsh criticism of the colonists' role in the triangular slave trade that fuels the brutal Caribbean sugarcane plantations.

Things start to get out of hand. Cook-offs are scheduled and then abruptly cancelled because the participating colonists keep dying. Finally, an emergency meeting is called to settle, at the very least, the most pressing issue: who will get the credit for inventing this distinctly American dish.

The great tribal leader, Weeps with Great Fury, speaks on behalf of the Native Americans, with smooth-talking settler, Manny F. Destiny, representing the colonists' interests.

Manny: So, we want the pudding. (*loooong pause*) That's our final offer.

Weeps: Offer rejected.

Manny: Okay, okay. Tell me what it would take for us to walk away with the pudding.

Weeps: That's our corn you're using. You yourself call it "Indian meal."

Manny: Cornmeal, Indian meal. We're splitting hairs. It's not like you invented corn. We can grow it, too.

Weeps: That's not what you said last year.

Manny: How about now? Can we have the pudding now?

Weeps: You need to offer something in return.

Manny: Fine. How about some blankets?

Weeps: We're not cold.

Manny: Trinkets?

Weeps: They *are* very shiny. But, not shiny enough for pudding. You can have pemmican.

Manny: Pemmican? What's that?

Weeps: Dried meat with berries.

Manny: …(*dry heaves*)

Weeps: It's good for long journeys…

Manny: I think we might be here a while.

There's a long pause in the proceedings, and the two

parties seem to be at an impasse. Finally, the colonial elder, at a whopping twenty-four years old, pushes to the front of the crowd and offers up the following compromise:

Elder: How about this? Whoever ends up with this country, the other gets the credit for the pudding.

Colonist 2: (*yelling from the crowd*) You can HAVE this stupid country.

Weeps: So, if we win, you will leave and take only the pudding?

Manny: And maybe a few lobsters, too.

(*Brief consultation*)

Weeps: We accept. As a gesture of goodwill, here is some pemmican.

Manny: Mmmmmm...chewy. (*gagging*) And for you, some trinkets. Look, I'll even wrap them up for you in this nice, warm blanket.

The rest, as we say, is history. At least, the Native Americans got to keep their pudding. If only the American copyright office had gotten the name right.

Indian Pudding: A Compromise

This tasty version of the American classic uses molasses and maple syrup in a tribute to both influences.

3 cups milk
¼ cup cornmeal
½ cup molasses
¼ cup maple syrup
2 Tbsp. butter
1 tsp. salt
½ tsp. ginger
¼ tsp. cinnamon
¼ tsp. nutmeg
2 eggs

Preheat oven to 300°F.

In a medium pot, heat 2 cups of the milk until little bubbles form around the edges (do not boil). In a thin stream, slowly whisk in the cornmeal. Add molasses, maple syrup, butter, salt and spices. Whisk constantly over low heat until thickened, about 10 minutes. Remove from heat.

In a small bowl, whisk the eggs. Temper by slowly pouring about ½ cup of the hot mixture into the eggs while whisking. Add egg mixture back to the pot and stir well. Pour into 8x8-inch baking dish set inside a 9x12-inch pan. Pour water into the **outer pan** to a height of about ½-inch. Bake 1 hour. Stir remaining 1 cup of cold milk into pudding and bake for another hour. Remove from oven and let cool in water bath. Consistency should be a bit loose. Serve warm with vanilla ice cream.

II

Not By
BREAD ALONE

Ruth and Boaz by Hans Holbein II

Italian Kitchen-Woodcut from *Banchetti compositioni di Vivendi-*
Christoforo di Messisburgo-Ferrara, 1549

GABBOOT

Firyal Alshalabi

unset. Rushing to the courtyard was a must. The chirrups of chickadees and coos of *yamamas* mingled with the unified, monotonous calls of hundreds of congregating birds in the tall palm trees. Twisting and shaking their feathers, helping with their beaks to remove insects and tiny twigs from unreachable spots, the birds were getting ready for the big party.

With arms spread like wings, head held back, and face looking upward, Muneera twirled under the canopy of fronds like a tranced dervish, expecting at any moment to lift off and join the partying birds. She wore her sleeveless light-yellow dress to blend in with the clusters of dates that had just recently changed from deep green. And since the hem of the dress hardly reached her knees, she could swirl around easily or even fly. Her movement stirred waves of hot, humid air swelling with the faint fragrance of the skinny henna tree near which Muneera liked to twirl. A sudden breeze carried the pungent aroma of food, cooked with heavenly spices. Muneera inhaled deeply with a smile. The party must have started and she was ready.

"*Inshallah* the bird droppings will taste good," her brother Hemed said in Arabic, slamming the iron gates behind him.

"*Chub!*" Muneera shouted, still twirling.

A tiny stone, coming from Hemed's direction, hit her on the shoulder. "I'm your older brother; don't talk to me like that."

"*Chub!!*" Muneera reiterated. She picked up several hard dates from under her feet and began throwing them at him, one by one.

Hemed looked ridiculous dancing in his long white *dishdasha,* trying to avoid the hard dates. "Go do your evening prayers instead of acting like a *majnoona.*" He disappeared behind the brown wooden door of the house.

Muneera kept throwing yellow dates at the door. But the urge to learn what that mysterious, vaguely familiar food aroma was proved stronger than the desire to pursue her brother. The smell must have drifted from the outdoor kitchen of their only neighbors, the Kraishans. Going there would be easy; she'd done it many times. But she'd also been scolded by her mother many times. Now with Hemed in the house, her mother would easily find out even if it took only five minutes to run there, ask what the food was, and run back. Deep in her mind, however, perched the hope that within those five minutes, Om Ali would give her a taste. Muneera knew how much Om Ali liked her. Just a week ago, Muneera went to visit with her mother to congratulate her for her new baby. Om Ali said she wished her new daughter might look just like Muneera, "with soft black hair and big black eyes."

"But *inshallah* not as skinny," her mother said, lifting Muneera's arm and dropping it.

"Yuma? Why do you have to embarrass me like that?" Muneera complained to her mother as they walked back.

"So that you will eat better and stop jumping around," Yuma patted her on the head.

The bird symphony trickled toward the end of the day. The sky over the Kraishan's house turned to a pale orange with streaks of thin gray clouds. One of them, shaped like an arrow, pointed at an old wooden ladder leaning against the tall adobe wall that separated the two houses.

Muneera couldn't remember seeing the ladder before. She stepped closer. It looked ancient, as if it was an extension of the sky and clouds above. The delicious, mysterious aroma became stronger with each step, drifting through her nostrils, straight to her head, making her dizzy, lifting her onto the ladder's shaky wooden rungs, delivering her to the sky. She managed to avoid the rusty nails jutting from the two parallel poles, which weren't quite parallel any more.

With the last step, Muneera found herself on top of the world, overlooking the neighbor's backyard. She reached to touch the gray clouds above her head, oblivious of the ladder's swaying and trembling under her feet. The aroma was definitely coming from the Kraishan's outdoor kitchen, only a few yards away from the wall she was leaning against. Her father had converted their old kitchen to a *deewaniya* to meet his men-friends every evening, to the delight of her mother who preferred him nearby instead of going to somebody else's deewaniya. Yellow light seeped out of the small square side window of the kitchen, but huge pots and pans hung in front of it, blocking the view.

Suddenly, a black cat flew out of the kitchen with a loud, brazen meow, followed by another feline kicked by a bare black foot wearing ankle bracelets. A huge, tall, dark figure emerged from the doorway.

"Ehh," gasped Muneera, almost losing hold of the dilapidated wall. "*Afreet*," she whispered to her heart which fiercely thumped against her ribs. A trickle of cold sweat escaped her temples and fell to the ground. *Djinn*! She had heard stories of djinn from her mother, about people who saw these supernatural creatures in the old days when her parents were growing up in the old town of Murgab in Kuwait. Just a few nights earlier Hemed swore by Allah that he had seen one in their own courtyard, twirling around the henna tree where Muneera herself liked to twirl at sunset.

This djinn now stopped in front of the kitchen door holding a steaming pot, filling the air with its mysterious aroma, wafting toward Muneera, who inhaled it deep into her lungs. The djinn must have heard Muneera, because it turned its head in her direction. A shiny ring in its nose sparkled under a bare light bulb dangling from a wire over the kitchen door.

Muneera was just about to loosen her grasp on the wall when the djinn said in a female voice, "*Shinoo?*"

Swallowing hard, Muneera forced herself to speak, summoning her courage from somewhere out of a pool of fear she thought would drown her: "*Inti afreet?*" She remembered that knowledge rules over fear and that her mother had said there are good djinn and bad djinn. This one with a female voice and a colorful sari revealing her dark belly must be a good djinn. Otherwise, why would it give off such a good odor? It could have easily engulfed her in an evil stink and struck her with its magic powers. Muneera pointed at the food and asked in Arabic what it was, "*Shinoo hatha?*"

Still holding the steaming pot, the djinn shuffled closer to Muneera. "*Shinoo?*"

Exasperated but persistent, Muneera leaned over, resting her stomach on the six-inch thick wall, pointing at the pot. "That! Hatha, in your hand."

The djinn's tense face relaxed, the big kohl lined eyes glanced down at the pot then up at Muneera. In English it asked, "This food?"

"An English-speaking djinn?" Muneera thought. Her mind rummaged through all the English words she'd learned from Hemed when he studied the language in fifth grade just a year earlier. She still had to wait two years to learn it in the classroom. "Yes! This food. What? Shinoo?"

With something like a smile on its face, the djinn lifted the pot toward Muneera. "You want?"

"Yes! NO! What name?"

"Oh." It seemed at last to understand. *Alhamdu Lillah!*

Then suddenly, just as the djinn's lips began moving, as if forming a kiss with the name of the food, Muneera heard her name shouted from under the ladder, turned to see who was calling and the rung under her feet gave way. Her hand slipped. She swayed sideways with the ladder, tried to grip the wall, but all she saw before crashing to the ground were shiny stars in a pitch dark sky.

"Muneera. . . Muneera. . . ," voices called. The only answer she gave was, "*Gabboot*, gabboot."

"Muneera!" A gentle patting on her cheeks followed.

"Gabboot" She moved her head sideways to avoid the hand patting her cheek and some unpleasant smell. When she was finally able to open her eyes, her mother's anxious face was peering closely at her. Hemed's face appeared just behind Yuma's, watching. Was he really worried about her?

"Muneera!" Her panicked mother called. "Do you hear me?" She sprayed cold water on Muneera's face.

Gasping, Muneera tried to sit up, but a sharp pain pierced her left shoulder. Where was she? Whose white walls were those? The fan in the ceiling looked familiar. Oh and there was that green framed painting of a lonely boat resting on a white shore. She never liked the painting or understood why it hung crookedly in their living room. Who had carried her inside the house? Placed her on the Persian rug with her head resting on a pillow? She tried to sit up again, and when she couldn't, she began to weep.

"Hemed," Yuma said. "Call your father from the deewaniya. Tell him he needs to take her to the clinic."

"Nooooooo!" Muneera cried. But crying only made her shoulder hurt more. She whimpered, trying to calm down.

"I want to know what you were doing on the ladder." Yuma said. Her hand moistening Muneera's face smelled repulsive, as if she'd rushed out of the bathroom without enough time to wash.

Muneera pushed her mother's hand away and asked for water, "*Ebi maii.*" While Yuma got her a glass of water, Muneera managed to sit up and lean against the orange couch. With her right hand she grabbed the glass and swallowed the water in one gulp.

"Why were you on the ladder?" her mother insisted.

Muneera's father saved her from having to answer. He dashed into the living room without his headdress of *ghitra* and *ogal*, swept her up, carried her through the hallway to the courtyard, and through the gate to his brand new Chevy Impala. On the way through the yard, Muneera tried to capture the mysterious aroma again, but she could only smell the sweet fragrance of the frankincense her father liked on his clothes.

The clinic doctor sent them to the main hospital for X-rays. It was very late at night by the time another doctor inspected the pictures, wrapped her arm with gauze and placed it into a sling.

Muneera hoped that by the time they arrived home, her mother and Hemed would be asleep. Yuba was nice to her. He didn't ask why she had been on the ladder. He only insisted that if she had said "*bismillah*" before she climbed up, nothing bad would have happened.

To Muneera's disappointment, when they arrived home, not only were her mother and Hemed awake, they were waiting outside the house in the yard. They sat on two old folding chairs, facing the wooden ladder that lay scattered on the ground. What was Hemed telling Mother? Was he the reason she fell?

"You two must be hungry," Yuma said, as Muneera and Yuba walked toward them.

"I'm going back to the deewaniya. I'll eat there."

"What did the doctor say?" Yuma asked.

"Muneera will explain," Yuba said, rushing toward the deewaniya in the back yard.

"It's not broken, only tears in the tissue." Muneera said sheepishly. "I'm hungry."

She followed her mother to the living room. Muneera was sleepy and sat on the flowery couch facing their first color TV set. The screen displayed scenes of men dancing with swords while others beat on big drums. Hemed turned up the volume, then sat on the floor, pretending to watch while stealing glances at her every once in a while. Muneera disliked that kind of music, with men's voices repeating incomprehensible words answered every now and then by a drum beat. But she knew if she asked Hemed to turn down the sound he would only turn it up. Yuma returned from the kitchen with a plate piled with steaming food. She handed it to Muneera.

A familiar aroma arose from the dish to awaken Muneera's senses. She forgot the noisy music. She placed the warm plate on her lap and, with the spoon in her right hand, investigated its contents. Two roasted pieces of lean lamb rested in the center surrounded by finger-sized dumplings and pieces of potatoes and eggplant, covered with thick tomato sauce. With the edge of her spoon, Muneera cut a dumpling in half and studied the white-and-green stuffing. Was it made of onion and cilantro? She brought the plate close to her nose, shut her eyes, and sniffed. That was it, she thought. An image of a heavenly party with fluffy feathers and happy creatures singing and laughing was forming in her mind, when she heard Hemed's voice.

"Look, she's like a dog sniffing food," he snickered.

"Chub!" Muneera yelled to shut him up, her eyes swelling with tears. Why did he have to ruin the best moments of her day?

"Hemed!" Yuma commanded. "Leave her alone." She turned toward Muneera who was still absorbed with the culinary delight in her hand. "Are you going to eat? Or just play with it?"

With a trembling hand, Muneera lifted a spoonful to her mouth. She closed her eyes as she slowly chewed. Yes, that must be it: cilantro and onion. Muneera swallowed and opened her eyes with a smile.

Hemed chuckled. "Majnoona."

"*Bas!*" Yuma snapped at him. "Enough."

"Yuma, I told you she's majnoona, *wallah*. Tell Yuba to take her to a mental doctor."

Yuma ignored him and glared at Muneera who was now devouring the food as if someone was going to snatch it away. "So this is the food you broke your arm for?"

Muneera shook her head. Between the last mouthfuls she mumbled, "It's not broken."

"Since when do we beg food from the neighbors? Ha? Since when?" Yuma sounded very angry.

"I didn't beg," Muneera said, wiping the edges of the plate with her fingers and sucking them clean. She'd eaten good food before, but never that good. That was when the female djinn in the colorful sari popped in her mind. Should she tell them about it?

"The neighbor's cook brought the plate and said you asked for it. How am I going to hide my face from Om Ali? They now think we don't feed you," her mother continued.

"Food beggar," Hemed said.

"Their cook?" Muneera asked. The djinn actually came to their house? Stunned, she looked at her mother in surprise. But then she began to recall Om Ali telling her mother about the new Indian cook they'd hired recently. Muneera and her mother had never seen the cook; they only heard her voice saying "shinoo" whenever Om Ali called her.

"Yuma, why don't you cook something like this for us?"

Hemed giggled. "Yuma, if I were you I'd hit her on her broken arm."

"Chub!" Muneera shouted.

"You two shut up, before you awaken your baby brother," Yuma said threateningly. She turned to Hemed. "Go to your room right this minute before I call your father to teach you a lesson in how to respect your mother and sister."

At the mention of father, Hemed dragged himself reluctantly out of the living room. Muneera stood to take the empty plate to the kitchen but Yuma asked her to come back and sit next to her on the floor, her favorite spot, where she placed a cushion between her back and the leg of the couch. Gazing at her mother's face, Muneera wondered if she was going to scold her again. But a gentle expression had replaced the previously angry look. Trying not to disturb her left arm while still holding the plate in her right, Muneera lowered herself to the ground and sat close to her mother.

Yuma brushed Muneera's disheveled hair from her face. "Do you remember the last time you ate this dish?"

Muneera shook her head. She only remembered that during the last two weeks every time she joined the bird party at sunset the same aroma was floating up there.

"You ate it two years ago when I gave birth to your brother Talal. But you were only five, so you don't remember."

"Allah! Two years and you never cooked it again?"

"I didn't cook it then either. Om Ali—may Allah increase her blessings—cooked it for me. It's a dish prepared and served only for women who give birth."

"What is it named?"

"Gabboot."

Muneera remembered the afreet's lips moving as if throwing kisses just before she fell off the ladder. Gabboot. That was the word she was repeating when she woke from her fall.

"Why is it called gabboot?"

Yuma smiled for the first time that day. "Wallah, good question. I don't know." She then held her hand in front of her face and made a loose fist, as if she was holding something she didn't want her to see. Muneera had always wondered at how tiny her mother's hands were. With those tiny hands, Yuma cooked and cleaned and swept and dusted and fed and washed and ironed and . . .

"Maybe it's called gabboot because when you make the dumplings you take a piece of dough, spread it in your palm, fill it with stuffing, and then close the dough on it, making a *gabda*, a fist. So gabboot probably comes from gabda."

"What makes it smell so good?"

"The many spices used in the sauce."

"Is it too much work?"

Yuma sighed. "So much work. Who has the time to make it? But it is a very nutritious dish to heal the wounds of the mother who just gave birth. It's supposed to tighten parts of the body that got loose with birth. That's why neighbors and relatives prepare it for women during *el nfas*."

"El nfas?"

"The forty days after a mother gives birth are called el nfas. During those days she's supposed to stay in bed, does not leave the house, and no one should see her doing anything, otherwise she'll get the evil eye."

Muneera calculated how many days were left for Om Ali before she was through with el nfas. But she knew Yuma would never let her ask for more gabboot. "Are you going to have a baby soon?"

"*Fal Allah wala falich!*" Yuma protested. "I hope not."

At that moment Yuba walked into the living room with a surprised look on his face. "You're still awake?"

"This daughter of yours keeps me awake with her endless questions."

Yuba switched off the television and the lights of the living room. "In one week she'll go back to school and ask her teachers all her questions. And no more staying up late."

"Can I ask you a question, Ba?"

"Just one. I need to go to sleep."

"Why do the birds call and sing together at sunset?"

"Sing? They don't sing, they pray and chant God's name in worship."

"But . . ."

Her father interrupted her, "and if you wake up at sunrise for school in a week, you will hear them chant Allah's name first thing in the morning, just like people do at mosques."

"*Lakin* . . . But. . ."

"*Khalas!* That's it. You said one question. *Tesbeheen alakhair*, good night." He switched off the last light in the hallway.

In bed, Muneera adjusted herself so she wouldn't crush her wounded arm while she slept. But she felt wide awake. Such a delicious dish should not be prepared just once a year, if that. And what if she decided she did not want to have children? Especially not boys like Hemed. Did that mean she would never eat gabboot again? No. She would learn how to cook it, and eat it whenever she liked, as soon as her arm healed. Inshallah.

She turned off the light on her night table and smiled. Birds might worship at sunrise, but at sunset, they have a party.

GABBOOT

Ingredients:
1 pound of beef or lamb meat with bone
1 large chopped onion
1 Tbsp. crushed garlic
¼ cup cooking oil
4 chopped tomatoes
1 small eggplant chopped in squares
2 medium size potatoes chopped in squares
¼ cup of tomato paste
1 tsp. Turmeric
1 tsp. allspice
1 tsp. coriander
3 cups water
Salt to taste

Ingredients for dumplings:
2 cups of flour
Water enough to make dough
1 Tbsp. cooking oil

Ingredients for stuffing dumplings:
2 large onions finely chopped
1 bunch of cilantro, finely chopped
½ cup raisins
1 tsp. black pepper and allspice
Salt to taste

Preparation:

Sauté meat with onion and garlic for a few minutes on medium heat, then add potatoes and eggplant. Cook for a few more minutes until tender, then add chopped tomatoes, spices and tomato paste. Stir well mixing all ingredients together. Add water. Bring to a boil, then reduce heat to simmer and let cook while covered.

To prepare dough for dumplings mix flour with water only. Set aside while preparing the stuffing by mixing all ingredients together. Take a small amount of dough, about the size of a tablespoon, knead lightly. Spread dough open in a greased palm. Fill with stuffing and seal, rolling it in one hand with the help of the other. Repeat procedure until all dough and stuffing are used.

Drop dumplings in meat and vegetable sauce. Cook together until dumplings are tender and fully cooked, about an hour.

Note: Some people cook gabboot with only eggplant, some with only potatoes. Experiment until you find your favorite version. Feel free to vary amount of water and spices to your taste.

PIONEERING THE "SPREAD ON TOAST" CONCEPT:

A Conversation with Louis-Émile Tartine

Barry Foy

t is easy to forget, in an age that takes so much for granted, that at one time the word "toast" meant exactly that and nothing more: a slice of roasted bread, bare and unadorned, unimproved by the application of fat or sweetening or any kind of condiment.

If the memory of this culinary equivalent of the hairshirt is now a distant one, we have one person to thank, the brilliant if somewhat quirky Louis-Émile Tartine. Born in France's Dordogne region in 1911, Tartine outraged his father as a teenager by refusing to follow him into the bricklaying trade, opting instead for a life in the restaurant business. From the beginning, he demonstrated a talent for food work, which led to a long and celebrated career as a chef and cookbook author, in the course of which he created innumerable new dishes, cooking techniques and flavor combinations.

But the milestone forever linked with the name "Tartine" is toast. That is because it was Louis-Émile Tartine who transformed the notion of toast by proposing, to an initially uncomprehending world, that roasted bread be spread with some sort of substance to enhance its flavor and palatability. This concept, the very essence of simplicity, generated a firestorm of reaction at first, both positive and negative. Once it caught on, however, it is no exaggeration to say the breakfast world never looked back.

I had the privilege of conducting the very last interview this culinary giant ever granted. It took place at Monsieur Tartine's home in Paris, just two weeks before his death at the age of 97 in February 2008:

Good afternoon, Monsieur Tartine.

Good afternoon. Is that chair comfortable enough?

It's perfect, thank you.

May I offer you a drink?

I wouldn't turn it down!

I'm in the mood for a Campari-soda myself. How does that sound?

Make it two.

Here. I hope that's strong enough.

I'm sure it's just right. Say, how about a "toast"?

I beg your pardon? Oh, yes, "toast," I see. Haha, very droll. You Americans! Cheers, then.

Cheers! Well, should we start?

Whenever you're ready.

All right. Unesco has declared 2008 "The International Year of Toast." But frankly, I don't see what all the fuss is about. I mean, it's only toast.

Get out of my house!

[*Unfortunately, Monsieur Tartine abruptly terminated our interview at this point, and within a month he was dead. The following is the conversation as I imagine it, had things worked out as planned. It combines questions I intended to ask with answers that, based on my reading of various other interviews, I feel confident Monsieur Tartine may well have provided.*]

Hello again.

Oh, it's you.

What a handsome ascot! Where did you get it?

I don't know. Something my wife picked out. She chooses all my clothes.

I see. Well, where should we start? Maybe you could begin by describing the toast of your childhood.

Certainly; I remember it as if it were yesterday. In those days, bear in mind, the word "toast" referred merely to plain, roasted bread.

Any particular type of bread?

It varied. Given a choice, obviously, everyone would have eaten fine white loaves, but in reality only the upper classes could afford them. Working families such as mine ate darker, heavier breads made of rye and other coarse flours.

Was it always eaten toasted?

Oh, my, no! Who would have had time for that?

I don't follow you.

Don't forget that this was long before the home kitchen was a showroom for all manner of gadget and appliance, as it is now. When I was young, only the rich had a ready means of toasting bread at home.

So how did you do it?

We didn't. That was the baker's job. His oven was the only reliable source of heat in town.

You mean you bought the bread already toasted?

No. It worked like this: You'd buy a loaf from the baker and take it home. Then, when you wanted toast, you'd cut off the desired number of pieces and take them back to him to be toasted. Being the youngest child, I was usually assigned this errand. As the bread toasted, I and dozens of other children waited in a cluster outside the bakery door. Many, many's the winter morning, I can tell you, that I spent shivering and blowing on my freezing fingers as I waited for the toast. The only compensation was the marvelous smell that filled the air.

I've always loved the smell of toasting bread...

No, not the bread. There was a perfumer across the street. Oh, the fragrances that wafted from that shop! It was an experience I'll never, ever forget, as long as I live.

How long did you usually have to wait?

I forget.

So then you'd take the toast home?

Yes. But one had to run as fast as possible, before it could cool. Unluckily for me, I wasn't a particularly fast runner, and I received many brutal beatings from my father for bringing him lukewarm toast. My father was a remarkable man.

Tell me more about your father.

Get out of my house!

[TWO DAYS LATER]

Hello.

I'm sorry—have we met?

Yes, I was here two days ago. You were telling me about bringing toast from the bakery as a child.

I'll take your word for it.

I'm curious as to why people wanted their bread toasted in the first place.

Why? Goodness knows. I've never given it any thought.

Were the breads of that era more flavorful toasted, maybe?

Not really. In fact, they were far tastier fresh. Come to think of it, I suppose it was a matter of texture.

Texture?

Good toast has a very pleasing *crunchiness* about it, wouldn't you agree?

I guess so, but...

People today have no idea how rare crunchiness used to be! It seems as if everything's crunchy now: potato chips, cookies, candy bars. There's crunch everywhere you look. But in those days, yes, we had *crispness*, plenty of crispness—celery, apples, that sort of thing—but real *crunch* was a scarce commodity, and toast was about the only affordable source of it for the common man. It was one of our few real pleasures in life. That and worshiping Satan.

Huh?

Haha, my little joke!

I see.

I had you there, didn't I?

For a moment, I guess...

Hahaha. You Americans!

May we continue?

Be my guest.

So, with your discerning palate, I gather the toast struck you as quite bland.

Not really.

I picture you thinking, "Something's missing here. Surely there's a way to make this more flavorful."

I can't say that occurred to me, no.

But such drab food...

Good Lord, man, it was only roasted bread! How delicious was it supposed to be? Let's not get carried away.

Well, then...

Yes? Spit it out!

What about the innovation you're internationally famous for?

Which one?

You know, spreading stuff on toast.

What about it?

It wasn't for the sake of flavor?

It had nothing to do with flavor—it happened by accident!

It did?

You Americans!

With all due respect, Monsieur, I'd appreciate it if you'd stop insulting my nationality.

What?! Get out of my house!

No. You gave me permission to interview you, and that's what I'm going to do. So just sit there, if you please, and answer the damn questions.

Hmmm... I'll say one thing for you, *mon vieux*: You have spirit. I like that in a man. You Americans!

Please describe precisely how and when you invented the concept of spreading fats and sweet substances and condiments on toast.

Fine, fine, Your Highness. Here's how it went: My father expected me to follow him into his trade, which was bricklaying. That's what a son usually did back then. But I had neither any interest in that work nor aptitude for it. And unlike many young men, I was bold enough to tell him so.

How did he react?

He beat me severely. My father was a remarkable man.

You told him you wanted to cook instead?

I *didn't* want to cook. I wanted to be an artist!

An artist?

Oh, yes. I was *obsessed* with art. I spent all my time drawing, drawing, drawing, night and day. I drew pictures of trees and people and tools and anything else that caught my eye. It was all I ever thought about. But we were not a wealthy family, as I've told you, and drawing paper was expensive. So I drew on anything I could get my hands on: walls, eggshells, even my own skin. It was a kind of mania...

Yes, and?

Well, one day, in June of 1927, I was sitting idle at the kitchen table when I was seized by an irresistible impulse to draw. A slice of stale toast lay on a plate in front of me, and apart from a little charring around the edges, it was entirely free of marks. Which made it, as far as I was concerned, a perfect surface for...

[Author's Note: At this point in the interview my recorder malfunctioned, creating a large amount of noisy staticups It was only when playing back the recording a week later that I realized the next three minutes of M. Tartine's speech had been rendered completely unintelligible. I sincerely apologize for the omission.]

...so, naturally, I took a bite. The combination struck me as strange at first, and yet something about it appealed to me. My father was at the table as well, engrossed in his newspaper, and I felt I should share my discovery with him. "Papa," I said. "Taste this."

How did he like it?

He took one look and flew into a rage, scolding me for not only spoiling a perfectly good slice of toast but also wasting expensive lard.

Would he taste it, at least?

Not even a nibble. In fact, he broke it into pieces beating me with it. I ended up with lard stains all over my shirt.

Your father sounds like a remarkable man.

He was.

Quite a tale.

Quite a tale, eh?

And the rest is history, as they say.

Yes. God knows, everyone's heard the story a thousand times from that point on. There's no point in going over it again.

I agree. There is one aspect, though, that in my opinion has never gotten the attention it deserved.

Which?

The reaction of the Serraters.

Oh. Most unfortunate! The Serraters Guild—*Les Denteleurs,* as they were called—were the union that specialized in cutting serrations—teeth, you know—into knives. They didn't like the spread-on-toast idea one bit. Up to that point, you must remember, knives had been for cutting only, and the idea of using one to spread soft, rich substances on bread struck the Serraters as effeminate and demeaning. Not only that, but they feared that a sudden demand for dull, toothless butter knives would drive them out of business.

Why did their opinion matter?

Why did it matter?! Sir, the Serraters were a very ancient and prestigious guild. They had been serrating the finest French knives for nearly five centuries. And they had connections: the ranks of honorary *Chevaliers de la Dentelure* reached into the highest levels of the government.

I see.

Those were frightening times. Threats were made against me and my family, and *Denteliste* vigilantes stopped many bakers from toasting bread altogether. Which, well, you can just imagine what that meant for the working people of France.

No more crunch?

Precisely. Almost overnight, the average Frenchman's life was drained of what little crunch it had.

My God.

Dark, dark days—it pains me to recall them. Eventually, barricades went up in the streets of Paris, and soon the government simply ground to a halt. It went on like that for days; thousands perished.

What finally broke the impasse?

You Americans!

I asked you to stop that.

No, I'm saying one of you solved our problem.

An American?

Certainly!

Who?

Why, Josephine Baker, of course. Every French child over the age of eight knows this—what on earth do they teach you in American schools?

Josephine Baker, the nightclub entertainer?

Bien sur—she was an absolute sensation! She'd been in France only a year or two, but she had the country eating out of her hand. Those breasts!

How did she manage it?

Her beautiful voice, her dancing—so, so *sauvage*—and those breasts! My God, what marvelous breasts!

I mean how did she manage the toast problem?

With unbelievable ease! One day, some fans of the new style of toast paid her a visit, hoping to win her to our side. They brought samples, and when they offered her a taste she was very impressed; she thought they were marvelous. Right then and there she decided to incorporate a song about toast into her nightclub act.

That's it?

Not quite; there was one more step. In a brilliant *coup de grâce*, she offered to perform a concert exclusively for the Serraters Guild. What a thrill; what an honor! Within hours, every last bit of resistance had evaporated!

And that was all it took?

Listen, *mon ami*, that was plenty! In those days, one word from Josephine Baker could move mountains! People said she was the greatest thing since sliced, oh, sliced *something*—I forget what they compared her to. And those breasts! The first time I laid eyes on them, I forgot who wrote *Les Misérables*!

Impressive.

But don't think she stopped at toast—not on your life! Less than two years later she worked a similar miracle for my latest creation: whipped cream.

You invented whipped cream?

The outcry! Ferocious! People called it sacrilegious, an unforgivable insult to the traditional runny cream. They tried to hound me out of the country!

I had no idea you...

And even that pales in comparison with the unrest of November 1936, when I introduced the hamburger.

Hamburger?!

—she snuffed out the clamor as if it were a candle on a birthday cake! She was a goddess!

You invented the—

All I can say is, thank heaven for Mademoiselle Baker. Without her, I would have... She...[*breaks down*]...she...I could never thank her enough.

I really had no idea.

Good Lord, those breasts!

Really, the hamburger?

Sheer perfection! It's such a shame you weren't around to see them.

Well, Monsieur Tartine, I hardly know what to say. This has been a real education. I appreciate your taking the time to speak with me.

You're most welcome.

I hope it wasn't too much of an inconvenience.

Don't mention it. The pleasure was mine.

I guess I'll be going, then.

No, wait!

Yes?

Before you leave, I'd like to say I'm, uh, sorry for kicking you out of my house.

No problem. I guess I could have been a little more polite.

Not at all! It's just, well, one gets short-tempered in one's old age...

I completely understand...

And I am, as you know, French...

Yes.

May I tell you one other thing?

Certainly.

I want you to know that you are without a doubt the brightest, most insightful interviewer I've ever had.

Oh, now…

I'm not joking. Your questions, they were so well thought-out. They really got the wheels turning in my mind. Very refreshing!

It's nice of you to say so.

And so good-looking, too!

Monsieur Tartine, please…

But I suppose you hear that all the time…

Now and then, I guess.

In fact, you know, I have a good mind to…

What?

Yes, by golly, that's what I'm going to do: I'm going to call your boss and insist—*insist!*—that he pay you double for this interview. At *least* double.

You're embarrassing me, Monsieur…

No, don't even *think* of trying to talk me out of it! I can be very stubborn when I've made up my mind about something. Just give me your boss's phone number.

But…

Immediately!

Oh, all right.

[*A Note on the Translation: French is a language replete with poetry and nuance. It is possible that the word translated here as "hamburger" was actually intended to refer to "cassoulet" or "crêpes suzette."—B. Foy*]

ORFEO'S OYSTER

Marjorie Sandor

be loved the sea—does anyone know that about him anymore? It's music this and music that, the woodland animals coming his way and children following in a dance, when the truth is, he only dreamed of water. Not just any water, either, but the kind between fresh and salt, and the first briny taste on the tongue. That was what gave him hope, for it was in such a place that he saw his bride go out, playfully waving, then disappear for good. It was in an estuary like this, with its deceptive calm, blue herons lifting their heads, then gazing back down to something darting beneath—something he couldn't see—that he felt it most possible to begin his search. Here was a threshold; a place where one world might falter before the pull of another.

So it was that he floated on his back and let the water lift him. Musician that he was, he understood that a lift must necessarily lead to a fall. He lay on his back and waited, and, as he did, the brine settled on his tongue and sang her own little melody to him, a melody of blue autumns, of ancient beds where a story so old nobody knew it anymore still played its melancholy song of waiting, of the hope for reunion and return.

So the brine seduced Orfeo, gathered him to herself just as the dark distance once angled for Eurydice and took her away. Eyes closed, he floated and listened—was this song real? Was this the song that would help him bring her back? Maybe it was, because he swore he heard a strange, high keening. Then the world went greeny-black, and he seemed to sink.

They say he didn't recognize her at first. Her pink skin had gone a silvery-gray from being down there so long, and she wore a frilled and scalloped collar of black. She wore it like a slave, her head hung down, but all of her shining, nonetheless, in that watery light. Once she lifted her eyes, but they'd gone silver too, like polished candlesticks reflecting dim flames, from where he could not tell. But he also knew where he'd seen that light before. It had been in her blue-grey eyes the day they met, oh even on the day they wed. It was always there, and now he understood. Something had been waiting for her down here, just the way he waited up there.

He was told, and absolutely understood, the conditions of the deal. The rules, the required discipline, the likelihood of failure. Who can blame him for trying? He held on longer than any of us could have. But on the journey out, the mortal part of him began to rise, to hunger. He'd never felt more alone, more lost, even the sound of her breathing disappeared, and all his cherished memories, one by one. But he was stubborn, and as he threaded his way through passages that wound like dark arabesques, he heard a new music: one with corners and detours and sudden drops where there should have been a rise. It refracted and dappled and the melody vanished for days at a time. He'd been a musician a long time, and had some faith in the return of melody. He'd heard longer journeys than this on land. There—on land—the melody always came back, eventually. But this—this was different. This was something else.

Is that what made him turn, just a little too soon? Was it the lure of a new music, a kind in which melody didn't have to come back? A music that his bride, for all her tenderness, must have known about and kept secret, a seed in her heart?

Or was it that other sound, the terrible keening that grew now, a chorus of all the dead, wanting to take advantage of an opening, and rise along with her?

Everyone knows what happened next. How, leading her out, he couldn't resist a backward glance. And, for a second, there she was: a candlestick of silvery grey with her fading hint of flame. Her little ruffled collar of black. Then blackness, all.

And Orfeo stood, dripping and alone, cloaked in estuarine mud, his hands empty but his heart damp and full of weird new music, the color of herons, autumn, grief.

So the oyster waits in its shell, sometimes with a seed made against grit and desire, let in by the smallest breath. It's no accident that there is always music playing when you approach an oyster—if you dare approach at all. Nor is it accident that the oyster is not for everyone. It's a peculiar taste, a silken worry to the tongue, so tender it seems wrong.

But this won't stop you from hurting yourself, trying to pry one open at a party. And it's why, in the company of friends, you might feel suddenly alone—melancholy and ecstatic all at once. Take a moment. Notice that you hold in your hand a knife, and in your blood a startling, unreasonable urgency. And that when at last you put your tongue to the ruffled collar, you feel first a shudder of longing, and then an unaccountable desire to close your eyes.

Angel on Horseback

Wrap a petite oyster in a 2-inch piece of
bacon and secure the bundle with a toothpick.

Roll it in breadcrumbs, and broil till
bacon is done, turning once.

HEART, CHOKE, LEAVES

Jill Foulston

I.

While it was still dark and damp one morning I struggled out to the kitchen garden, expecting the mud to suck at my boots. About a week before they'd felled my favorite tree, one my father had told me about, one his father's father had planted. I cried when they cut it down, because I'm sure there are none left now. Not in this country, perhaps not in the whole world.

The fruit of that tree was the thing. Cup-shaped, smooth and wildly unsweet. You think of a fruit as being something to eat after a meal, but this was more like something to start it with. The flavor was watery, bitter and good with pulses, stews, even certain types of game.

I'd slip it into a bird and the tongue would find its velvet against the stringy flesh, the caramelized onions, the sauce-drunk bread and sage. Or I'd boil it whole, and reward its hollow with melted spiced butter. Some said it didn't mix with wine, but then what goes with what is always a personal view, and one that I, as a cook, rarely share. At this stage, it hardly matters. The tree is gone, and with it its fruit.

I took my hoe to the ground, not yet frozen, and wondered about a landowner who could order such an act, and a gardener who would follow it through. This walled patch full of herbs and salads, fruits and vegetables, the odd flower, is my territory, really—and yet the gardener marched in and took the one plant I couldn't replace. My most cherished growing thing. It was *not* a mighty tree, *not* one that grew to great heights or could be climbed. It did *not* demand much space. Its bark was strong but its structure weak. In the autumn, silvery grey disks hung thickly over its limbs like plaintive moons open to the sky, the leaves having dropped to the soil below, weeks earlier, to mix with the earth.

How could he do it? It took little or no time to fell. What had it become, then—part of the new barn? Firewood? A fiddle? Cradle for the next illegitimate child? Until that morning, I had refused to look at the scar where it used to stand.

I leaned my hoe against the garden wall and collected the rake. I dragged the rake through clots of earth as rain began to seep through my woollies. I wiped my leaking nose on my sleeve and shivered, scanned the clots for anything edible, something left at the tag end of the year. Harvest over, the dead season stretching into infinity, almost. Although the sun was up, it wasn't light.

A stone caught in the teeth of my rake. I shook the rake, but the stone wouldn't budge. I wasn't in the mood to argue—my back was already aching (I'd be no good the rest of the day) and I couldn't bend over to remove the thing, so I went to bash the rake against the wall. In anger. In hope that the stubborn thing would go flying.

The rake clanged against the brick and the stone plopped to my feet, soft as a bird's nest. My toes curled in expectation, fearing to take the brunt of its force, before I knelt to the ground and felt around.

And I knew that damp texture. It was the feel of my cat's tongue.

I cradled it, ran my fingertips round the disc's rough edges, put its chunk to my nose and took in the scent, still crisp and living.

I looked around, trying to detect through the secret fog any moving shape. I saw none. If I put my prize back where I found it, what then? Was it possible that the tree might grow again from this, its fruit? No harm in wishing.

At my side hung a bag of coarse cloth, its sides collapsed instead of bulging, as they do in spring, summer and autumn, with jewels of the underworld. Into it I placed the silver-grey wodge, rubbing my thumb against its dented flesh like a talisman. Planning my last meal.

II

Dearest Isabelle,

It was a horrible journey, with the carriage jolting all the way, the other passengers smelly and rude. Our parents have sent me to my cousin's house to keep me from unsuitable attachments in town—and also, I think, to hide their misery from me—. The quiet here in the country is immense and unendurable, used as I am to the street cries, the traffic of the city.

There were several days of rest, and settling in, before Emmeline took me to the village, where the country folk gawped at us, tugged at our dresses. We threw sweets at them and carried on our way. They frightened me somewhat.

It is a huge house, with so many servants that I am prompted to wonder if my cousin's family have not more money than ours? But I tell you, Cook is the oddest creature. Emmeline started giggling one evening after supper, didn't stop until Uncle scowled at her. She told me later, it was because of something she had discovered in Cook's room.

"Do you often enter the servants' rooms? At home, we prefer to stay in our own portion of the house."

Emmeline guffawed, most unbecomingly. "Here? If you don't show them their place, they'll soon show you yours! They'll take over, front and center. Believe me, dear cousin, they're used to it. And anyway, their property is our property, is it not? What do they have that we haven't given them?"

Which made our discovery all the more shocking.

Emmeline had decided that Cook needed humbling. She'd gone exploring in her tiny room a day or two before I arrived and now took me by the hand to show me what had made her laugh, in that tiny cupboard under the eaves. (In our house, sister, Maman has stopped putting her old hat boxes in that space because of the mice.)

I felt uncomfortable. The house was dark and complicated, unfamiliar to me, and I didn't like what we were doing. But I am stuck here with Emmeline for months to come, and I could not see a tidy way of objecting.

We pushed open the door, and Emmeline fairly skipped over to a low chest of drawers under a skylight. The bottom drawer moaned as she teased it out, slowly, carefully. She reached toward the back, in the left corner. Held out a knitted sock and asked me to feel inside and guess its contents. I was not allowed to look.

My hand squirreled down the flaccid woollen tubing—a bedsock, by the looks of it—and my fingers met a cold, pasty thing. Goose-fleshed, moist and rounded, with a sort of feathery roughness to the edges. It was not nice to touch. I was unhappy in that cramped room, pawing through Cook's festering property (luckily there was no smell as such). The game was fast losing its charm.

You remember what Emmeline is like, don't you? She became impatient, flung the sock away. She shoved a grey disc under my nose (I swear she touched me with it! foul girl) and now her laugh was nasty.

"What do you think this is, silly!" Her eyes spat at me while her fingers scampered nervously over the bristles of

Cook's hairbrush—, collecting loose hairs. She took these, curly and dull, wound them round and round the disc, ran back through all the dark corridors. Ran with it, fast, beyond the stone walls, down to the brook that borders the property, her manic laughter trailing her like dirty laundry. I followed until I saw her fling it into the water and then I turned back, ashamed and angry, not knowing—

Shh!! someone's coming. I must stop!

III

I've had enough, you know. One moment you're sleeping peacefully, the next someone's tugging you from your loamy bed. It gets worse.

It wouldn't have been so bad if I had stayed hidden in that woolly tunnel. At first I felt myself on the verge of expiring there, but at least it was warm and quiet. Then other fingers began smudging me, interfering with me, pressing at my yielding flesh. Not like the first fingers, which pulled me up from my dreams. These would rough me up a bit, toss me back in the tunnel, rough me up again. There was no denying it. I was beginning to molder. My shape was changing.

Perhaps I had begun to smell. At any rate, one day I was clotted and bound with, what? some sort of flaxen thread? and hurriedly thrown into running water. An odd cackle accompanied the toss. I guessed from the motion and the icy puffs of air that I must be outside again, and after I got over the shock of the chill, I thought to myself, *Ah, I can relax now, it won't be long before I'll sink to the bottom of this stream and melt into its bed.* I wasn't too frightened of nourishing a fish, either. One stomach's as good as another, in my book. I settled in to float for a while.

But no. The next thing I knew, a spike punctured me, a leaf with a thorn—whatever! and it stuck. These things are random. Yet now I realized that instead of moldering, I'd be suppurating. The idea did not appeal.

Somehow, though, the dart-that-stuck had the effect of calming my movement, of slowing me down. I nudged against the bank once, twice (who was laughing at me *now*?), and then the water surged drunkenly, and I found myself lying on a flat jetty of earth above the stream. It was dark, and the eyes of beasts burned into the deep space all around me. Droplets rilled over my ruff.

I wasn't having any of it. Lord knows, I'm not afraid of the dark, but I was not about to put up with any more meddling. I shifted. (Okay, I *am* afraid of the dark.) I wanted something round me—to veil me from others, to shield my sight. To protect me.

I started rolling. Little by little, softness clung to me. Leaves pale and tender, almost transparent at first (matter most decayed?), so that I could still peek out from between their veiny skin. Then firmer, clutching me more tightly, each tipped with a tiny spine. Like a pinecone.

I kept nosing the mossy soil, my strength gathering even as I disappeared from view. I rolled and I rolled. At times I fell asleep, I'm sure of it, the gentle rhythm lulling me on.

Stillness finally woke me. Or the sound of the waves. I could smell the briny water, hear it pounding the shore,

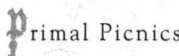

even if I couldn't see for beans. And oh! the mist. I knew its color—violet-blue—like I knew my own heart.

It was here I'd put down roots.

Artichoke and Lemon Pesto

6 artichoke hearts
⅛ cup rich, fruity olive oil
2 fat cloves of garlic
¼ cup ground almonds
rind from 2 or 3 lemons (to taste)
salt and pepper
dried hot pepper (optional)

Take 6 artichoke hearts, preferably just boiled or roasted and not canned or marinated. Mush by hand or blend in a food processor until not quite smooth. From the olive oil, take a tablespoon or so and sauté the garlic cloves over low heat, taking care not to brown them or they will taste bitter and ruin the pesto. Add the ground almonds (holding some back if the mixture seems dry), the rest of the olive oil, the rind of 2 lemons, salt and pepper to taste.

Makes enough sauce for 2-4 servings of pasta (depending on greed) or to feed a week's surreptitious filching by spoon from a container in the fridge.

SOFT PRETZELS

Lisa Stock

Once upon a time in a dark, foreboding forest between the borders of two kingdoms was an old woman who lived in a house made of candy. Its red licorice roof, and yellow lollipop windows were not dulled by the shade of the trees. Its gingerbread doors and cookie dough walls overcame the smell of moss and fungi growing on the forest floor. And every child who ran by was drawn to its delicious trap. But it was brittle, and sticky, and every time the door slammed a chunk of candy cane gutter would fall to the ground shattering like the children's hopes of ever finding their way out again. Then one night when the old woman lit the fire and fell asleep, forgetting about the veritable fondue she lived in, the house melted down to a lump of hard sugar and was pecked away by blackbirds, escaped from a pie on her windowsill.

Yet, her neighbor could do no better. She was a lonely widow caught up in her mourning and misery. Her house was a log cabin that coughed soot from its chimney the same sickly grey as her skin, veiling the sky above. With no sun, the widow's garden wouldn't grow. It was overrun with weeds, and guano from the birds that ate too much sugar. Her cupboards, therefore, were bare. And the only company she ever drew were the hungry, stray dogs circling outside her door, waiting for her to come out.

But wait, look there, just skirting through the trees—a house being carried on its hinges! Even amidst the shadows of the forest, it is almost too grotesque to glimpse! Its walls are made of *human bones* and they say the woman inside has eaten every person who ever walked over her threshold. We dare speak no more of it, lest the hag within should hear, and run our way seeking our skulls for doorknobs.

A sad, dark forest you say? Perhaps. But there is one more house. Across the brook tucked away from the stench of deceit is a house where every queen must venture to give birth. Every child born to a king has breathed their first inside this cottage and left with their fate intact.

Its moist, stone façade is blanketed with ivy, and ropes of woven poppies. The windows are shuttered against the sunlight and opened only when the moon is full. This is when the queens arrive barefoot, alone, and with no map to guide them. They walk from their bedchambers in trance, unseen by sleeping handmaids, and disappear into the wooded land between their world and the next. They pass under the watch of the stars, and over the paths where wolves have followed little girls, and cats have lain in wait to rob them. Two hearts inside her body leading her on in the night.

And it was just past the widow's garden when Marta, Queen of Plaquemine, awoke.

She couldn't take another step. The pain in her back was unbearable, the child was as heavy as her husband, and she thought she'd give birth through the crack splitting her head in two.

Then it all went away.

The breeze cooled the sweat from her brow, and for a moment she heard her mother's voice.

A curtain dropped in the window of the widow's house. Marta was thirsty and tired. She made herself walk to the door and knock.

No answer.

The wood around the garden sank into itself, disappearing into the dark, as the moon dropped lower in the sky. She didn't know where she was, but knew enough not to press the matter if a ghostly house wouldn't let you in. As she tiptoed past the sleeping dogs the house knocked back from inside, but never opened its door.

Marta headed deeper into the forest, the beating heart inside her growing stronger with every step. When once she strayed to the side, following the light of fireflies, the baby's heart skipped and stopped. She rushed back to the path she was on before and it started to beat again.

She slowly walked on into the darkness until she heard the splash of water. A brook cut through the trees, enticing her to drink. Oh, what a cruel joke the gods played putting the vessel to quench her thirst at her feet—no longer within her bending reach. Instead, she sat on a fallen tree and let the sound of the water wash over her, carrying away all thoughts she had of thirst and pain. She hadn't been alone since she was a child, and suddenly found herself grateful for the solitude. Why did she feel no fear? Why was she not panicked to find her way home?

The baby's heart inside her fluttered.

Marta stretched her legs and felt the tall grass at her hips as she ran through the field after her brother. Her little feet unable to keep up with his bounding stride, she gave up to lie down in the grass and watch the clouds go by. This one a horse, that one a rabbit and that one the prince she would one day marry standing in front of the castle they would live in with its moat and drawbridge and chickens and tower of magicups All in one cloud. All in one dream. But as soon as it drifted away she jumped up and started running through the grass again.

What would the child she carried see in the clouds? What would it dream for? Perhaps more than she. Perhaps it would want to see more of the world than what is brought to it on platters, or pulled through the sky by the wind. She heard her mother's voice again, but it was drowned out by the pain promising to split her womb in two, while at the same time digging its claws in to hold it together at all costs. Back and forth. Back and forth. It came in waves of light and dark until she gave out a cry to wake every slumbering spirit under the earth!

Then all fell silent. And this time when it all went away, everything else did too. Marta could no longer hear the water, or feel the breeze, and the moon hid itself deep in the branches of the trees. Standing across from her on the other bank of the now still brook was a house picked up on its hinges, chicken feet reaching to the ground, and every eye socket of every skull of its walls turned to look at her.

She dared not breathe. The tiny heart inside her slowed not wanting to call it any closer. The house swayed where it stood. It leaned over the water then back toward the bank. It turned to the trees and back to the moon. Perhaps, she thought, the empty eye sockets couldn't see. But then it took a step toward her. One clawed foot at a time, down the bank into the water and up the other side. It wavered in front of her, tipping its face to the moon. Was it smelling something? Her sweat? Her sudden choke of fear?

The house looked back, dropped its walls and settled down in front of her. The door scratched and rattled and pried itself open; the odor of rotting meat and days-old fish expelled itself from within. Nausea overcame her worse than the pain had before and she retched over the tree where she was sitting.

The baby's heartbeat was so faint. Her own beat twice as hard. Never had she known such fright. She was alone and lost, and wanted her mother's protection now more than ever. The canopy of the forest fell in and their lives were about to be snuffed out. One before it even began. "Enough," she said aloud to the house. No. This is not what her child would find in the wood. They would not succumb to its hunger. She covered her stomach with her hands, and mustering every ounce of courage, looked into the mouth of that foul refuge of death and said, "Leave us."

The house sat quiet. A candle flickered on a table throwing the echo of a perverted figure on the back wall. Pipe smoke blew out at Marta, the door slammed, chicken feet rose again, and it was gone.

The forest breathed once more. The water in the brook trickled on and the moon leveled itself to the horizon. Marta blessed herself—an afterthought of protection— then pushed herself up from the tree. Behind where the house of bones had stood was a cottage, shutters open, and the smell of fresh baked bread filled the air. She gathered her strength, crossed the brook and made it to the door— which opened before she could knock.

"Come in," an elderly woman with a kind, plump face and thick, silver hair, said, gently pulling her to a chair. "Come in, come in. Marta of Plaquemine, you've finally made it! We've been waiting all night for you."

Marta looked around. The room was small and cluttered with stacks of chairs and sacks of flour dangling from the ceiling. A fire, over which a pot of water boiled, crackled in the corner. Sitting in chairs against the walls were a dozen other expecting queens—panting, sweaty, glaring at her and each working a ball of dough in her hands.

"Were they made to wait for me, too?" Marta asked the old woman.

"No!" the woman laughed. "A child to be born waits for no one. They'll pop when they're ready." She laid her hands on Marta's stomach and closed her eyes. "Oh my dear! You've been through much. It's no wonder you woke early. Near the widow's cottage, I think—that's a good sign though. It means longevity for this one."

A long life, Marta thought. That's good. She wished her mother had had the same. But she was gone before Marta had even taken her own first breath. Before she could know the difference between cloud princes and real ones. So many days lost, so many times she thought she heard her voice.

"Look at me, Marta." The old woman's eyes were full of pride. "You have waited for joy long enough. Your mother's namesake is inside you. You have a girl."

"A girl," she repeated to three women who suddenly appeared near the fire. They were all statuesque with long red hair like the fire, and serene expressions that immediately put Marta to ease. The old woman held out her hand and one of the three placed a ball of dough into it.

"Here," she gave the ball to Marta, "squeeze every time your belly does."

"What is it?"

"Your child's fate, get to work." The old woman went to tend another queen. Marta looked at the fire, but the three redheads were gone. The dough was cold and stuck to her fingers. A sudden pain pulled at her stomach and she sank her hands into the dough.

A flash of green before her eyes. Then the vision of a tree on a hill.

"This one's ready!" called the old woman as she led another queen to a room in the back.

Marta twisted the dough in her hands. Another glint of the tree, and the sound in the room went dead.

"What is this?" she asked the old woman when she returned. The woman patted her hands and wiped her brow, but Marta could not hear her words. She began to roll the dough into a rope—a girl trapped in a tower. No. She molded it back into a ball. It stuck to her fingers again, and she started to pull it apart in long strings—a girl sleeping among the vines and thorns. No. She quit kneading and the room came back. The queen across from her sat with the same long strings of dough, but hers had turned into golden threads.

"Keep working, my dear," the old woman encouraged Marta. She took the queen with her golden threads to a room in the back.

Another pain gripped her stomach and Marta clutched the dough—the tree raced toward her. Its vibrant green leaves shimmered under the sun. She pulled her hands out of the dough to wipe her brow and the tree disappeared. She worked it back into a ball—an apple and a girl. No. She threw it on the table and pounded it with her fist. The dough splintered into a thousand shards of glass—a girl running down a flight of steps away from a castle, one shoe left behind in her haste.

"Come my dear." The old woman put her arms around Marta and led her away from the others. The dough lay in tatters in her grasp.

"Wait, no," she said. But the old woman took her into another room. The dirt floor smelled faintly stale though the shutters were still open to the twilight of dawn. A small bed took up half the room next to a fireplace, and a table the other half.

"Would you like to lie down?"

Marta sat at the table. The old woman reached for the strips of dough.

"Wait." Marta held on to them.

"Work out what you see. And your daughter will make it come true."

Her womb wrung itself around the baby and she gripped the dough tighter than before. The tree again, but leafless and dead. Its branches twisting back on themselves in a mass of knots. A prince placing the slipper on the girl's foot.

"No." She dropped the dough on the table and scraped it off her fingers. "I will not mold that fate for her."

"You must, my dear!" The old woman handed the dough back to her.

"I cannot!"

"You must sculpt what you see. It is her fate and therefore yours too. If you deny this to her, you deny it to yourself and you will die. A mother lives to see her wishes for her daughter realized."

Marta held the formless mass in her hand. The baby's heart beat strong, but hers was uncertain and began to weaken. And suddenly, she heard her mother's voice more clearly than she ever had before.

(Her mother had died refusing to shape Marta's fate.)

But Marta wanted to live. She wanted to see her daughter grow to womanhood and cast her own potential.

"You must work what you see!" The old woman pressed the dough further into Marta's palms. "Please, my dear. For your daughter!"

The tree returned, twisted branches and glistening green leaves burned into Marta's eyes. She threw the dough down on the table and began pounding it flat, then rolled it into a strip and began twisting it back on itself, like the branches.

"What I see is a fate with no beginning or end, just infinite possibilities." She handed the shaped dough to the old woman. It was a heart with the ends crossing the middle and uniting the sides.

The old woman smiled and took it to the fire to bake.

The next day there was a grand banquet in the land to celebrate the birth of the princess. Lords and Ladies from neighboring realms came to pay their respects. Dukes and Duchesses arrived with lavish gifts. Beggars, jesters and monks visited her cradle one by one. And when it came time to feast they say the queen's cooks presented each guest with a spiral of baked dough. In honor of her daughter, she wished to bestow them all with courage, that each might live away from the shadow of the forest and in whatever house they wished.

Save, of course, for the children who wandered into the houses made of candy.

Ancestral Celestial Cocoa

½ cup sugar
1 heaping Tbsp. flour
1 heaping Tbsp. unsweetened cocoa powder
$^1/_3$ cup water
butter—optional

*In a small saucepan combine all dry ingredients and mix until
blended, no clumps. Add water and stir over LOW heat
until thick. As it begins to thicken remove from heat. Mixture
needs to remain liquid.*

Pour into a bowl and add butter if desired.

*This is a very rich sauce we called "Cocoa" in my family.
Some people call it chocolate gravy, but we served it in a bowl
like soup and broke our biscuits up and dropped them in.
It's not quite a fondue either, as you get the
whole bowl to yourself. Enjoy!*

KASHK-E-BADEMJAN

Aphrodite Désirée Navab

he fourth century BCE was a bad time to be born both Greek and Persian. The Persian-Greek wars devastated both sides of the empire, burning capitals and leaving distrust all around. My father was advisor to the court of Xerxes. He gave counsel on matters of state, but also on philosophy and medicine. A captured Greek singer stole my father's heart. He freed her and asked for her hand in marriage. She was frightened at first, but his kindness and earnestness slowly won her over.

I grew up in a home where Greek and Persian were both spoken but talk of war was forbidden. In times of peace we visited my mother's family in Athens for three months and lived with my father's family in Persepolis the rest of the year. We were four children, two boys and two girls. I was the eldest. We grew up with fairness and love.

One day, when I was eleven years old, a Greek stranger came. He had heard in town that he would find hospitality at our home. I did not trust this man. It wasn't just his blue eyes. Among both Greeks and Persians, blue eyes are rare and therefore feared to be signs of a dark force. There was also something sinister in his smile, which quickly turned to a scowl, when he thought no one was looking at him. But I was. I studied him. I was small. I was only a girl. Big men like that did not see me.

He is not who he says he is, I thought.

My parents were raised in each of their cultures to treat the stranger as family; to treat the guest as a god (for there had been gods in disguise, time and time again).

"What a lovely home," he would say.

I spat. My mother taught me to spit every time someone complimented us, to chase away the evil eye.

"But one has to do it discreetly," she said.

I saw my parents turn away, look over their shoulders, and spit silently. My younger siblings were not interested in the evil eye at all. They thought it was something that my parents invented to stop them from doing the things they liked. So they did not take heed.

"What a beautiful family," the stranger continued.

I spat again.

"How lucky you are. How fortunate I am to know you," he concluded.

I spat profusely.

The stranger noticed what I was doing. "Why is she spitting so much?" he asked, turning to my parents.

"Does she think I'm giving you the evil eye? I am only a traveler who needs rest and company," he added.

"Oh, don't mind her, she has a problem with her tongue," my mother explained, winking at me as the stranger walked toward the window.

"What fertile land you have," the stranger observed.

The back-to-back compliments seemed so insincere, as if he wanted to own everything he saw. *And this, and that, and this, I want.* I don't know why I was the only one noticing it.

As if she could read my mind, though, my mother came and stood next to me at that instant. She squeezed my elbow. I looked at her face and she winked again. Later that night, while the stranger was in the guest quarters, she went around the house with our house servant burning *esfand*, wild rue, which is used to chase away evil spirits.

Sometimes the stranger sat in the flower garden in front of our house and wrote on a leather scroll, while my mother was in the women's quarter and my father was busy at court. I climbed on a chair and peered onto his scroll.

"What are you writing?" I asked.

"Oh, just drawing things here and there," he said, pulling his scroll closer to him.

"What are you drawing?" I continued.

"Something in Greek that only grownups would understand."

"Can I take it to my mother, so she could read it to me?"

"No!" he yelled. He looked embarrassed at how loud he protested.

"You see, it's actually a surprise for your mother. You don't want to ruin it, do you?" he asked softly. Like his smile, his voice changed quickly.

He hid his scroll, almost holding it to his chest. This man was concealing something. What could it be? With the help of our house servant, I started protecting my home. I persuaded the cook to give us raw garlic from the kitchen and we hid it behind objects in every room. I wore my evil-eye necklace, which has a glass bead in the shape of a blue eye. Inside the large ceramic pots on the shelves against the wall, the house servant put water, oil and sugar for protection and sweetness in the home.

But how to discover the intentions of this man? My Greek grandmother taught me that eggplant is loved by both Greeks and Persians, and rarely would anyone on either side of the empires refuse such a dish. My Persian grandmother taught me that garlic wards off evil spirits, by the smell and by the increase in blood circulation.

"It has chased many an ill-meaning spirit from my home," she said to me, as she arranged the garlic around her house.

My father taught me that if you combine *kashk*, whey, with garlic and oil, it sits in the stomach like a king on his throne.

"Truth settles, solid and steady," Baba liked to say.

Armed with these teachings, I decided to test this man whose compliments and sly smile left my mouth dry.

A week had passed since the uninvited guest first arrived. My parents took him into town to introduce him to their friends. This is the day, I thought.

I gathered my brothers and sister and held a meeting in the kitchen. "Today is the day we find out what this stranger, who has camped out at our home, is up to," I announced.

"Why, what's the matter?" one brother asked.

"He seems odd, but have you seen him do anything bad?" asked my other brother.

"Well, he has a scary smile," my sister said.

"It's not that he is strange, and yes, he does have a fake smile, but it's what he's about to do that I want to figure out. I just don't trust him. This plan will prove me right or wrong."

"What are you up to, big sister?" one brother asked.

"How can we help? Do you want us to put insects in his shoes?" my other brother asked.

"No, it's about food. If we put gross amounts of garlic, kashk and oil in an eggplant dish, maybe if he is evil, we could chase him away."

"But what if our parents try it first and get sick? They will punish us all, when you are to blame, really," asked my sister.

"We will taste it first. Have I ever led you wrong?" I added.

"Yes!" they all replied. Then they giggled. Usually they are the ones who get me into trouble.

"Will you be serious? I do not have a good feeling about this man. Please help me put together something so potent that it will chase him away if he really means to do us harm. If it works, we save our family. If it doesn't work, well, our parents will be happy that we made a nice dish for them. I dare you. Are you mature enough to help me with this very secret mission?"

"Secret? Mature? Mission? We can do this!" my siblings agreed excitedly. "Count us in."

We divided up the labor. The house servant went with my brothers to the marketplace nearby and bought half a cup of kashk. With the gardener, my sister gathered thirteen cloves of garlic and three large eggplants from the vegetable garden, behind our house.

"The garlic will tell the truth, just as Baba says. If the guest is good he will stand it and stay, but if he is bad he will be sent away to the outer limits of the empire," I explained.

With the help of the cook, the four of us peeled and cut three large eggplants into thin slices. We chopped the garlic and mixed it in the olive oil. We poured the garlic-oil mixture into a cauldron over fire. We then threw in the eggplant. We covered the cauldron and let it cook until the eggplant turned very soft. We stirred the cauldron, chanting: "Evil spirit go away. Come again when goodness reigns."

After an hour, when the stew looked soft and brown, we threw in half a cup of kashk. It is salty and creamy, and turned the stew greyish-white. We stuck our fingers in it, one by one, and tasted it.

"What have you concocted, my dear sister?" one brother asked with delight.

"This is delicious," my other brother added.

"Mmm, mmm," my sister joined in.

I was last to taste it. "Oh! There is a lot of garlic! But none of you seem to be getting ill from it. It seems to work, but we will only know for sure once we try it on the stranger."

We hugged each other, jumping up and down. We poured the eggplant dip into a large ceramic bowl, and shaped it like the mountains which surround our home. My siblings and I topped the eggplant peaks each with an olive. We used my hairpin to make a rippling pattern up and down the eggplant mound, like the raked fields of Persepolis. We set the bowl on the table with warm naan, the flat bread curling at the edges from the heat of the oven.

Then the gardener, the cook and the house servant cleaned up all the clues, and were sworn to secrecy.

An hour later, my parents and the stranger returned.

"We made a dish for you while you were away," I said aloud, hugging my parents.

"Yes, we thought you were tired," my siblings joined in.

"That is so sweet of you, dear children," my parents said.

"What wonderful children you have," the stranger said.

I spat again. My siblings and parents did, too, over their shoulders.

"Please help yourself," my father said. "Guests go first."

"Are you sure? I've imposed on you enough," the stranger said.

"Yes, go ahead, there is plenty to share," my father insisted.

"Thank you, I don't mind if I do," the stranger replied.

He took a large piece of naan and dipped it into the eggplant. We stared at him, intensely, without blinking. He smiled broadly, chewing and smacking his lips in delight. But then his smile turned into a scowl as gurgling sounds arose from his belly. He grabbed his stomach, his face turned red and then his entire body jerked and quivered as if he was on fire. In fury and confusion, he glared at us. My parents moved to help him, but he turned, without a word, and ran out the way he first came in. We all stood staring at the door in stunned silence.

The stranger had left behind a small leather bag in the guest quarters. I fetched it from beside his bed and gave it to my father. He looked inside, trying to find some information about him. There was the scroll he had been working on in the garden. Baba unrolled it carefully. It was a map with Greek writing and he handed it to my mother. She was an unusual woman in that she could read and write. We watched her face turn to horror.

"It is a military map. There are notes on how to enter the town, and capture it. There are suggestions on how best to torch Persepolis!" she said.

We all rushed to hug each other.

My father said, "He was a foe, not a friend. He meant war, not peace."

"This explains why he was constantly complimenting us," I said. "He wanted to bring the evil eye into the house!" I said.

"And what was in that eggplant dish, my children?" our father asked.

My siblings pointed at me: "It was all her idea."

My parents smiled and my father sat me on his lap.

"Yes? What did you do and why?" he asked gently as my mother took a small bite and licked her lips.

"I put eggplant and garlic and kashk and olive oil together and hoped that it would chase any evil spirit away," I explained.

His look reflected all the tenderness and trust with which my home was blessed. "Good for you," he said. "We will call this dish: *Kashk-e-bademjan ma ra nejat kan* (eggplant with whey, please save us), and teach the recipe to all our people, so that they can use this simple remedy to sift the evil from the good."

Postscript

Centuries have passed and no one remembers that a young girl invented this eggplant dish in order to protect her home. Today, from Asia to North Africa, from the Middle East to the Mediterranean, variations of this eggplant dish exist: *baba ghanoush, melitzano salata, imam bayaldi, baigan ka bartha, chana baingan, gulla bhajji…*

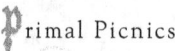

Kashk-e-Bademjan

Serves 6

3 big eggplants/*bademjan* peeled and thinly sliced
13 cloves of garlic peeled and finely chopped
½ cup or more whey/*kashk*
pinch of salt and pepper
6 Tbsp. of olive oil
1 kalamata olive

*Peel and cut the eggplants into thin, vertical slices.
Heat oil in a large frying/saucepan. Add eggplant and finely
chopped garlicups Cover and let fry for one hour on low heat.
Check and stir with wooden spoon, regularly. When eggplant
is soft, add* kashk. *Stir well with spoon and let fry for another
15 minutes uncovered. Remove from heat and put in ceramic
bowl to cool. Add salt and pepper to taste. Place kalamata
olive on top and use a fork in a downward motion to add
a raking texture to the mountain of food.*

Noosh-e-joon! (*May your soul enjoy*)

STARLIGHT MINTS

Gloria Frym

tarlight Mints sucking candy (as my relatives used to call all wrapped hard sweets) are peppermints with a taste and flavor akin to Christmas canes. For everyday use, they are a superior pick-me-up. They aren't food and yet serve causes far higher. They pack their punch in a diameter smaller than a quarter and larger than a nickel. A quick Google search will yield:

"Starlight Mints are an indie pop band from Norman, Oklahoma. The quirky quintet is nationally renowned in the indie scene for their creative juxtaposition of classical and pop elements in their musicups The band was formed in the '90s and has varied in size between four and seven members. The current lineup consists of Allen

Vest (vocals, guitar), Andy Nunez (drums), Marian Love Nunez (keyboard), Ryan Lindsey (keyboards/guitar) and Javier Gonzales (bass). Two previous members contributed to their sound on violin and cello. After releasing *The Dream That Stuff Was Made Of* in 2000 through the label See Thru Broadcasting, and *Built on Squares* in 2003 through Pias America, they signed with <u>Barsuk Records</u> in December 2005 and released their first album with the record label (*Drowaton*) on April 25th, 2006.

"Drummer Andy Nunez owns and operates the Polis, an indie rock venue in Norman, Oklahoma. The venue hosts both local and national acts."

I am deeply out of touch with most contemporary indie pop bands, especially those hailing from Norman, Oklahoma. Yet, there exists for me an uncanny conspiratorial connection between Starlight Mints, Oklahoma, poetry and my enduring love for these confections.

The affair dates back to the early part of the last decade of the last century when I was scheduled to read at the St. Marks Poetry Project in New York, second on the docket. Because I would present from my first published collection of "stories," nearly everyone I knew in the immediate area came out for this debut. Plus my co-reader had his audience. The Church was packed.

What amazing fortune to sit next to the poet Ron Padgett. He's from Oklahoma, where he teamed up with poets Ted Berrigan and Dick Gallup. Ron writes my idea of perfect poems. Utterly comprehensible and thoroughly mysterious. They aren't fancy. They are just so. Reading them, I always discover a place for the genuine.

During the first and what seemed like a long reading, as many readings seem to those who wait to serve, I did try to pay attention. Perhaps the metal chair squeaked a few times as I adjusted myself. However, nothing but instinctual kindness can explain Ron turning to whisper,

—Are you nervous?

—Oh yes, I whispered back.

—Sometimes this helps, he whispered back and reached into his coat pocket to hand me a peppermint Starlight Mint.

One of the world's oldest treats is the humble mint. Today we use mints as after-dinner breath fresheners, candy flavorings and in toothpaste, however mankind has been using mint for a variety of things for ages. The word mint is derived from Minthe, the mistress of Hades, the God of the Underworld. Legend has it that Hades and Minthe were romantically involved, which didn't make Hades' wife, Persephone, very happy. Persephone's anger led to turning Minthe into a plant, the sweet herb known as mint. The ancient Greeks were known to scatter mint leaves on the dead for two reasons. One: to cover the smell. Two: to remind Hades of his past.

Since Ron Padgett's loving gesture, I've carried Starlight Mints (or some knockoff) everywhere I go and offer them to those in need. Kindness, as the Dalai Lama says, is my religion.

Mint was also used by numerous cultures as a medical remedy and for cooking. Today mint is still used for these purposes. Peppermint is a popular remedy for colic, indigestion, headaches, gingivitis and rheumatism. It also has both anti-viral and anti-bacterial properties. You can also use mint leaves around the house to freshen smells and even repel ants. Mint is an easy herb to grow ...

Not beyond the scope of this account is a recent visit to the Bob Marley Museum, the Graceland of Reggae, in Kingston, Jamaica. Unlike Graceland, it is a modest two-story Victorian bought by the famous Rasta after growing up in Trenchtown, several miles away. Trenchtown cannot be compared to any place known to any person in the United States except maybe the homeless. The museum is located on Hope Road.

The guide was young and serious, as guides in historic places think it's their duty to be. She only knew what she was taught to know. After the tour of the rooms—Bob Marley's studio wallpapered with the musician's performance posters, Marley's upstairs private kitchen with a special blender for vegetarian Rasta food—we descended to what could have been a sun porch, except who needs sun porches in Kingston, Jamaica? The walls were pocked with bullets from an assassination attempt on Marley. We stepped even more lightly and mournfully into the garden.

This is a replica of Bob's Herb Garden. The pretty, dreadlocked guide pointed at two skinny marijuana twigs

about a foot high and some anemic mint growing in half
the size of a single bed. It was July. The three Italians and
two Germans on the tour snapped some shots with nice
single-lens reflex cameras.

—Mind you, said the guide, Bob used these herbs for
medicinal purposes.

Of course, we six nodded, sweating in the shade. It
is so hot in Kingston on a summer afternoon that the
only things moving are highly air-conditioned vehicles.
On Hope Road, in July, ants stay underground. The most
tended gardens wilt in the post-colonial sun. You have to
ascend to the lusher heights for giant Brobdingnag mint
growing by streams. There you will also find mangos the
size of watermelons hanging from trees north of Spanish
Town near the village called Time and Patience.

Don't forget our favorite use of all for mints—candy!
Nothing beats a cool, refreshing piece of mint candy.
Freshen your breath and enjoy the minty flavors you love.
Use individually wrapped selections at your establishment.
Customers always appreciate a tasty treat and who doesn't
love mints? These candies offer a refreshing "pick me up"
any time of the day, not just after dinner. Dentists, you
will love our assortment of sugar-free mints! Stock up and
hand these out as a sugar-free alternative.

My dentist does not hand out candy of any sort. He's
certainly very knowledgeable about the product Xylitol.
When I was under the drill a while back, my mouth duct-

taped open, he told me how this natural vegetable-base sweetener could actually remove plaque and remediate tooth decay. And how the sugar cane lobby has effectively monopolized artificial sweeteners. I like my dentist. He's down with all the latest research, he pays his assistants and hygienists decent salaries and gives them vacations in exotic locales, and they've all worked with him for at least twenty years. After we last spoke, I rushed out to a health food store and bought some gum with Xylitol. The first bite was the sweetest. By the third chew, all sweetness disappeared. I unwrapped a Starlight, popped it in my mouth and created the perfect cocktail.

Real sugar works like no other product. Sometimes some of my fabulously glamorous and perpetually fatigued art students rest their artistic heads on the table, snug in the crook of their elbows during class. Understandably, they work on projects for their studio courses until dew visibly coats the shrubs outside their dormitories. All I have to do is throw a Starlight Mint at a sleeper, and voila! he perks up, relieved to receive this modest gift of the gods.

Use them in recipes:
21. White Chocolate Candy Cane Fudge
22. Peppermint Four-Layer Cake
23. Chocolate Mint Layer Cake
24. Peppermint Ice Cream
26. Make your own Peppermint Ice Cream Sandwiches
27. Chocolate Candy Cane Sandwich Cookies
28. Candy Cane Chocolate Chunk Cookies
29. Candy Cane Brownies (these are vegan!)

30. Chocolate Peppermint Pinwheels
31. Peppermint Meringues
32. Add to Rice Krispies Treats
Candy Cane Cheesecake

Who among us has ever tried these remarkable concoctions? How often did Julia Child crush Starlights into slivers with the bottom of a sturdy French café glass? What average New Yorker would indulge in Candy Cane Cheesecake? New Yorkers may balk at the term "average," but surely not a single denizen among the many millions who live and work in and among the boroughs does not know cheesecake. Show the untutored one to me and I will enter him in the Guinness Book of World Records.

I put that first Starlight Mint into the deep side pocket of the Vietnam army surplus pea coat I wore then. Today the coat is hanging in New York while I am living in Berkeley. It is hanging in New York in a closet at Westbeth in an apartment where the great artist Helene Aylon lives and has lived since perhaps Ron Padgett decided to leave Oklahoma and make his way in Manhattan, where he doubtless knows her. Surely they know *of* one another, though given the way New Yorkers are, they could live on the same street and never meet.

About the pea coat from the Vietnam War, or as the Vietnamese call it, The American War, that's a story from another era. Era spelled backwards is are. All wars are not alike; some wars kill more people and keep inhabiting the future. It could be that one war leads to another.

Last time, I brought the coat to New York for another winter reading at St. Marks, but it just wasn't that cold, so I didn't wear it and that's how it came to hang in the closet. When I packed up to fly back to California, I left it, confident that the next time I took a winter trip to New York, it would be there, my friend would still be my friend, and snow would silence those charming cobblestone streets of the West Village.

The name of the owner of the pea coat is printed nicely on a piece of cloth well-sewn onto the inside back lining. Where did he learn such sturdy, basic stitches? Why would he need such a heavy coat in a tropical country? And what about the boy to whom it was issued?

We should not leave off without a body count: a hundred Starlight mints make a pound. Recently, on account of an about-to-expire gift certificate (given to me by a student at whom I'd thrown a Starlight), I visited a store, whose name shall not be spoken, whose structure has nothing to do with architecture though perhaps non-Euclidean geometry, with a friend who had lived abroad for almost a decade.

My dear friend and I roamed the aisles like terrorists. Cameras poised high on every post; there was really nothing we wanted and nowhere to hide. Near the checkstand, I grabbed a ten-pound bag of my favorite confection. It was on sale, as was everything in the store that called itself a city, a depot, a bunch of fabulous guys. We exchanged the gift certificate for the bag, and cantered out past the security guard who commanded us to have happiness that evening.

We descended to the parking lot with vertigo, amnesia, headache. Where was the car? When was dinner? Ten pounds of Starlights sagged through the thin plastic bag. Across the horizon stood the towers of Extended Stay Homes: Short Term Living at Its Best!

Hiking into the deeply parked distance, where the purple sky embraced the San Francisco Bay, we approached the car. A click of the remote and we climbed in. My friend slumped over the steering wheel. He moaned, he groaned, I was about to offer him the salutary mint.

—Oh, no, no. No. How did it come to this? How did America come to this—he kept repeating, his voice muffled by his muffler.

What could I say to such suffering? He persisted. Young persons drove up, squealing the brakes of their boxy yellow vehicle with tires the size of restaurant stoves. The familiar pounding bass only enhanced our mutual distress.

—O, my companion lifted his head. Oooo … oh …, oh no.

I ripped apart the tenacious plasticups Starlights spilled onto the car floor. Dusk had fallen during my companion's slumping phase. The dark was specked with clear stars. I shook him, he murmured, —Mmmm, Oo, oh … wha?

—Here, I said, as I unwrapped a candy. Here, try this, really, it will revive you.

—Cinnamon, he moaned, dropping his head back onto the steering wheel. Spearmint, he lisped and picked up his head and turned to me: not peppermint. Never peppermint.

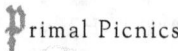
Starlight Mint Tea

Drop a Starlight Mint into a mug
with a bag of peppermint mint tea.
Pour in boiling water.
Sip. So sweet!

Euro Starlight Mint Tea

Pop a Starlight Mint into your mouth.
Drink a cup of peppermint tea while holding the mint
between your tongue and palate.

ROZHINKES MIT MANDLEN/ ALMONDS AND RAISINS

Lisa Trank

he house was freezing. A chill rose from the top of the blankets, which she held up to her chin. Meg took a deep, cold breath. At least she could smell that coffee was made. She pulled herself out of bed and slid her feet into slippers. She grabbed a sweater and knocked the temperature up five degrees. A game they played. He walked by and turned it down. She walked by and turned it up. This morning she could knock it up as high as she could stand it. He'd awakened early and taken the kids for a ski trip. She had the house to herself.

She poured a large cup of coffee, stirring in sugar and cream. Settling into the living room loveseat, she cradled the cup behind her right knee. A blanket was wrapped around her feet, which the dog shared. She planned to spend the entire day like this, a dog, hot coffee and uninterrupted time with the Sunday paper.

A brown truck screeched to a stop in front of her house. Out popped a delivery guy who was wearing shorts, despite the severe cold. He was built like a runner, lean and fast—the type to never turn the heat on at all. Meg chuckled as she watched him heave up the back of the truck and pull out the largest crate she'd ever seen. At first she thought it looked like a coffin, it was so large and substantial. She stared at it for a long time.

The delivery guy hoisted it onto a flatbed dolly and headed across the street toward her walk. She watched the delivery guy struggle up the walk, covered with snow. He gave one last yank up the front step to the porch and nodded his chin in her direction. She waited for him to ring the bell.

She stood at the large picture window for ten, fifteen seconds before she realized the coffin-sized crate was intended for this house. Her house.

She opened the wood door and cracked the storm door a couple of inches.

"Sign here, please."

"Are you sure this is for here? This address?"

The delivery guy pointed the pen for the electronic pad at the computer-produced address label. She lifted up her glasses and peered down at it. Her address was right there after "To." She scanned the "From" side to see an address in California she had to think about. Her brother.

"Can you sign for it? I'm already behind on the morning because of this thing. It weighs a ton."

"Sorry," she said as she scribbled her name across the pad. She opened the storm door to prop it open and started to direct him to take it into her living room, but he was already heading back to his truck.

"You should really shovel this walk. It's dangerous."

She pulled her sweater tightly around her waist and sipped her coffee. It was cold.

***

"H-he-hello?" A very sleepy voice slurred on the other line.

"Seth," she said. "It's Meg."

"Meggie, what's time is it?"

"Seven my time, which makes it…?" she waited for Seth's answer.

It was a game they'd played for years. Whenever they left each other messages, they'd always let the other know the difference in their time zones.

She was glad she'd waked him. She knew he rarely got up before ten.

"I got an interesting delivery this morning. Wanna fill me in?"

"Let me make some coffee and I'll call you right back," he yawned. "I promise."

Meg stared at this thing which took up most of the length of her porch. It was a good thing the delivery guy didn't try to bring it in. It wouldn't have fit through the front door and she was glad to not have to bear the weight of that inconvenience. Her mind drifted to a lifetime of crushed boxes and she put down her coffee. She grabbed the shovel and started to heave snow off the walkway.

"Hey, Meg, when you finish that, you want to do mine?"

It was their next-door neighbor, Dave. They'd lived next door to him for almost ten years and she'd never really had anything to say to him.

"Sorry, Dave, I only do one walk a day," she said as the phone rang.

"How's your coffee?"

"Black and sweet, just like I like it," Seth said, taking a big gulp. "You still drinking it like a girl?"

"You want to tell me what is going on?"

"You remember those crates Mary brought with her from South Africa?"

***

Mary was their grandmother, their mother's mother. They never called her *Grandma*, or even the more formal *Grandmother*, because she didn't like them to. The sound of it made her feel old, so it was always just Mary.

A friend of their mother's had called from South Africa to relate that Mary was losing touch with reality. Their mother, an only child, flew to South Africa, and fetched her from an apartment in Johannesburg and brought her back to a ranch house in Southern California. About two months later, the crates started arriving. They came in twos and threes, but after all had been delivered, there were forty-two of them. They were kept on the back porch, in the garage, anywhere they could be put. And they were huge. Substantial.

Mary wouldn't let anyone touch them. When their father threatened to burn the crates in a backyard bonfire, their mother was finally able to convince Mary to begin going through them. She gave in, but only in her room and only by herself. Every weekend, Seth and their father would drag a crate into Mary's room, but she never could manage to get through it. She'd close the door and the family would hear her weeping, muttering away in Yiddish.

"Of course, I remember Mary's crates," Meg said.

"Well, I guess there was one crate that was never opened. Mom discovered it when she closed the house."

"Okay," Meg said. "But why is it here, on my front porch?"

"Mom said to send it to you. She said you're supposed to have it."

***

Meg slid a flathead screwdriver under a corner of the crate. She worked slowly, afraid to splinter the old, dry wood. Once that corner came up, the rest were easy. But Meg hesitated before she lifted the top off.

The cat sat with its front paws perched on the crate, ready to take ownership.

"What do you want?" Meg said as she pushed her off and raised the lid.

The first layers were pipe cleaners, piles of them shaped into dolls and little animals: rabbits, dogs, cats, birds. Black, red, white, green, blue.

Under the pipe cleaners lay her mother's childhood drawings, rippled with dried watercolors and streaked pastels. None of them were signed.

Two hours passed. The front porch was scattered with a pile of shredded paper, now occupied by the cat. Paper dolls had been taped to the front window. A pink dress with a pinafore hung on the back of a chair.

Meg peered into a corner of the crate. She pushed away some scraps and saw a small blue satin bag, tied with faded red ribbons. She lifted the bag from the crate and held it in her hands, feeling something granular inside. She opened the bag as gently as she could, but the frayed ribbons disintegrated at her touch. She held the bag by a corner and tipped some of the contents toward her right hand.

A cluster of yellow rice and brown flecks fell into her palm. At her finger's touch, the rice crumbled into dust. Meg looked back into the bag and saw a small piece of paper, about as yellowed as the rice. She opened the bag as wide as she could and extracted the paper. She was afraid to unfold it, afraid it, too, would dissolve. She lifted one corner and then the next until the small square opened to a rectangle. She held the paper to the sun, which was just slightly poking through the clouds. The edges were slightly torn. There was writing on it, a fluid script that moved from right to left. The script followed a form Meg was familiar with. At first she thought it was Hebrew, but then realized her grandmother wouldn't have been able to write Hebrew. None of the women of her grandmother's generation were allowed to study Hebrew. With the little she could make out, Meg recognized the script as Yiddish, written in Hebrew letters. The distinct smells of cinnamon, ginger and smoke seeped from the paper. Meg held the bag upside down and poured the last few grains of rice and spices into her hand. She put them into a small glass bottle and set it in the window.

***

Mary couldn't keep anything down. The doctor and her husband pushed her to eat more for both her and the baby's sake, but nothing seemed to want to stay in her system. She wasn't hungry for anything, except for rice pudding. Her mother's rice pudding. She nearly drove Boris crazy as she nagged him to search through their steamer trunks to find the blue satin bag. It took him three days and long nights, but finally, he emerged triumphant with the bag held high in the air.

Mary made Boris leave the room before she would open the bag. She took out the thin piece of paper. She held it to her chest, then down to her small, bulging belly and took the first deep breath in weeks.

Boris spent the rest of the afternoon running all over Frankfurt in search of the ingredients. No substitutes would be accepted, Boris knew that much. And since it was the first time in their married life of eight years that Mary had ever showed a domestic inkling, he didn't want to jinx it. His search took him to the dairy for a quart of the freshest and thickest cream and even fresher eggs. From there he went to the spiceman for freshly ground cinnamon, ginger powder and vanilla beans. The ginger had to be from China and had to be the color of a lemon. Lemons! He'd forgotten the lemons. Where would he find lemons at this time of year? He asked the spiceman if he knew where to get lemons and was told of a location on the other end of town. But it would close in less than thirty minutes, so Boris paid and grabbed his bags.

The owner was just about to pull down the chain fence when Boris turned the corner. He pleaded with the owner to let him in to buy the lemons. The owner shook his head, but when Boris offered to pay double, as well as two tickets for the troupe's new show, the owner let him in.

He proudly checked the list. Cream, whole milk, eggs, cinnamon and ginger, honey, vanilla. Lemons. Golden raisins and almonds. Plum wine.

Mary was pouring hot water into a bowl containing white rose petals (from last night's theater bouquet) when she heard Boris coming up the stairs, huffing and puffing. The stove, never used before, warmed the small flat and was bubbling with boiling water in pots. She inspected the parcels and pointed to where they should be stored. She nodded her head and Boris put them down, neither of them saying a word.

She warmed the honey jar in her hands and poured just the right amount, stirring constantly as the warm water, saturated roses and honey mingled. She cut and sliced, adding the rest of the ingredients with her eyes almost closed, as if in a trance. She poured the mixture into a large white ramekin and set it in the oven.

Less than an hour later, Mary carried the pudding to the table, wrapped in a muslin towel. She took out two bowls. Boris looked up from his paper and came to the table without a word. With a simple sense of ceremony, Mary spooned two generous heaps and sat down. She waited for Boris to take the first bite. He held the spoon up to his nose and inhaled the flavors. It was as if all the places they'd ever traveled to, all the cities they'd performed in, were contained in this little white bowl. He took another bite. This bite contained not only where he and Mary had been, but all the places his or her people had ever lived in, and been forced to leave. He smiled at Mary and she smiled back. They slowly ate one spoonful after another, then one bowl after another, until the pudding was gone.

"Where did you learn to make that pudding?" Boris asked later that night. He was curled against her back, his favorite way to fall asleep; his nose nestled in her hair, his hands on top of hers, both pairs on her belly.

"I'll tell you, but only once. Then, never ask me again."

***

The morning was foggy with the melting of a late spring snow. Mary loved to run across the field before her mother and sisters were awake. She played a game of cat and mouse with them, hiding in trees while they did the morning chores. She knew they would never stay angry with her, the blue-eyed fairy of the family. She was the youngest and the family favorite, especially of her mother, Racheli.

She was climbing down her favorite tree when she heard what sounded like distant thunder. She saw a cloud of dust that seemed to grow larger with every second. She ran across the field and to the back of the house. Just as she was opening the door, a hand reached and pulled her behind the huge black stove that took up almost one wall of the kitchen. Two of her sisters were crouched there. She was just about to ask what game they were playing, when the thunder came closer. One sister clasped her hand over her mouth and Mary knew from the look in her eyes to not say a word. The hand slowly dropped and the three breathed in rhythm with tiny, shallow breaths.

She heard the sound of breaking glass and the boom of the front door being broken down. Mary could see through the grates in the stove what looked like a sea of dark boots. Some of the boots stomped upstairs and then she heard her other two sisters and her mother screaming as they were being dragged down the stairs by their hair.

One sister's hand pushed down hard on Mary's shoulder. Her other sister had one hand on Mary's knees. They both tried to cover her eyes, but Mary shook their hands off, coming close to biting them. Her sisters dropped their hands to their sides.

Even though she was not yet fourteen years old, Mary understood what she saw next, her sisters' and mother's dresses being cut off with sabers, the men's trousers falling to their knees and more screams. Her mother jerked her face away to the side and squinted to catch Mary's blue eyes staring at her from behind the stove. A gloved hand grabbed her mother's face back and Mary watched as a line of blood trickled from her neck. The screams stopped. The boots left as they came, breaking whatever hadn't already been broken.

Mary and her sisters sat frozen behind the stove. When the smell of smoke began to choke them, her older sister pushed Mary out. Mary wanted to stay behind the stove and go up in flames with her mother, but her sister dragged her by her hand toward the back door. Mary broke free of her sister's grasp and ran toward her mother's limp and bruised body. She covered her with her own body and waited to feel the flames. Her sister pulled her off their mother's body. As she was being dragged to the back door, her eye caught the sight of her mother's tin recipe box above the stove. She wrenched her hand once more and reached up to grab it. The roar of the fire was so close she couldn't hear her sister's pleading to leave. The tin box was too hot for her to hold. Mary quickly opened the box and pulled out a small blue bag. Dropping the box to the floor, she shoved the bag into her apron pocket and pushed her way out the door, choking on the smoke. She and her sisters stood in the field and watched their home burn to the ground.

"It was just two months later we met up with you. My sisters didn't know what to do with me. The troupe was looking for an ingénue and I was so young. They knew you had always been in love with me, so they made the arrangements that I join the troupe and you'd look after me until I came of age to be married. So there it was."

Boris always knew Mary had suffered great loss, but he knew to never ask about something that was unspeakable. The only time he ever got a glimpse of it was on stage, when a certain look would come over her face. A look that had made her one of the great actresses of the Yiddish theater, one that moved audiences to tears all over the world.

"Mary-ela," Boris began, but Mary closed her hand around his and pulled both their hands up to her mouth. She pressed his fingertip to her pursed mouth.

"Sshh," she repeated over and over again until both were deeply asleep.

The next morning, he woke to the same smells of rose water, honey and cinnamon that had lingered during the night. He found Mary standing before the stove humming and stirring, humming and stirring. He held the blanket close to his face and closed his eyes, hearing his own mother's voice: *Rozhinkes mit Mandlen.* Almonds and Raisins.

In dem beis hamikdosh,
In a vinkl cheider
Zitzt di almoneh, bas tzion alein
Ihr ben yochidl yidelen viegt zi keseder

Zingt ihm tzum shlofn a liedele shein.
Unter yideles viegele,
Shteit a klor vaise tzigele
Dos tzigele iz gefohren handlen
Dos vet zain dain beruf
Rozhinkes mit mandlen
Shlof-zshe, yideleh, shlof.

Under little one's cradle in the night
Came a new little goat snowy white.
The goat will go to the market,
And Mother her watch will keep.
He'll bring you raisins and almonds
So sleep my little one, sleep.

***

Meg folded the paper and slipped it back into the blue satin bag. She tipped the small glass bottle toward the mouth of the bag and the few grains of rice tumbled into the dark blue. She tapped the bottom of the bottle where the spices had gotten stuck against the cold glass. The cinnamon and ginger loosened into the bag. Meg began to gently pull what was left of the red ribbons together, pausing before closing it. She held her breath as the smells lingered on the back of her tongue. She swallowed and closed the bag with a simple, frayed knot.

Rice Pudding

Custard
1 cup cream
1 cup whole milk
½ cup honey
2 large brown eggs
2 large brown egg yolks
3 cups white rice cooked in 2 cups water and 1 cup red plum wine
¼ each tsp cinnamon, ginger powder, fresh lemon zest and grated
vanilla beans, or pure vanilla extract
½ cup golden raisins soaked in ⅓ cup honey rose water*

Topping
½ cup brown sugar
2 Tbsp. water
¼ cup sliced almonds (toasted if desired)

Honey Rose Water: *Bring one cup of organic rose petals and
one cup of cool distilled water to a boil, slowly adding a heaping
tablespoon of honey, and let boil for 10 minutes. Cover and
steep overnight (to retain the intense fragrance) and then strain.
Refrigerate in a tight-lidded clear glass jar for up to two weeks.

1. Bring two cups of water and one cup of plum wine to boil. Add
one and a half cups of medium white rice and bring to a rapid boil.
Cover and turn heat to low and let cook for twenty minutes.

2. Preheat oven to 350°F. Place sliced almonds on a lined cookie
sheet in the oven, being careful to just lightly toast them.
Line the bottom of a large flat-bottomed oven-safe bowl with the
sliced toasted almonds. Put aside.

3. Place the brown sugar and water in a small, thick-bottomed saucepan. Heat on medium heat. As the sugar begins to melt, gently stir with a wooden spoon to break up any lumps, until the sugar and water begin to turn light, then darker brown. Remove the pan from the heat, pour over almonds and coat the bottom of the bowl. Place the bowl into a baking dish.

4. In a small saucepan, on medium heat, mix honey, cream and milk until the milk is warm to the touch and the honey has completely dissolved (about 120°F). Do not let the milk boil.

5. In a separate mixing bowl, whisk together eggs, egg yolks, vanilla, ginger, cinnamon and lemon zest. Add to the egg mixture, ¼ cup of the warm milk mixture, then add the egg mixture back into the pan of milk, cream and honey. Slowly stir the cooked rice into the milk/egg mixture, then gently add the golden raisins soaked in honey rose water, until the rice and raisins are completely folded into the liquid.

6. Gently pour the rice custard mixture into the bowl, trying not to disturb the layer of almonds. Pour hot water into baking pan as far as one quarter up the side of the bowl.

7. Bake on the middle rack until the center of the custard is set, about 45 minutes. Insert a knife into the center and if the knife comes out clean, the custard is ready. Be sure to not overcook. Transfer to rack and let cool to room temperature. Can also be chilled and served cold.

8. To serve, either dip a spoon in hot water and ladle out servings into smaller bowls, or run a warmed, non-serrated knife around the edge of the bowl to loosen the custard. Place a flat plate over the bowl and gently turn the bowl over. Spoon remaining almonds and caramelized sugar over the top and cut into generous slices. Serves 6.

III

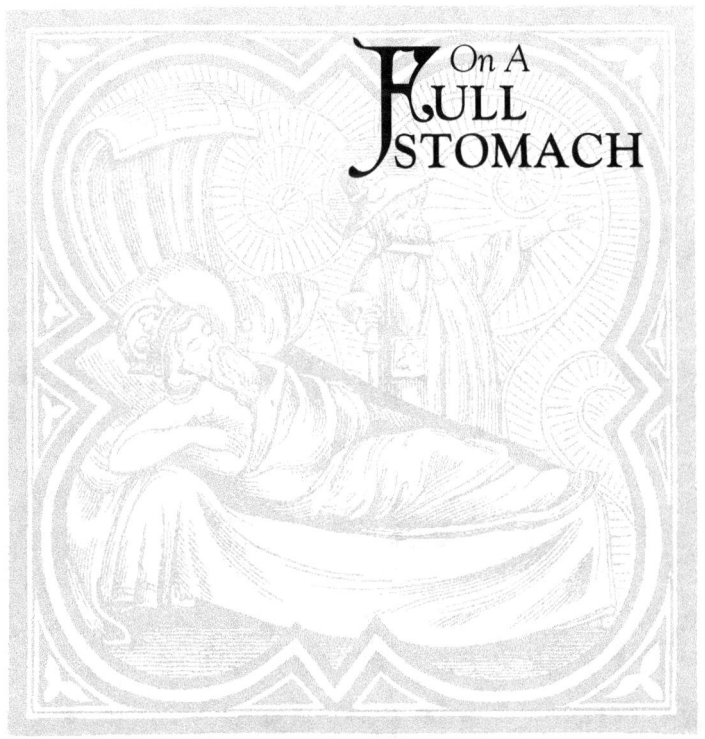

On A Full Stomach

Charlemagne after a good meal

STEAK-UMMS &
BBQ POTATO CHIPS

(A Meal with a Side of Urban Legend)

Vinnie Penn

it was a collision course as preordained as that of the Mayflower and Plymouth Rock.

Moreover, it was the byproduct of a carefully conceived plan, hatched by young minds capable of working a high level of government today, perhaps even CIA or FBI.

There were no arrests. No permanent marks on records.

There were only hushed tones immediately afterwards, fingers pointed accusingly during church on the Sundays that immediately followed, or from the bleachers at subsequent home games. Everyone pretty much knew who was involved, but it could never be proved. No different from a stink-bomb in the girl's bathroom, really.

It all began with a poster in the cafeteria. The year was 1981, and "International Foods Week" was coming. The regular menu would be bumped for five days in favor of "delicacies" from around the globe, faux lamb en route to the school, along with heretofore unknown veggies, maybe even Shepherd's Pie, which the students surely didn't realize they would love. All they knew was that their stand-bys of steak sandwich, hotdogs and meatball grinders would not be served for five miserable days and, what's more, brown-bagging it for the week was less than enticing (Mom's PB&J?—be serious) and would be equally less than appreciated by a gung-ho principal.

A casual conversation in the locker room after gym class escalated from flip, joking comments about sabotaging deliveries to references to a recent storyline by Marvel Comics, involving Nick Fury and S.H.I.E.L.D., to a full-blown "we can actually do this" hands-in-the-circle moment.

Keep in mind that this predates the personal computer, so simply hacking into the system and deleting requests, invoices or what have you, was not an option. Today's kids are punk-ass. Back then it took ingenuity, lock-picking skills and more than a little bit of guts (fence-hopping was also a huge plus).

The first step, it was decided, would be to see what was coming from where and when it was due to come. As luck would have it, one in this elite group had semi-access to the cafeteria as part of a work program. Again, it is important to note that this was all before fax machines, photocopiers, cell phones that could take pictures of the order forms; merely destroying paperwork would only succeed in delaying things for half a day at best. The guy who suggested this was immediately invited to—and the guest of honor at—a Noogie Party.

The second suggestion was to get all of the necessary telephone numbers and cancel the orders via a muffled voice and fake name. That, too, was ultimately vetoed, as it could lead to an investigation, the type that results in canceling end-of-the-school-year festivities.

This all had to look like one gleeful accident, pure happenstance with only a few choice foods surviving the catastrophe.

But what foods?

Steak sandwiches and meatball grinders tied for the top spot. The hot dogs, boiled rather than grilled, were a distant second (plus they elicited too many homosexual jokes at this all-boys Catholic school). The steak had gotten significantly better in the past few years; the stringy, semi-tough meat that soaked through the already mushy rolls had been replaced by a brand new, sheet-like, icy, faux-steak. Faux as it was, though, sizzling it up on the kitchen grill in an enormous pool of pseudo-butter turned it into Bliss-on-a-Bun, plain and simple. This faux was not the foe we were certain the lamb would be.

Where side dishes were concerned, the school's french fries were downright horrible, especially compared to

McDonald's, so potato chips won pretty much unanimously (there may have been one lone Funyons vote).

Once the top foods of choice were identified, and it became clear there was more than enough already of one on campus, things really fell into place. You see, there had been a huge pre-order on the steaks, thanks to their popularity and the fact that they could survive Armageddon. The meatballs were on a decidedly different ordering schedule.

Thus, the idea was to simply prevent all these bizarre foods from countries no one had any interest in visiting, so all that would be left were—at the risk of being redundant—the steak sandwiches. A week of steak sandwiches and nothing else! Let the drooling begin.

Next up: determine what road the delivery trucks would most likely use. But, sabotaging the main one leading to the school might result in every student having to march in unison behind the gym teacher's shrill whistle. It not only needed to be determined which way the International Food Week trucks would be arriving, but a road needed be picked that was as far out as possible yet still accessible to the group. Disabling the truck a block or two or three away wouldn't stop the delivery. But, six blocks? Eight?

After guessing the road, the plan was to smash dozens bottles of soda, peppered with thumbtacks and whatever else could provide an assist.

There were only two road possibilities. Obstacle: not a driver's license among us...er, I mean...the Elite Squadron. (Okay, quick question: what's the statute of limitations? Can a high-school diploma actually be revoked?)

Sure, there were older brothers who could be called upon, and there were even cars that could be snuck out under cover of the night, but that was more than daunting—it was *unthinkable*.

The outlook became momentarily bleak. There could be no "heading off trucks at the pass" as originally hoped, forcing them deep into snowdrifts, much as the resulting press would have been kickass...something only boys this age could truly appreciate. (Imagine, newspaper articles laminated for posterity, even if only the police blotter!)

That is, until the weather reports came in. Apparently Mother Nature had picked sides.

Local meteorologists had begun calling for a nor'easter, a minimum of six to eight inches of fluffy, white snow, and heavy winds to boot. How fortuitous! Could it possibly not be looked upon as the gods themselves joining in to assist in the mission? No, it could not; the God of Good Food Himself was surely aiming his trident (four-pronged, like the fork) at this gaggle of steak-sandwich lovers.

It was common knowledge that whenever a band was coming to play at the school and inclement weather loomed, they took a secondary route to ensure a safe arrival. It was a route much more accessible and familiar, through hilly backyards and across makeshift bridges over ponds. Best of all, we, er...they could do it on foot! Things were (potentially) getting much easier. If the snowfall even neared four to five inches, chances were good the trucks might use this route, in which case sabotage would work.

The snow began to fall late afternoon. In under an hour more than two inches of half-dollar-sized, ultra-fluffy flakes covered the landscape. The telephone calls from rotary phones mounted on kitchen walls began right away. According to the pilfered paperwork, deliveries were always made later in the afternoon, directly after dismissal. The best agents were dispersed, four rough-and-ready "regulators," each prepared to spout nothing but name, rank and serial number. One soldier's older brother's snowmobile was trotted out of the garage, while said older brother played an away basketball game. Another soldier rode shotgun (which, on a snowmobile, translates to "like a girl"). The other two walked their tour of duty.

The nails and thumbtacks wound up being few really; a cardboard box nabbed off a workbench in one kid's garage. Too many would raise eyebrows anyway. As for glass, digging up a half dozen empty bottles of soda was easy enough. They were promptly stomped into bits and shards beneath workboots, the arsenal was soon full and soon the road was literally littered with the glass.

Right now you're probably thinking, "But wouldn't other vehicles suffer the same fate as the delivery truck? Didn't the possibility for an absolute tragedy exist?" The answer, of course, is yes. And when does the possibility of casualties not exist when it comes to a greater good? Sacrifices sometimes need be made.

"Operation: Steak for Christ's Sake" (ah, the Catholic school sense of humor!) went off without so much as a snag, not a hitch—the ambitious lads never even missed dinner.

Sure enough, by the time the evening news rolled around, one of the lead stories was about several vehicles that had blowouts. A refrigerated truck was one of the casualties—which surely led to a few muffled cheers from living-room sofas and bottom bunks—as were three cars, one of which was carrying two nuns straight from Rome who'd be pulling double-duty teaching Italian at the school for a week plus educating the boys about some of the alien foods they were supposed to be sampling.

The elite squadron splintered. Heated four-way telephone exchanges took place, threats were levied, termination of friendships dangled like twitchy bait. One—the weakest link of the lot from the get-go—was certain this development cemented his afterlife residency, a studio apartment in Hell. Another, a bundle of nerves— the dumb jock, i.e., muscle of the group—seemed poised to spill at the slightest provocation. Still another—arguably the brains of the outfit—began concocting escape routes and alibis. But the fourth—the best-looking of them all— ate his dinner that night guilt-free.

By Monday of International Week, the "Fearsome Foursome" were barely interacting. Teachers shot side-eyes. Rumblings about an investigation reverberated, but nothing came of it.

The disabled refrigerated truck proved to be the one carting all the international fare. Word was there were skewers plunged through chunks of some repugnant meat, patties of lamb and mystery peas, and even more indeterminable abominations. The delivery personnel did manage to get the packages to the school kitchen, but they were judged a health risk.

By lunchtime there were slim pickings: bologna-and-cheese sandwiches, steak sandwiches and chips. No international fare: no goulash, or souvlaka, no pesto or gnocchi. The ratio of BBQ to regular chips was also off-kilter. A shipping error in favor of BBQ. The Good Food God, perhaps, checkmating?

There was also a plethora of cookies, and milk was always a lock, a nearby farm distributor having the school account.

The mission could only be declared a success.

High fives! Back pats! Touchdown!

And then *she* entered the cafeteria.

Sister Donna Bagatelli, visiting from Rome, walked with a cane and had a patch over one eye. No one was sure if this was a recent development thanks to the car mishap or an earlier condition. Nor did anyone want to know. She proceeded to lead the entire room in prayer.

Then the lunch bell sounded. Sister Donna looked down at her plate skeptically. The pickings were so slim she had no choice but to imbibe, wisely choosing the hot lunch over the skin-on bologna. She took a bite of the steak sandwich and followed it fast with a BBQ chip, ostensibly to "chase" this odd sheet steak with something—anything. She moaned deeply from her gut. Everyone looked at her cautiously. The fearsome foursome tensed over their plates. One elbowed another in the gut. Their time had surely come. This "meal," after all, could not be acceptable to a patch-wearing, cane-toting nun from Rome. There would be...well...hell to pay.

A pause so lengthy it put to shame the quiet that followed belching in homeroom, while Sister Donna stared at her plate. The conspirators held their breath. Visions of summer school danced in our...their...heads. Her mouth agape, the masticated remains of this sandwich steak everyone adored, and some potato chip shrapnel, too, was visible along one stretch of bottom teeth. Sweat formed on their already oily foreheads. It felt like minutes before she finished chewing, raised her head, blinked with her one good eye and declared:

"This is what fish and loaves of bread must've tasted like to the Apostles."

A sigh of relief went around the dining hall. Everyone tucked into that delicious wafer-thin sandwich steak, which would soon find its way into freezers across the country forevermore known as Steak-Umms. Some even put the BBQ chips directly on the sandwich, a variation on lettuce, a nod to the gods.

The Ultimate Steak-(Umm) Sandwich

1 Steak-Umm (a knock-off or even minute steak will suffice)
2 slices of Swiss cheese
8-10 BBQ potato chips
Pinches of oregano, garlic powder, and salt and pepper
Pat of butter or some substitute (optional, as, interestingly,
the Steak-Umm generates its own cooking oil)
2 slices of bread, preferably white or wheat

*Insert bread into toasting apparatus. In the time it takes to
toast your bread, your Steak-Umm will be done (Approx.
4 min.). Put stovetop at medium heat, either adding pat of
butter or not; immediately place steak into pan. It will cook
quickly. Upon flipping over, add pinches of salt and garlic
powder and then crush BBQ potato chips in your hand. Then,
generously sprinkle chips atop the cooked and seasoned meat.*

*Lower heat. Place slices of cheese over the crushed chips
covering the steak. Cover. By the time the toaster "dings"
take the top off the frying pan and you will see what I refer
to as "melted goodness." Dash the oregano and pepper onto
the cheese, gingerly remove from frying pan and place on one
slice of toast. Then top with the other slice and prepare to be
transported to a place where you work part-time at the
mall and "Saved by the Bell" is on 24/7.*

BURRITO

Elizabeth Robinson

i

Blanket

When she was very small, she had a blanket. The central fact of the world was: blanket. It swathed her everywhere she went, pale and fleshy as a skin. First, she had plucked the fuzz from it, rubbing it before her nostrils: the smell of skin and hair, of transit through the day. The blanket bleached in sunlight, grew thinner, grew almost transparent. She began to wad up sections and suck on it. In her sleep: dreams. A dream of divine hunger. Various dreams of terror and succor. One morning she woke with a mouthful. The blanket was in her mouth, malleable and moist between her teeth.

ii
Fingers

The left fingers were the beans, and the right fingers were the rice. "Ah, do not intermarry," said the grandma, but the little girl felt for her own impulses. Coyly, she said, "Here's the church, and here's the steeple." "That's right," said Grandma. "Open the door," said the little girl coaxingly. And Grandma fell asleep in her chair, while the little girl set out a plate on the table. White grains, the sheen of the black beans, the union that makes complex proteins. Grandma makes a hushy snore. The girl pulls up the chair, places her fingertips across the bare plate, prepares to eat.

iii
Blanket and Fingers

She likes best the sense of the blanket around her shoulders when she is just out of the tub and naked. Far too late into her childhood she sucks her fingers, wraps herself in the blanket, dreams at night that God's mouth fills with saliva when he looks down on her. This dream is so persistent that it becomes fact, reshapes her biology.

iv
Loss

As a grown-up, she will wish to regain this. What she later lost. The feel of God's hand definitely upon her, and the sense that she is not indigestible. The divine world wishes to hold her, wrapped and salty, in its mouth.

v

Adolescence

This is a difficult time. During this period, when she is hungry, she must eat herself. True, this is not new to her, but the pleasure is gone. She carries a smell of frying pan around with her, of old oil and fried onions. Her teeth are crooked from sucking on her fingers, so her fingers are taken away. That first blanket, see-through, thinning, sheers away into nothingness. God, laughing at his joke, makes her grow breasts and hips. Then no blanket, floury or otherwise, can surround her.

vi

Fat

She makes up for all this by becoming enormously fat. She is herself from the inside out, the savor of shapelessness. She will confound God with her free will. Him whose tongue she still sees from a distance. The day she leaves for college, she is a warm mound of body draped in a dress the color of blue corn masa. In college, she reads a kind of a bible that tells her to make sacrifice: to send a pleasing aroma before the nostrils of God. Subversively obedient, she smiles.

vii

Flaca

Alternatively, she might dry the tears of God's hunger and starve herself. There could be no temptation toward what does not exist. A universe liberated from fragrance. The tongue is now an organ oriented only to making words, and lacks the sense of other texture. Wandering through the Southwest, she finds potsherds. They are strangely decorated, the design of appetite is upon them. She becomes a performer balancing their bits on her ever-thinner fingers.

viii
Or

The glory of body wrapped in body. Blur of thigh wrapping thigh, spice and the bowl of armpit. Her mouth opens to make nourishment. "Psyche," he breathes; he clasps her ear in his teeth and she can, that way, smell his cumin and lime. When she lights the lamp in the dark, the oil splashes back on her, sizzling, and they are both delighted.

ix
Recipe

She reflects idly that more could be added. The tortilla, the rice, the beans. Her fingers intertwine. The meat. Her teeth straighten. Cheese, avocado. Her hair acquires a shine. Chili. Sour cream. The very idea. Now whom will she feed? Breath wrapped in voice.

x
Pregnant

She lies flat on the horizon, not to tan her skin, but to purify it. Light bleaches the color from the blanket she is. God admires this intimacy of distance. Her flesh is pliable at its work of wrapping. The hump of her belly broadens the landscape, smells smoky. Her thighs part. God sniffs the almond of the mandorla. God sends an angel with a cup to succor her thirst, and she sips, recognizing the sweet clarity of his saliva.

xi
Birth
When her son is pushed out from her, she wraps him hard in a blanket so he cannot move his arms and legs. Little lump of meat he is, God's dew on his forehead. She takes his left fingers, his right fingers, and interweaves them, then wedges his hands back into the swaddling. She takes the blade to her corncob and sheers off the kernels, feeding him with their milky residue.

xii
Refrain
Awake, he cries and cries. She puts a bean on one eyelid and a grain of rice on the other: he sleeps. In his sleep, she can tell by his happy moans that he knows by whom his is eaten. Awake, he cries and cries until the neighborhood children fall upon him, rolling him this way and that. "Our baby burrito!" He blushes, gasps, when their teeth sink into his fleshy little thighs. God's spit lapping his cheek. She sees this, that her child is not indigestible.

Bean Soup

This is simple to make, but very tasty and satisfying.

3 Tbsp. vegetable oil
1 onion, peeled and chopped
2 cloves garlic, peeled and chopped
2 fresh chili peppers, seeded and chopped
(using canned chilis works too)
1¾ pounds canned or cooked red kidney beans, drained
14 ounces canned tomatoes, chopped
2 pints chicken or vegetable stock
juice of one lime (sometimes I add more)
freshly ground black pepper
handful of fresh cilantro, washed and chopped

Heat the oil in a large, lidded pot. Fry the onion, garlic and chili peppers until soft. Add the beans and tomatoes, mix well and simmer for 3 minutes. Pour in the stock and lime juice, season and bring to a boil. Cover the pot, reduce the heat and simmer for 30 minutes. As you prepare to serve it, you can process the soup to make it smooth if you want to; I don't.

Stir in the cilantro just before serving. Serve also with lime wedges, sour cream and crushed tortilla chips.

A RECIPE FOR DISASTER

Kate Bernheimer

ink Chiffon & Pink Lace
Pink Lady's Slippers
Pink is the best.

We the undersigned will write all of our poems on pink paper.

We the undersigned will write our poems on pink paper for now and forevermore.

We the undersigned promise to think pink

We the undersigned forever pink

We will wear pink every Saturday

We will wear pink every Monday

We will only write our poems on pink paper

We the undersigned:

FOREVER PINK!

Once upon a time there were two girls. One had blonde hair, one had brown. The girl with blonde hair lived in a house made of stone. The brunette's house was made of wood. Both of the girls lived in houses surrounded by trees. Next to the wood house was a creek they called The Fake Creek. Its water came from a pipe. Across from the stone house flowed The Good Stream. The two girls had names for everything. Out by The Fake Creek or by The Good Stream they would clasp hands and sing children's songs, though they were fourteen.

Oh jolly playmate,
Come out and play with me,
And bring your dollies three,
Climb up my apple tree,
Slide down my rainbow,
Into my cellar door,
And we'll be jolly friends,
Forever more.

At the stone house, everything was brown and was grey. Not just the stones: the light, the walls. Sweaters the blonde's mother wore. The wood house was technicolor. Yellow. The blonde girl, named S—, envied the Apple Pie Family that lived inside there. (That's what she and her mother called them.)

The brunette was named K— and preferred the stone.

It was K—'s first girlhood friendship. Her only other friend, D—, she had made friends with in nursery school.

(K—'s friendship with D— was to live forever, etched in The Book of Childhood Dreams.) With S— she felt herself growing older each day. This was an uneasy feeling. It contained danger. Was unknown.

Summer evenings, they watched television in the attic of the stone house. The television sat perched on a wooden table, its rabbit ears cocked to the side. In twilight they watched a show about supernatural things that happened in a strange, murky zone. The blonde girl's mother had forbidden the program. But the two girls really loved it. Its music began with a forbidding tone...and the actors seemed to stare out at them. With evil eyes, it seemed to them.

Oh jolly playmate,
I cannot play with you.
My dolly has the flu,
The mumps and measles too.
I can't slide down your rain barrel,
And through your cellar door.
But we'll be jolly friends,
Forever more, more, more, more, more.

Other times they would ride on a green train to downtown and buy colorful earrings made of feathers— from peacocks and from other birds. Green, blue, black and brown. And jackets made of green wool, dark green faded to nearly brown.

K—'s mother was kind. She packed K— lunch every day, and put it in a brown paper bag. Even in summertime (which it was when this story took place), she would pack a lunch for K— to take with her to S—'s house when she went to play. Sandwiches wrapped in wax paper. S— and K— would eat the sandwich up in the attic while they watched TV, or sitting together on the green train while they went downtown to buy feather earrings.

"Drink me," they'd say to their glasses of water, dripping red in—they'd vowed to eat everything pink in the summer of 1983.

On the train sometimes they'd plug cords into a yellow box that played music. Their friend P—, whose parents allowed her to drink vodka, had made some cassettes.

> *And her name is*
> *P-I-N-K-Y*
> *P-I-N, no lie*
> *K-Y, me-oh-my*
> *She's $69.95*
> *Give her a try*
> *P-I-N-K-Y*
> *P-I-N I cry*
> *K-Y don't be shy*
> *$69.95, boy*
> *Give her a try*

It was the hot summer, once upon a time, and they made themselves drinks to take into the woods or by The Good Stream. Silver thermos, crushed ice and the reddest of wines.

Once upon a time, the girls (one blonde, one brown) were wearing pink skirts and pink checkered sneakers. They had recently seen an episode of "The Twilight Zone" in which a wife had woken up and forgotten her name. They were replaying it down by The Fake Creek. S— stood in the mud and spread her arms to the sky. "I will now recite a poem about pink!" she exclaimed. Then she recited a long story-poem in which two girls (one blonde, one brown) stood by a creek in pink clothes and invented a world in which no mothers went mad. S—'s mother had recently entered the hospital, for "forgetting to blow out the candles at night" (i.e., trying to burn the stone house down). Then the two dear friends walked back to the yellow wood house, where S— was also now living. The entire Apple Pie Family was home. K—'s mother welcomed them in with a smile and some ice cream—it was white ice cream with red hots inside. It became pink—the pinkest ice cream you ever saw.

The girls fed each other. Pink dripped down their throats.

Say say my enemy
Come out and fight with me
And bring your weapons three
Climb up my torture tree
Slide down my razor blade
Into my poison pit
And we'll be jolly enemies
Forever more more
Shut the door.

Once upon a time, in a town that was part of a city, two girls grew up who loved pink. They promised to be friends forever. They exchanged letters on pink paper, and then when electronic letters came into vogue, they learned to turn the background of e-letters pink. They invented a dessert called The Pink Lady Slipper. At the Waban Market, you bought some Lady's Fingers. These were yellow cakes made in the shape of tiny boats—or fingers. Then you filled them with Cool Whip into which you'd swirled red drops of dye.

Many years later, one of the girls died. By her own hand; she leapt from a building. Once upon a time in a magical land, everything was gone.

Think pink.

Drink pink.

The disaster is now.

Pink Pimm

Makes 2

(Serve in tiny glasses so each party has four drinks.)

4 shots Pimm's No. 1
1 cup raspberry ginger ale
¼ cup freshly squeezed lemon juice
1 dash Angoustura Bitters
2 cucumber slices from a very small cucumber, cut very thin

*Pour Pimm's No. 1, lemon juice and ginger ale over crushed
ice; add dash of bitters, and top with cucumber. This beverage is
best had in a teeny little pink glass as an apertif to a Pink Early
Supper, at which smoked salmon sandwiches, sour-salt roasted
beets and pink macaroons would also be served.*

PAUL CEZANNE AND THE MYTHOLOGY OF APPLES

Mary Kite

inally, the white linen was cleaned and gathered. Chickens in the dappled woods were fed while shadows grew. If not for the zephyr in the room where the woman was giving birth, it would have been unbearably hot.

As she slipped in and out of consciousness, verdant leaves on cottonwoods made her world; the bed, her midwife, the geometric wallpaper and the dark furniture... illuminated in emerald. All of this created a close-knit synthesis. Apple blossoms scented the room with the rhythms of birth.

He slowly submerged his right hand and then his left into the warm copper bowl. Cupped his fingers together, then removed the placenta as if it were alive. He found it possible to place the burgundy mass into a deep hole. A sapling from the original tree stood nearby. It had transformed itself into a sentinel of ceremony and was promptly planted on top of the afterbirth. This tree faced the window where baby Paul could observe his surrogate sibling.

II

In the 1800s, not everyone could be wise. During clear nights, trees grew far more than people noticed. Moonlight helped them through spiritual realms of what the trees called "saint petals." They produced the finest fruit in all of Provence. If a dendritic spirit became ill, a robin was sent to nest in the tree. This bird gave it "cooing council in the fresh world" or a world without harmful insects.

Partial shadows between regions of complete darkness looked into the eyes of young Paul Cezanne and saw that his tongue, ears and hands had a connectivity with the apple sapling outside his window. As the summer months rolled by, he listened to its leaves play into the wind with an audible…"ashhhhsloughsho," then…"ahhhhshinlishhhheeeeyoooooo," to a fairly discernible…"AHHH LOVE YOUSSSSHHHH."

During a pensive moment, Paul put his right hand flatly to his forehead and in complete stillness, closed his eyes and took this in. These transitions were translated into a synaesthetic axis of emotion between the tree, the boy and back again. It was a passage from a common planar influence into something volumetric: human-plant love. An understanding grew. Alone in his room he'd listen to the rain and watch his tree delight in the downpour. Such happiness was exhibited by the gentle change in color gradations of its leaves.

III

There is a time of night when very little moves and dew is tranquil. Just before dawn the apple tree senses the breath of the child is now deeper. He has slipped into adolescence. In response, its roots thump chants. Cyclical torrents of sound provide a means of following water back into Heaven. It was during this time that the apple tree was able to flower or visit "sugar Saint Eden." All the while, there was an irregular chorus of airborne creatures who celebrated its growth. These decibels hit Paul Cezanne as if infinity had set out to condition him into the lives of what other people called "objects."

These glasses, these plates, these apples…they talk
amongst themselves. Interminable disclosures!

—Paul Cezanne

Paul understood "things" as peopling dark voids around us. The tree was "appling" its limbs with luxurious fruit born from something placental. The connectivity between this plant and the baby who had grown to become a painter was undeniable.

At noon, he picked fruit. The kitchen throbbed magenta…extra-spectral apple color in space. The scent pouring from the vine-woven basket was overwhelming. He wanted to open the window to invite the orchestra of seasonal sound in, but his strength began to weaken. Paul's blue boot scuffed the pine floor with a peel that he had allowed to fall. The collision with the floor resonated a percussive clap that was oracular in its tonality. Tim-tom sound coupled with owl hoot bounced from the white ceiling to the floral print walls, down the floor and back again with deeper amplification overlaid with these words, "Flower buds, offshoots and tenderness, plant milk, sap and dew." He felt a swish of air and fell into a state of unconscious suspension. In the distance, a donkey brayed.

IV

If time is a garden where flowers speak to windows, where petals wilt and bud into apples, then the serene wavelengths that Paul recomposes this moment in time speak as additive consonance within coexistence. Only one red apple can extend above the horizon. And, what of the apples? The footprint of a paintbrush in "todayness" locks in formal interaction with itself and Paul Cezanne. He paints himself as an apple and uses formal Aristotelian restraint. These apples possess the memory of himself as an infant. The apple is in a state beyond memory; reduplicative paramnesiac floatation. The artist only answers with the identity of a sensation or the resemblance of separate moments in taste, olfaction, color and the texture of emotion. Waters of life connect all living things, just as it is the truth of blood that links Paul Cezanne with these apples.

From another viewpoint, what does the apple feel to exude its extraordinary "appleness"? It has a name, "red delicious," but it, because of its unique history, has organized the countenance of something special. Further, the apple can recall energetic embraces of its tree to the afterbirth...and cannot forget to reconstruct its inner molecular composition.

Doubtless, it must feel very difficult for the apple to communicate. Conscious distances between apples and men seem immense. Even sensitive men, such as Paul Cezanne often fail to interpret certain signs. What is the essence of inter-species teaching? What can be learned from a plant which provides food? And, what... under what conditions can mythologies...the love of Paul Cezanne to the love of an apple tree to the love of image...become reality so that each time he decides to partake of one of these fruits the apple can arrange the perception of sound within bites clearly heard as, "Ahch chursough chyou" or "Ah luveh chiyou" to simply, while in a dark room, "I love you."

Each apple from the tree demands apprehension and interpretation. Love and homage must be paid to the apple. Its existence remains sensuous. Each leaf on the tree offers rhythm and specific relations to sunlight; extraordinary joy emanates throughout a day's uncoiling.

V

The translation of thought is action. When young Paul Cezanne became close friends with Émile Zola they found themselves in matching uniforms consisting of blue tunics with gold palms on the collars and fancy red piping. For their pants, they wore white duck canvas. Émile and Paul were inseparable. Even after Zola moved with his mother to Paris, Cezanne's letters to him arrived all at once, like sparrows having alighted under a tree; as emersions within song, short stories and poetry. Émile responded to Paul with this poem:

Songez, mais dites-vous que vous faites un songe,
Que ce ne vent que joux, qu un amusant mensonge;
Et si, sans le vouloir, vous vous perdiez au
Ciel Point de pleurs, en voyant la beauté du réel!

—Émile Zola

Émile Zola, now old enough to travel alone, decided to make the trip from Paris to Aix-en-Provence to visit his dear friend. It was late one summer afternoon when the two lads found themselves laughing underneath the apple tree. They were in the middle of constructing a play called "Naked on the Viaduct." It went something like this:

Z: Awkward by private inclination...

C: ...landed him in weak tea with only a little sugar and no...

Z: ...beaten silver or cream, just a small vessel as a lifelong schoolroom; for he was...

C: ...a balloonist. In doleful charm, he calmly smoked next to leaky fuel tanks.

Z: Like all good fashionistas, such a man was fragile. Slightly unhinged.

C: His narrow face projected...

Z: ...a visual topography that bordered on abstraction.

C: The air that surrounded him was imperceptible. It was obvious that his spectacles were blurred with apple juice.

Z: Vertiginous collapsed space...

Émile then placed his right hand high above Paul's left knee and met his eyes. Tree limbs above them began to quiver. Feathery fans of leaves whipped away from branches and fell in an enormous verdigris curtain. In the distance, a gramophone played Donizetti's *Lucia di Lammermoor*...scene 2, act 3:

Dalle stanze ove Lucia
tratta avea col suo consorte,
un lamento, un grido uscia,
come d'uom vicino a morte!
Corsi ratto in quelle mura:
Ah! Terribile sciagura!
Steso Arturo al suol gioaceva
muto, freddo, imnsanguinato!
E Lucia l'acciar stringeva
che fu già del trucidato!....
Ella in me le luci affisse...
«Il mio sposo ov'é?» - mi disse.
E nel volto suo pallente
un sorriso balenò!
Infelice! Della mente
la virtude a lei mamcò.

There was a deafening crack as a large (apple heavy) limb directly above the couple's heads, unhinged itself from the trunk and crashed down on Émile's left shoulder with its ragged edge just missing his exposed chest by a gasp. Slightly shaken, this demonstrated to young Paul the unmistakable passion the tree held for him and confirmed that there is indeed a language of action. At this realization, the young man's face became flooded with a rush of blood. Sudden silence was regained in his rediscovery of primary emotion. Paul Cezanne finally recognized himself within wood's scent. He raised his index finger to his nose and sniffed. It was the same.

VI

In order to decipher secret languages, one must transcend the order of the mind, categories of matter, and skip playfully down the halls of obscurity. For the fully initiated, color opens the door to this alphabet. Ribbons of diverse hues swirled around his palette knife. He spoke to each apple as it were a paramour. His lips brushed against their skins while he whispered, "Beauty is always simple." Clouds fell to the ground. Visions appeared to him in the night. With hands like spoons, he caressed the ripe fruit into his water-filled eyes. And, during the morning, he arranged these apples with such perfection that the darkened corner of the small room glowed. While Paul painted, the left edge of the wall squared with the edge of his canvas to allow these matched perspectives to fit his emotions; for painting provided the only clear manifestation of truth in imagery. From the window, his apple tree observed with pleasure.

Heavy Step Apples

Pare, core and dice
2 large tart apples
sauté them in a large skillet under medium heat
with

2 Tbsp. butter
1 Tbsp. cinnamon

until they are a little soft.
Add

½ cup raisins
and
2 Tbsp. honey

Stir.
Serve hot over
a large scoop of vanilla ice cream
per person.
Serves 4.

PEANUT BUTTER
A History

Jack Collom

Used to be there was no peanut butter. Lightning yes, giant ferns yes, dramatic crags yes, but, well, just picture if you can, a world without creamy or crunchy brown stuff. O silver, blue and orange birds flew; flowers bloomed like rainbow handfuls; photosynthesis tripped the light fantastic everywhere; it was a world without *palpable* beauty. The earth in extreme slowness forged itself into being, out of benign death and rot—but it found no expression of its soul save through the metamorphosis into more glamorous life forms. There was no substance, yet, that leapt out of earth and said, "Look at me; taste me! Me, Earth! *I* am no hothouse pink, no golden pheasant, transcendent melon nor shrinking violet! No platinum-sheened vodka to suck you into the abyss! Nor am I fatty-bloody-beefstuff immortalizing slaughter! No, I am none of these—I am earth! I am earth *as* earth." End quote. No. There was no such speaker....Until the moon did a turn and Spirit of Earth slipped out at last, into the open, unadulterated, through the cunning yet sincere "nut" of that southern leguminous annual herb (*Arachis hypogaea*) with showy yellow (sun-color) flowers, the one having a peduncle which elongates and bends into the soil, where the ovary ripens into a pod containing one to three oily edible seeds—the one known as peanut.

Then Spirit of Earth stood up, squinted, scratched her butt, ran in place, showed her coffee teeth. Thunderbolts flashed and thundercracks rolled. Rainbows wrestled themselves to dirt. Crumbled rock had sex with liquid extracts. Texture played with itself, from crème to crunch, crushed and churned and back again. The peanut pod became a little round god, grinning, grinding, "Eat me!" (as gods are supposed to do). Spirit of Earth bent over, waved her hazel hands. Shells went flying. Nuts were born, and borne into the nitrogen-rich broth of air. Hearts removed! Sun-roasted. Gently pounded, pulverized, shattered and smashed. Then mingled, commingled, commixed, intermingled, entangled, combined, compounded, interlarded, stirred, amalgamated, fused, coalesced and merged. Not to mention jumbled, scrambled, snarled, socialized and evolved, into a party, a divine mahogany-colored mess. It lay there vibrating, like everything.

Suddenly the wind licked a little bit, mmm. The sun sucked up a taste, mmm. Hummingbirds delicately probed, mmm. Some grizzly bears gobbled, mmm-mmm. Oxygen osculated nose and mouth, mmm. Even the moon sipped a gleaming droplet, mmm. The wood partridge drummed: "*Peanut Butter Peanut Butter Peanut Butter,*" on and on.

Then, when history was nearly used up, branching bulbheads called "people" busted into the act. Pioneering peanut paste as base for Nahuatl molés, powdering peanuts into palpitating stews (Africa, fifteenth century), concocting creamy protein sauces for people with bad teeth (China, Ming Dynasty), producing peanut porridge (American Civil War). And Metal! Steam! Hydrogenation! Emulsifiers! Committing research! G.W. Carver figured out/crafted three hundred wonderful peanut uses! We had goober peas, peanut gallery, small-seed oilrich, Runner Types, Spanish Types, etc., etc., but ah! Susceptible to the mold *Aspergillus flavus* (carcinogenic—don't agglomerate it!). Peanut butter: the material of materials, the very substance of having it both ways. That taste: like chocolate's down-to-earth mom! Serious texture! Color: the everyday version of orange!

Peanut Butter takes over. "Taste of Earth" triumphs. Tawny glass jars rattling in railroad cars coast to coast, covering the nation with their quotidian elation. A new division of post-Freudian psychology into creamy and chunky personality types gains vogue with the intelligentsia. In politics, Axis of Grits fights Axis of Glossy. Art museums vie for postpostbuttery. Commerce: a single peanut sells for $77,777!

Spreading, spreading, to Fluffernutter / Koogle / Nutella, Jif, Skippy / Elvis Sandwich / Sun-Pat.—Civilized Earth Spirit dons Hawaiian shirt, as it were. Quote from ambitious Science: "Using high pressure and high temperatures, it is possible to transform peanut butter into diamonds." Perhaps into stars!

But at last, at present, two people happily simple, natural, under a bridge, gazing at the moving muddy water spotted and crested with cinnamon teal: a girl and boy each chewing (but not too much) a peanut butter and jelly sandwich (and this is just one of legions of similar stories). ...Rebirth of the Earth Spirit! Simple, natural! Deep whiffs through nose into brain fill the mind with pungent, salty-brown, Gaia-esque integration, such spirit leading to—just maybe—earthsaving reaches, outreaches into gray, not-yet-real time.

Can Earth substance inspire sustainable Earth?

(Also great with celery.)

Heaven-on-Earth Sandwich

1 half-full jar chunk-style peanut butter
2 semi-thick (manually sliced) pieces European rye bread
2 Tbsp. densely textured south-of-the-border hot sauce
2-3 leaves fresh spinach, approximately 4"x4"

Lay pieces of bread on bright black plate, adjacent to each other.

*Dip table knife into peanut butter jar and scoop out
hefty dollop chunk-style peanut butter.*

*Spread peanut butter onto one piece of bread in a manner
nicely balanced between rough coverage and thoroughness.*

*If necessary, repeat Steps 2 and 3, until peanut butter
averages at least ¹/₈" in thickness.*

*Wipe any excess pb remaining on table knife back
into peanut butter jar. Seal jar.*

*Dip knife into hot sauce, spread carefully onto second piece of rye
bread until prescribed amount has been distributed thereon.*

*Place spinach onto peanut butter-covered
piece of bread, cross-veining the leaves.*

*Gently clap the two pieces of bread together in such a manner as
to frontally unite covered sides. (NOTE: Experts differ on the
importance of matching the bread slices by shape. Heaven-on-Earth
feels that interesting effects can be attained by turning
piece #2 180°, then placing it facedown onto piece #1.)*

Pick up sandwich, preferably with both hands.

Eat it.

Reincarnate as golden eagle.

MANGO SNOB

Maliha Masood

When I was growing up in Karachi, there was no such concept as being grounded. But I knew what punishment meant when Dadijan deprived me of the taste of *kairis*. As raw mangos, kairis were mostly all hard seed surrounded by bits of unripened flesh that I used to dab with lemon juice, salt and crushed red chilis. Kairi eating was mostly a matter of chewing off the softer edges of the seed and sucking it dry. The tart, spicy juices would set my mouth on fire but I wouldn't have it any other way.

My grandmother knew my weakness and she exploited it to the hilt the day I accidentally punctured her hot water bottle by using it as a football. Okay, I admit it was a sorry state of affairs, but Dadi's injustice was downright evil.

My beloved kairis mysteriously vanished and searching for them became a full-time obsession.

Every day after school, our modest Karachi kitchen turned into a war zone as I flung open cabinets, cluttering up counter tops with plastic bags of spices, bottles of oil, tea tins and half-opened packets of flour and legumes. No kairis emerged.

"*Bechari, bechari!*" The servants felt sorry for me and pleaded with my granny to let me have just one little kairi, just this once, but Dadijan was no bargainer. I had to resort to sneaking away on the rooftop when Dadi took her afternoon naps on the verandah. Sonia, my favorite servant girl and playmate, smuggled me a half dozen supply of illicit kairis. My stomach ached from eating so many all in one go.

According to legend, mangoes, also known as the king of fruits, have been around for at least six thousand years. In ancient India, princes prided themselves on the possession of large orchards. The Moghul emperor Jehangir was particularly enamored of mangoes, as was Alexander the Great when he traipsed into the Subcontinent. Despite this royal pedigree, the word for mango in local parlance is *aam*, which means common, or masses.

During the summer holidays, when I went to Bombay to visit my mother's family at peak monsoon season, the choicest mangoes were bought in bulk, wrapped in old newspapers and stowed away in tin trunks at the foot of my uncle's bed. He kept the key on a massive ring, safely pinned to his plaid-printed *lungi* (a kind of sheet wrapped like a sarong, a sort of rundown male skirt) that my uncle wore when lounging at home.

It was always a messy business to eat a fully ripe mango. I would grab a stainless steel plate and announce as if taking a vow of seclusion, "Going to eat a mango." My aunts and cousins knew what this meant. Do not disturb. Leave her alone. She's busy with a mango.

It took up to twenty minutes to finish one clean. I sliced it lengthwise and nibbled until I got to the best part, the fleshy seed with sticky juices dribbling down my forearms that I chased off with my tongue. It was heavenly stuff. So heavenly that my training in mango culture suffered a cruel blow when I moved to America as a teenager and confronted in the local Safeway what passes for a mango at ninety-nine cents a pop.

It wasn't so much the squat puniness of the fruit that offended my sensibilities, but the taste, rather the lack of any discerning taste to my South Asian palette. When it comes to mangoes, I am, for all purposes, a real snob. Mango snobbery, my cultural birthright. There could be offenses far worse.

Kulfi
Mango Ice Cream

1 liter whole milk
1 Tbsp. flour
1½ cups canned mango pulp
1 tin sweetened condensed milk

*Heat the milk, condensed milk and flour together and bring
to a boil. Do this over a low flame and stir continuously as
the condensed milk has a tendency to stick to the bottom
of the pot and get burnt. Cool completely. Mix the mango
pulp into the milk mixture. Fill popsicle molds with this
mixture (in Bombay we ate this out of little clay pots) and
freeze until set. When set, dip the molds in warm water,
unscrew and hold over a plate to slide out the ice cream.*

THE PRIESTS

Rebecca Brown

We used to play priest.

Whoever was the biggest would tell everyone to go to mass or you'd get in trouble. She'd have a towel and she'd wrap it around her shoulders and make it hang down in front like that thing I now know is called a "surplice" and make us kneel down in front of her as if we were at the altar and bend our heads and she'd touch us on our heads and say "the body of Christ" and give us a Necco wafer. She'd put it on our tongue and hover over us until we swallowed it. You were supposed to chew it but I didn't. I kept it on my tongue and let it soften, thicken, melt, slough apart from papery to gluey to sticky and soft, like frosting, but also gritty, like powder except wet and that is when it really started to taste.

It tasted like vanilla.

Though only at first because we used the vanilla first because it was white, beige actually, like it was in real life, whereas after we ran out of white it tasted like grape or cherry or chocolate or finally orange. It tasted even more when it was sliding, warm and slippery, down my throat.

She'd listen for you to swallow and watch the movement in your neck then put the Dixie Cup of Kool-aid or Hawaiian Punch or Tang to your lips and say, "the blood of Christ," and you'd feel this little pressure against your lips, the waxy edge of the Dixie Cup, and she'd push a little toward your teeth, and you'd open your mouth and your head would go back and she'd tip the cup toward you and you'd drink.

The priest made up the rules and what would happen. The priest told us what everything was, what everything meant and all about sins. Sins were bad but some were very bad.

The priest said there were other things, secret things and signs we weren't ready to know yet but might be someday. The signs would tell you who was who, the secret things to do.

A lot of us kneeled like this at first, then later only me.

She always was the priest, I never was.

Sometimes for the altar she'd pick the sidewalk, not the real sidewalk but that ridge of concrete where it goes up from the street to your yard. I had to put my knees on the concrete. The top parts of my knees could be on the grass with my feet turned up like the soles of my shoes were looking up at Heaven. If I was wearing sneakers this wasn't so bad, but if I was in flip flops or sandals, the street felt awful although I liked those feelings some.

I also felt the end of the towel, the tips of her "surplice"—or was it "chasuble"? Maybe I'm not remembering right, oh! what have I forgotten!—swaying against my shoulder or head or along the back of my exposed bent-over neck.

We only played outside like that in summer.

In the winter we were in the house, alone, her mother still at work, my father somewhere, and she'd tell me to put a cushion from the couch down on the floor and kneel and wait while she left the room—she was going to the sacristy to prepare—then came back with communion.

At first she'd just step into the hall and, almost as soon as my head was bowed, come back and touch my head with her sticky hand and say "the body..." "the blood...," etc.

Later, however, she took her time.

Did she go to the bathroom and look at herself? Did she comb her hair, again, in front of the mirror? Or call on the phone to one of her friends, a popular girl or a boy? Did she saunter off to 7/11 to buy a Coke? Or go out back and throw the ball to their chained-up whining dog? I don't remember. But I do remember her doing that before it died, throwing the ball to tied-up dog. She always threw it just a little out of reach.

The "real" priests, in the church were men,
but that didn't stop her.
And it didn't stop me from believing in her
and in whatever it was we did.

Later it wasn't a Necco
and later it wasn't one.
Later it was two
with creme to hold them.

(Creme: American: a whitish fake food designed to pass
for cream. Invented because it was cheaper and could have
a shelf life of millennia. It fell from favor during the natural
food boom, but later was reclaimed by liberal-minded
vegans, vegetarians and Persons of Lactose Intolerance.)

Two crisp and dry but sweet and round, so that your
tongue, if you ran it around them, or them around beneath
it, could lick along the edge like a curious cat. The bottom
and top, though separate, were two, were similar, alike,
the same.

The two, that is, were *homo* (etymologically from the
Greek for *same*), they were not *hetero* (etymologically
from the Greek for *other, different*).

They were, that is, a sign.

The two were not alone, which priests, that is, "real"
priests, the ones in church, were meant to be.

Although we wondered.

Real priests were supposed to be like Jesus, who was celibate.

Although we wondered.

For though He didn't procreate, He said "this is my body" and he told us it's "a temple." There was also all of that with the disciple whom He loved, who lay his head upon His breast, who stood at the foot of the cross and did the things the women did, like weep and mourn and grieve, be fair and pretty, whose name was John.

Of course we wondered.

We wondered about them, all of them,
We wondered about ourselves.
We wondered if there were others,
then who they were,
then how to find them.

We found us in our history,
a hidden one,
read secretly in signs.

By the eleventh and twelfth centuries, many Christians in Southern France had come to despise the official Roman Catholic clergy as insensitive to the lives of regular people, excessively materialistic and disgustingly wealthy. At a time when peasants starved, priests and monks were pudgy and pink as pigs. They looked like little Neros, all ruddy-faced and mincing in their swishy robes and pointy, pretty shoes. Their teeth were dark with too much wine and their breathing stank of sausage, booze and boys. Despite all their babbling about purity, they were promiscuous. They slept with boys and women, too, and girls and with each other. Sometimes they called the other one the "wife."

No wonder, then, that when two idealistic young clerics on their way home from a pilgrimage to Rome encountered the excesses of the church in Montpellier, they set out to reform all of Christendom. Dominic, better known to us today as St. Dominic, the founder of the Dominican order, and his long-time companion, Diego, began a program of scripture study, introduced a new austerity into the church and even founded, in 1206, a religious school for girls.

Dominic and Diego were not, however, the only reform-minded believers running around the south of France at the time. Long before the two friends arrived, the Cathars (from Greek É»ÉøÉΔÉøÉœÉÕ› [Katharoi], meaning "pure ones," a term related to Katharsis or Catharsis, meaning "purification"), were spreading their own anti-materialist gospel. Also known as Albigensians, because their twelfth- and thirteenth- century incarnation was centered near the town of Albi, the Cathars were a neo-Manichaean sect whose ideas may have been introduced to France by an unnamed woman from Italy. (Unless it's something cool or even great, in which case it's attributed to "anonymous," it's always the woman's fault.) Or via Eastern European trade routes.

Neo-Manichaean thought was inspired by the ancient dualistic religion of Mani, which was based on the idea that Good and Evil—God and Satan—were two separate and equally powerful forces continuously fighting one another, and that our struggle here on the earth is the battle of material Evil versus the immaterial Good—i.e., our bodies versus our non-bodies. Mani (b. 216 AD), it must be said, was from Persia (now Iran, Iraq), an Eastern locale whose very existence, not to mention its sexually liberal practices, had troubled to the point of obsession, the West.

We have had it out for them for centuries.

In any event, for Cathars the worst thing in the world, the temptation you really had to watch out for, was procreative sex. It not only brought two bodies together, it also could lead to the creation of another evil, sinful, suffering, carnal beautiful body.

In order to help save the poor souls drawn to the heterosexually married state, God, the Albigensians believed, created *parfaits* ("pure souls"). Parfaits were elite persons who, like Roman Catholic priests, neither married nor procreated. However, unlike Catholic priests, parfaits were encouraged to create a life with another human being who, in the interest of avoiding the temptation of procreative sex, was to be a person of the same or homo gender.

Parfaits led and taught the larger number of congregants or *croyants* ("believers"), who did have heterosexually procreated families. Though croyants, too, it was hoped, would participate, before they died, in the *consolamentum*, a form of baptism that would render them almost as pure as the pure parfaits.

Cathar thought may have been introduced to France via an unnamed Italian woman, or it may have come via Eastern European—including Bulgarian—trade routes. So when people incited by the Church started harassing, then persecuting Cathars, one of the things they called them was "Bulgarians," transliterated into English as "buggers," which later meant men interested in sex with other men.

Ways Cathars were persecuted included being beaten up, run out of town, burned, bashed, called sissies or, worse, "women," and having sticks rammed up their asses, the latter a wry commentary on reputed Cathar practice.

In addition to renouncing heterosexual marriage and procreation, the Albigensians also forbade the eating of any form or product of the flesh, even in the symbolic form of wine-as-blood and wafer-as-flesh.

A doctrine that forbade the eating of animal products was difficult to impart to a nation of gourmands. Nonetheless, the Albigensian parfaits journeyed extensively to spread their gospel, traveling, as they later dwelt, together in same-sex pairs: women with women, men with men, other with other.

Albigensian practice, unlike that of the Roman church, allowed women full participation, even as parfaits. In fact one of the reasons Dominic had founded that girls' school was because he didn't want to lose all the Roman

Catholic females who wanted to do something with their lives besides make babies to the Cathars.

As is often the case with missionaries, the parfaits adapted rituals practiced by the people they wished to convert. In the Roman Catholic eucharistic supper, one man served many, kind of like the wealthy wife of an industrialist doling out soup at some feel-good social service project, and the believer ate the flesh and drank the blood of a single person, Jesus. The Albigensians' sacred supper, on the other hand, was *shared*, two believers feeding each other. It was also two believers feeding two things, for the single wafer of flesh had become a happy pair and the water-wine had turned to creme that bound them. This sweeter meal required neither death nor cannibalism. Plus, you got chocolate.

When word got around about how tasty the Albigensian sacred meal was, people started showing up at their revival meetings less to learn about the pure life than to eat. Almost overnight the delicious biscuit(s and creme) became France's number one snack food!

A good thing too. Because after St. Dominic, even better known to us today as the founder of the Inquisition, got wind that his reforms were less popular than those of this truly popular religious movement, he further decided, in the way only a dog of God can, to deal with the Albigensians. (Dominic's followers were known as *Domini Cane*, i.e., Dogs of God because they protected, like shepherds' hounds, their flock, but also, like rabid curs, went after different others with their fangs.)

The Albigensian Crusade became official in 1209 when Pope Innocent III, a swishy-robed, pointy-shoed, immaculately coifed and boy-attended pontiff who was obsessed with *vir cum viris* (Latin for males who copulate with males) and *femina cum feminis* (Latin for females who copulate with females. See also females who do not wear swishy robes or pointy shoes or have immaculate coifs or fuck boys), authorized the genocide of the Albigensians and anyone else they thought a bit suspicious. The first campaign was the siege of Beziers and it was a doozy. Refugees fleeing the crusaders, whose shock-and-awesome fame had gone before them, had holed up in the church of Saint Mary Magdalene (a whore). The holy warriors dragged the people out of the church and slaughtered them all—men, women, others (especially others) and children. Villagers were dragged behind horses, hatcheted, mutilated, used for target practice, fired from their teaching jobs, waterboarded and given electroshock treatment. When the Cistercian abbot Arnaud, the local FEMA representative, was asked how to tell Albigensians from Catholics, he answered, *Slay them all. God will know his own.* (Latin: *Caedite eos. Novit enim Dominus qui sunt eius.*) After the levee broke and everyone was dead, they burned the city down.

When the Inquisition became official in 1229 many of the remaining Cathars went underground. All across Europe, witches, weirdos, perverts, darkies, commies, trannies, punks, panhandlers and occasionally even liberal democrats were burned at the stake. Also, buggers/fags. (From Latin *faggot* meaning little stick, kindling, the stuff they used to start the fire to burn people at the stake. Heretics, in fact, soon became identified with the faggots used to burn them. Some faggots [the men, not the sticks] who refused to stop being faggots [buggers] even embroidered symbolic faggots [the sticks not the men] into their garments in defiance like they were saying, I know you're going to get me, but I'm not going to be closeted by you fucking Nazis. [See everyone who ever wore a yellow star, a scarlet "A," an HIV tattoo. See also, a century later, Joan of Arc, later sainted, though earlier roasted, for the crime of transvestitism. Wait— that sounds like she was sainted for being a transvestite, which she wasn't. I mean she *was* sainted and she was a transvestite, but she was not sainted for *being* a transvestite. For being a transvestite she was burned at the stake like a faggot, with faggots. What she was sainted for was having visions that today we would put her away forever into a mental institution though at least in that case she wouldn't be homeless.] Also, colloquially, a cigarette.)

Joan of Arc didn't smoke (cigarettes, I mean. Though she herself, that is her body smoked, that is her flesh, hair, fingernails, bones, etc., produced smoke when she/it/they was/were roasted at the stake.) In prison Joan ate, before she died, smuggled in by true believers, girls who dressed like boys and others, at the risk of their own imprisonment, and with them, with their tongues tonguing the ridges, their mouths licking off and sucking out the creme, her last supper.

France had no idea its favorite snack food was the sacred feast of an outlawed sect, it just knew it was scrumptious. Nor did the savvy Cathars tell the general public they couldn't eat their cookies. In fact they encouraged people to eat them, because how you ate the cookie could signal to other secret Cathars you were one of them. Then you could go with them, or they with you, and together you could enjoy your own communion.

The stake-burning megatrend was helped along by Thomas Aquinas' (1225?-74) declaration that homosexuality was one of the worst worst worst of the "sins against nature" (Latin: *peccata contra naturam*).

Whose nature?

Fortunately, not all of our forebears were burned at the stake eviscerated ripped apart by horses (their arms and legs having been tied to four poor unwilling different animals) crushed inside an iron maiden hanged pressed to the width of an envelope by stones thrown into the river to drown had their tongues cut out balls cut off twats mutilated sentenced to hard labor chemically castrated made to undergo aversion therapy or fired from the Boy Scouts. Fortunately, some of them were only stuck into ships' galleys and forced to work like slaves. (For actual slavery see: American History.)

Some of them got to America.

Then some of them made us.

OK, I don't mean "made us" in the carnal sense (though they did so, and happily, some). I mean "made us" by keeping the faith, by carrying on the way they did and dressing the way they did, by doing things they knew we'd recognize, though others wouldn't, by leaving us signs like bread crumbs in the woods that told us we were not the first and that we weren't alone. They kept our secret and passed it on in hopes someday we'd see.

Though the Albigensian movement was suppressed by the crusades of the mid-13th century, believers continued to have faith and meet in secret. A look at the map of the south of France will reveal the lingering presence of Cathar culture in village names such as Queribus (Latin for Queer Town); Montsegur (Latin for Mountain Man Town or Daddyville, a town still occupied by large hairy men and their cubs); Foix (Latin for fag); and so forth. Gertrude Stein, a parfait, and her parfait wife, Alice B. Toklas, lived in Perpignan for many years and hostessed American military boys who traveled to see them two by two, initiating them into the cuisine, culture and unnatural practices of the Cathars.

(Stein, who, though Cathar, was famously misogynist, was not much interested in other communities of female parfaits, such as the one centered around Natalie Barney in Paris.)

Toklas was also the early twentieth century Keeper of the Recipe. Among Toklas' contributions to Cathar/ Albigensian culture were her insistence on the purity of the cocoa and the addition of optional other ingredients for particularly visionary rituals of worship.

Stein, for her part, was not only the authoress of the modern version of the Albigensian Liturgy of the Supper, but also actually The Giver of the Name to the cookie that had remained heretofore, for reasons of security, unnamed. The brilliant linguistic play for which Stein is known can be seen in the variety of sources, puns and interpretations of the simple four-letter name she created:

(From Latin (or) meaning gold, (re) meaning King and (o) meaning Oh). Starting and ending with "O" the omega, the beginning as/is the end, the completion of the whole, the roundness of the world, the lifted belly, the shape of the mouth in ecstasy, whether erotic or cuisinic, middled by the injunction to "re-ad" my (that is, Stein's own) books, to re-ad the signs you see around you everywhere, to re-peat what bears re-peating, to re-peat with all the earnestness of love, over and over re-peating and re-peating until you get it right, but also not only toward any end but just because the re-peating is exciting, lovely and peaceful. To start with "Or," thereby acknowledging that everything is only and infinitely possible, an either/or, a maybe else.

Then further, ore, the mass from which you mine the streak, the seam of what is hidden, what you want, the richest, sweetest thing.

A nod to the Or-phic mysteries, which or-iginated with Orpheus, the Singer! Whose poems could charm the pants off one.

Also, the song the slaves in *The Wizard of Oz* sing when they are slaving away because soon they'll be released: "O-re-O. Oo-oh! Oh. O-re-O. Oo-oh! Oh."

The food of children everywhere!

The sustenance of us.

Stein also told us how to read the secret meanings of both The Parts and of The Ways.

The wafers being hard and two are boys. They rub each other up and get that creme. The creme sticks them together like they're married, like if you pulled them apart before their time it's sticky and wrong, little frosting tips poking up like peaks, them crying out on both sides, ripped apart. Or if one side gets all the creme, like "getting the girl," as they say in the other history, like when you get to marry her, the other one, the other side is brown-black mostly sort of bruised-looking because no matter how clean you lick it away or scrape it with your teeth, a teeny little bit of it, like snow that's melting into dirt, remains. Some of it has seeped into the inside of the biscuit and it will not be removed, no, never, it's a stain, it's like a person who cannot forget a way he was, the way he should have stayed.

The two are also a woman's thighs, and the creme between—oh, the creme between!—is Heaven's invitation.

Oh, to approach the thighs of the Madonna! So firm and dark and clutching. It clutches what there is within but waiting to be out, and clutches you and what you want and what you want to give, to get from her, what is inside, both her and you, the moist and white and opening.

Her darkness spliced by mystery! Her cloven self both opening unto and pouring out, the thing you bring, the thing that you desire.

The white of sap, the thick of creme, like mothering of milk.

The Manichean meeting of the Evil and the Good, of black and white, of dark and light. Inside and out, the hard and soft and dry and moist, the chocolate and vanilla: cookie(s) and creme.

The mystery of the 3 in one: the biscuit Father, biscuit Son, and creme-y center Ghost.

A secret writ in Braille that you read out with your tongue.

The way you opened it, then what you did, would tell you and your fellows who you were.

If you ate it fast or whole, a bite and a break and a chew like it was just a snack, then you were clueless. We knew you were not one of us and we might then be careful what we say or do around you.

The rest of us knew what to do and how to do it right.

If she slowly, slowly twists it nice and even, one hand beneath and turning clockwise, and the other hand above and turning counter, if she holds her hands both openly but firmly, if she takes her precious time, then cracks it open, opens them and waits. Then if she brings it to her face and looks, at it and then at you, then breathes in like the ocean or the sky, the whole outdoors, if she breathes in deep the it of it, then, with her tongue or with her teeth, begins to lick or scrape or press along the white, if she leaves tracks of tongue or tooth around, across or down, into the creme then to the chocolate, then she stops, then takes a moment, looks again, as if she's looking at the dawning of the world, as if she's looking at a miracle, then starts, as slow as before, then gradually unslowing...if she removes the creme by slow firm tooth- or tongue-ful, then, finally, when the creme is gone, her mouth is sweet, and something's moist and melting, warm, then slipping down her throat like oil, wine, some thing divine, and then hands you the other.... The chocolate is supple, bending, nearly limp. If then she puts one in her mouth and one in yours, and sucks or tongues or presses, nibbles, bites, you know that she is one of us, parfait and pure and yours.

> We watch to learn the way we are
> and see we always were.
> We tell the stories that we must
> and see what we believe..

NOTES

Some of the historic stuff—and all of it's true, with the obvious exceptions of what I invented because I fantasize—comes from:

Rictor Norton, A History of Homophobia, "4 Gay Heretics and Witches," 15, April 2002. http://www.infopt.demon.co.uk/homopho4.htm.

You can read a lot about the historic residue of the Cathars, et al, in Montaillou, by Emmanuel Le Roy Ladurie. This book is based on records of a heresy trial in the south of France from 1319 to 1324.

The Catholic Encyclopedia is where I got the specifics about Dominic and Diego, Pope Innocent III, the Crusades, etc. But I've also been fascinated by Dominic and his Dogs for years, and, ever since I was a kid, the Crusades.

I began reading Stein in high school on the advice of a deliriously, to me, androgynous camp counselor. A few years later, my mother gave me Janet Hobhouse's biography of Stein, Everybody Who Was Anybody

(Putnam, 1975) for Christmas and then I found *The Autobiography of Alice B. Toklas* at the library and then, at college, the poems and lectures and the Modern Library and Black Sparrow editions and I made a Sunday afternoon salon with my writer and musician and painter pals in the old brownstone where some of us lived.

Other stuff comes from recent American history and the backs of snack boxes.

IV

A What the NGELS EAT

The Vegetable Kingdom mark of Guillame Merlin

16th-century Paris bookseller

THE TELL-TALE TONGUE
FOR EDGAR
"...of rather delicate and slender mould..."

Jennifer Heath

RUE!—hungry—very, very dreadfully hungry I had been and am; but why will you say that I am mad? The hunger has sharpened my senses—not destroyed—not dulled them. Above all was the sense of smell acute. I smelled all things on Heaven and Earth. I smelled many things—roasting, baking, broiling—in Hell. How, then, am I mad? Obsessive? Compulsive? Nervous? Hearken! And observe how healthily—how calmly I can tell you the whole story.

It is impossible to say how first the idea entered my brain; but once conceived, it haunted me day and night.

Object there was none. Passion there was none. I merely wanted to be slim. Is that so wrong? I think it's in the eyes. The eyes of those models in periodicals and on television; the dark-rimmed, piercing eyes peering from bony starlet faces, eyes wider than their waists, filmy, hungry eyes. I did not yet know that was the look of hunger. I thought only that those eyes were beautiful and that they told of languid strength and womanliness, so different from the famished, hollow eyes of children in Africa or Afghanistan. Whenever I looked into the eyes of twiggish girls on magazine covers at grocery stores—where I purchased bags and bags of foods to sequester and admire, but never to let my lips devour—I longed, too, for ribs exposed, for legs and arms like toothpicks, knees and elbows sharp as stones; I yearned to be gloriously hung with silks and satins, woollens and leathers. And those eyes, those eyes—my blood ran cold as I touched my own soft belly, felt my thighs rub together when I walked. One can never be too thin. Never too thin. Never, I told myself as I gazed in the mirror and observed the chubby cheeks that nearly obliterated my own eyes when I smiled, the double chin—oh! I shuddered and hated myself and so, by degrees, very gradually, I made up my mind to reduce, to disappear this puffy flesh, to rid my soul of envy, cleanse my heart of desire and, like those slinking lank and lovely creatures, gape at the world with that eye, that hungry, defiant, confident, glamorous eye.

Now this is the point. You fancy me mad. Anorexics know nothing, we are weak-brained and brittle.

Withdrawn and irritable. But you should have seen me. You should have seen how wisely I proceeded—with what caution—with what foresight—with what dissimulation I went to work. I counted every calorie. I sneaked, clever and undetected into the territory called bulimia and purged when I was forced to eat in public or counted out my laxatives—one, two, three, four…ninety-eight, ninety-nine, one hundred—so as not to maintain a single morsel in my shrinking belly. I cut every scrap on my plate into tiny pieces, I exercised for hours each day—you say I am weak and that my bones are shrunken? How many hours can you run on a treadmill? How fast and long can you pedal a stationary bicycle?

Oh, but I was still and ever vexed. I collected cookbooks with the most delicious illustrations. I copied sundry recipes precisely onto three-by-five cards and tucked them into a silver box. But concoct these dishes? Not once did I oil—or soil—my pots and pans. Yet nightly my eyes consumed lyric instructions for confections and casseroles, roasts and raviolis, layered and luscious dishes fit for royalty. And—after awhile—how proud I was!—I no longer hankered or drooled, but studied each method— basting, braising, folding, whisking, whipping—with cool objectivity, my eye as aloof as those of the cover girls whose blank faces stared at me from the walls of my sparkling, unused kitchen, for I collected them, too, and pasted their photos upon my walls.

Lettuce and zucchini. Tomatoes, cucumbers and radishes. All too, too fattening. Yet every day a victory:

another ounce gone, another pound evaporated. Oh! But I must contain my feelings of triumph: to think that I was losing weight, little by little, and nevertheless I am fat, so fat, too fat. You say my bones rattle under my skin, but do you not perceive the lumps and bumps and plump that linger? That will not go no matter how determined I am, no matter how disciplined?

You would have laughed to see how cunningly I shopped. In the morning, I visited the butcher and the dairy; in the afternoon, the baker and the greengrocer. I inched through the aisles picking cheeses, meats and mixes, choosing—oh so carefully!—dressings and sauces, spices and herbs, fishes and fowls, fruits and creams and cakes and cookies. Gooey, slimy, mashed or marinated. Fresh or frozen. Packaged or bulk.

And when I returned home, I hid my treasures, gently— oh so gently! pried open the floorboards, slowly—very, very slowly (for floorboards creak), so that I might not disturb the neighbors. I hoarded it all, though my fridge was empty and my cupboards bare. I stuffed my bounty behind the walls, in nooks, in crannies. I fattened the house, though I ate not a bite and all the while the starlets watched me, never smiling, always watching, watching with those vulture eyes, as cautiously—oh, so cautiously!—I might poke a tiny hole just beneath the molding and stuff it with olives, one by one from a jar, or pull apart a lintel and spread it with artichoke dip or loosen a light fixture and fill the glass bowl with honeyed donuts. Never before had I felt the extent of my own powers—of my sagacity, surrounded by all I craved and yet not letting it pass my lips. Why, I fairly chuckled with pride in my vigor and the girls, the skinny girls upon the walls, clucked back. What's that? I asked, What did you say?

And so it went. My house was permeated with a luscious fragrance that grew more pungent, riper every day, the sweet scent of rot as weeks passed and the house seemed to grow corpulent even as it seemed to shrink.

Day by day, the house ballooned. Day by day, it squeezed me until at last there was only a little crevice to move about. I must lose weight, I thought, more, for this house is closing in on me. And the eyes on the walls scowled at me, angry, give us space, they insisted.

And have I not told you that what you mistake for madness is but over-acuteness of the senses? Now I say, there came to my ears a low, dull, quick sound, such as a watch makes when enveloped in cotton. Presently, I heard a small groan, the low stifled sound that arises from the bottom of the soul when overcharged with awe. I knew that sound well. Many a night, just at midnight when all the world slept, it has welled in my own concave bosom, deepening into my gut, with its dreadful echo, the hunger that distracts me. My stomach growled and the women on the wall watched and now their blood-red lips began to move, first one, then another, eyes unblinking, framed in black kohl, large, and evil. Amid the dreadful silence of that house—as it simultaneously expanded and contracted—oh, but I could not breathe—there came a hellish chatter, quicker and quicker, louder and louder every instant. Feedfeed*feed*, the scarlet mouths moved slowly—very slowly—meme*me*, they pleaded, feedmefeedme*feedme*, louder and louder.

If you still think me mad, you will think so no longer when I describe the wise precautions I took to silence those voices and fill those mouths. I worked hastily, taking up planks from the flooring and scraping the composting foodstuffs from them, then rushing from one pair of sucking ruby lips to the next, first with a fork, then with my very hands, cramming the decomposing provisions into their maws, until finally the chatter stopped, the insistent demands tapered off and away. I glanced up, and the mouths, all smeared with putrid victuals were tranquil, all but one. Feedme*feedme*feedme, it continued, fat*fat*fat, it chanted. I shrieked. I could not bear the sound. I caught my reflection in the shiny refrigerator door, so seldom opened, and the mouth kept moving, *fatfatfat*!! Shut up, I screamed and banged it with a large slotted copper spoon. Shut up!! I yelled. Just then there came a knocking at my door.

I went to open it with a light heart—for what had I to fear? There entered a comely middle-aged woman—rather chunky, but motherly and mild—wearing a green apron on which was embroidered "World's Best Chef." She introduced herself with perfect suavity as my neighbor. She had heard a shriek and wondered if I was in danger.

I smiled—for what had I to fear? I bade the lady welcome. The shriek, I said, was my own in a dream. I did not dare invite her in, and all the while she stood at my door, her nose twitched at the bouquet within. Come, she said, come to my house. Perhaps a cup of tea to calm the nerves and bring peaceful dreams when you return to bed. Behind me, I could hear a rumbling, the clearing of throats, the licking of bee-stung lips. I've made a lovely gingerbread, my neighbor said soothingly, and took my hand. My ears were ringing, the voices growing louder, feedme*feed*me feedfeed*feed* fatyoufatyoufat*you*.

In the neighbor's kitchen, I was singularly at ease. She sat me down and while I answered cheerily, she chatted of familiar things. No, thank you, I responded meekly to her offer of cake, then wondered if the tea—consoling chamomile—might not have too many calories and so I raised the cup to my mouth but only pretended to sip.

The kitchen was warm and steamy, and upon the stove there bubbled a large pot that smelled of savory meats and herbs, sage and rosemary and perhaps a dash of red wine. My head ached. The deep and earthy aroma seemed to overwhelm me, but whether with comfort or anxiety, I could not tell. I inhaled the air close around it. It seemed to call to me. No doubt I now grew very pale, but I talked more fluently and with a heightened voice and yet the odor increased and with it came a low, dull, light splash, much the sound a wave makes as it laps the shore. My neighbor leaned toward me and touched my cheek. You seem so hungry, my dear, she whispered, how can I help you? Oh I'm fine, I replied, and began again to talk, more and more quickly, more vehemently; but the heady smell increased and the glubbing words from within the boiling pot grew louder. My neighbor reached across the table and placed a napkin, a soup spoon, and sliced bread in front of me. Come my dear, come help yourself, she said. Here is the ladle and here is a bowl. Open the pot and take as much as you would like.

I argued, but she persisted. Come my dear, come along now, you must eat. Nothing like a full warm belly to quiet the nerves…and she took me gently by the shoulders, guided me toward the pot. Go ahead, she said, take what you like. I clutched the ladle and for a moment wanted to whack her hard upon the skull and hand—let me go! I'm nauseous—but the lady had already lifted the lid of the pot.

There, within, floating atop a mass of onions and potatoes, celery and carrots, was a tongue. Rolling, roiling, undulating in the brown herbed water. And as it reeled and flapped in its broth it hissed: Never too thin. Never too thin. Never. Never.

I screamed. Oh God! What could I do? I foamed—I raved—I swore. I dropped the ladle and crushed the bowl between my hands. I swayed, my heart skipping and jumping, my breath coming in short bursts. Stop it! I begged, but my neighbor cocked her head at me with utter puzzlement. Was it possible she could not hear the tongue grow louder—louder—louder! Never too thin. Never too thin—it jeered. Why was she—why was it?—making a mockery of my horror? Oh, anything was better than this agony. Anything more tolerable than this derision. The tongue boiled on—never too thin, never too thin—it chorused louder! louder! louder!

Never. Never too thin. Never!

NOTE:

TRIALS, TRUFFLES, TRIBULATIONS

Anorexia is self-imposed famine, a sad phenomenon of modern, by-and-large Western, prosperity. Once upon a time, everywhere, to be plump was to be beautiful, for fat indicated abundance, well-fed wealth.

In times of troubles, we move down the food chain (and lose weight). Some foodstuffs have entered our cupboards via starvation. When crops or banks fail, when war destroys fields, humans have sought nourishment with provisions otherwise eschewed.* Certain grains, such as barley or oats, which in good seasons were only fed to livestock, and various kinds of root vegetables, such as turnips, which were scavenged when meat was unavailable, have today become staples, even culinary treasures.

Truffles, now expensive commodities, were once taboo, fungi, dug out from under trees in forests—in certain areas of Spain they are called *criadillas de tierra*, earth testicles—and eaten by the poor only as a last resort.

Famine foods are of course related to wild foods such as those Euell Gibbons, author of Stalking the Wild Asparagus, *espoused, and on which he claimed to have survived during the Great Depression, when he and his family would otherwise have gone hungry.*

Recipe for Famine Foods
Barley Risotto with Truffles

2 Tbsp. unsalted butter

1 tsp. olive oil

1 large shallot, minced

1 small clove garlic, minced

$\frac{1}{3}$ cup dry white wine

½ cup pearl barley

3½ cups chicken stock, heated

1 truffle, sliced—if fresh—into matchstick sizes

Melt 1 tablespoon of the butter with the oil in a large heavy skillet over medium heat. Stir in the shallot and cook for 1 minute.

Add the garlic, cook 4 more minutes. Stir in the wine, scraping bottom and sides of pan.

Heat to boiling; boil until slightly syrupy, about 4 minutes. Reduce the heat to medium-low, add the barley and stir until well-coated with shallot mixture. Stir in 1 cup of the hot stock. Cook, stirring frequently, until all liquid has been absorbed, about 15 minutes. (Reduce heat if liquid absorbs too quickly.)

Stir in another cup of stock and continue to cook, stirring frequently, until all liquid has been absorbed, about 15 minutes.

Add a third cup of stock and continue to cook, stirring frequently, until all liquid has been absorbed, about 15 minutes.

Add the remaining ½ cup of stock and continue to cook until the barley is tender and all liquid has been absorbed, about 15 minutes. Raise the heat slightly if the mixture is too wet. Lower heat and cover.

Melt the remaining tablespoon of butter in a heavy pan. When butter has frothed, add truffles and toss over heat for 1 minute, no more.

Put barley risotto on warm individual plates and top with truffles. Serve with a side of mashed turnips.

BUG SOUP

COMFORT

Ellen Orleans

alfway between Minsk and nostalgia, across the not-
yet-existent border from Chelm, long before the
Shoah and a full two years since the last pogrom,
Alter ben Fischkel threw bread into the water, casting off
his sins for the year.

*For the sin of scheming. For the sin of talebearing. For the
sin of impure thoughts.*

Alter was an impatient man. Fractious. If asked, his
shtetl neighbors might have termed him a misanthrope. All
of which likely explained why, on this slate grey morning,
angular, patchy-bearded Alter was tossing his sins into
the most stagnant corner of the shtetl's cold lake instead
of walking a quarter-mile to where the waters narrowed

and current quickened, promising a clean conveyance of his yeasty transgressions.

For the sin of coercion. For the sin of deception.

Alter spoke the words mechanically, threw his offerings like an automaton. His burdened bread sank as if exhausted, lodging itself in the invisible murk deep below the surface. If Alter had stopped to consider that nothing is invisible to *Ha Shem* might he have made the walk? No. Alter was in a mood to challenge God. After all, shouldn't it be God repenting? Alter's parents slaughtered in a Cossack raid, his brother, just twelve, dragged off to serve the Army. His sister, fourteen, dragged off to serve worse. And he, Alter, an ineffectual ten-year-old, hidden, cowering, seeing it all. How did God cast off his own failure to protect, his dereliction of duty?

For the sin of hardening the heart.

For that matter, Alter had asked, what kind of God created a world where such horror was *de rigueur*, the standard dull fare? Who among the Jews had not weathered such? His mind thus set, at age fifteen Alter left his cousin's crowded house to chart his own life, telling neither fellow travelers nor new neighbors his history. Who wanted their sympathy, or worse, to hear their own woes?

Alter tossed two more scraps. *For the sin of growing soft. For the sin of trusting others...*

While only God saw under the surface, passing villagers saw something else. Concentric circles on still water. The growing "O's" reminded Zisal of the mouth of Izzie, her ever-crying infant. Young Shimmel, who'd also been orphaned by Cossacks, thought of tree trunks and the cord of wood he was supposed to be chopping. Bina, tardy with her own chores, blushed hard, reminded of the forbidden circle between the widow Bluma's legs she had pleasured at dawn.

Mendel the Baker passed as Alter tossed in the final heel: *for the sin of insincere confession*. Mendel looked but did not see, was not reminded of anything. Yet, he remembered.

ii

God was great. Mendel's bread was not. Mendel was a timid baker, inspiration long ago beaten back. He baked the same blocky loaves his father had baked, never straying from the old man's measurements. But that afternoon, when Mendel should have been closing the drapes, wiping the cutting boards and climbing the stairs to his apartment above the shop, the *Shechina*, God's loving transcendent presence, slipped in through the closed door.

Oddly at peace, Mendel stayed put. He watched the large window panes grow dim, turn to mirrors, then, when his last lamp burned out, to ink. In the darkness, he saw Alter's bread hitting the water. His serenity dissolved. *Why bread?* he asked, uncharacteristically discontent. *Why my bread to carry the sin?* Why not Lazer's shoe leather, Toppel's tin scraps, or even pages themselves from Alter's dusty books?

Unbeknownst to Mendel, more than the divine had entered his shop. All day, Alter's bread, tumescent with sin, had sat at the bottom of the lake, until, swollen beyond capacity, its transgressions had swum upward. Surfacing, they'd become one, gaining breath, life and presence. Mendel's shop, its first stop.

Eventually, Mendel's indignant thoughts of Alter slid into to wistful thoughts of Ruchel, who, everyone knew, would someday be Alter's bride. Mendel thought unhappily of the shtetl's other couples, lovers old and young, even of the widow Bluma and spinster Bina. Mendel normally did not care to involve himself in people's private matters—why shouldn't one gather a little joy between miseries? Tonight, though, he felt infested with...what? Revulsion? Envy? Injustice? Why didn't Rabbi Macher instruct the observant ones to throw the golden-yolked eggs of Bluma's hens in the water? *Why bread, Lord?* he beseeched. *Why the taint, the stain?*

As the night stilled, the divine pushed out the devious, and Mendel reconsidered the concentric rings. The bread sank, yes, but not without a fight, not without sending out circle after circle of protest, of memory. *I was here. I was here.* Still in his bakery, without knowing or questioning or stopping, at the hour he should have been blowing out the last candle and pulling the goosedown around him, Mendel stoked the fire. He reached for his largest bowl, his longest whisk, his best bag of flour. Bluma's freshest eggs. His youngest yeast.

Following a soundless voice within, he stirred his lightest honey into the hottest water his fingers could endure. He sprinkled in the yeast which, unlike Alter's scuttled lumps, first lay pollen-like on the surface. Waiting for it to prove itself, Mendel hummed a wordless *niggun*. Soon the bakery filled with the sweet beeriness of foaming yeast. As he hummed, Mendel washed and scrubbed and rinsed. Thus cleansed, he added flour and salt to the froth, and ebullient himself, plunged in his hands.

Mendel kneaded. He kneaded and added handfuls of flour, then half handfuls, then just a pinch until he turned the bowl onto the floured block, where he stretched and turned the dough for as long as God wanted, listening, but not too intently, for the command to stop. It would come. When it did, Mendel oiled the bowl lightly and replaced the dough. Child rejoining the mother. Baker rejoining his creator.

With his finger tips, Mendel spread a fine film of oil over the top of the mound. Unbidden, he saw the smooth, round stomach of all-but-betrothed Ruchel. Mendel had only seen Ruchel's flesh once, unintended of course, as she hung laundry on a blustery day. Whispering an apology to Ruchel and God, Mendel lay a wetted cloth over the bowl.

Mendel waited.

For the dough to rise. For guidance. For what to do with the mass of warm, leavening dough, soon to breach the lip of the bowl. Mendel considered. Mendel hummed. Mendel breathed. Mendel, without realizing it, prayed.

Without knowing why, Mendel filled his heaviest pot with water and set it on the stove. Since it was nearly the new year, he tossed in malt for sweetness.

When the dough had doubled, he returned it to the board and pulled off a small section. He watched as his hands rolled it into a cylinder, a tube, into Eve's snake. He worked the mountain of dough this way until an Eden's worth of snakes inhabited his bakery counters. Looking at them, he remembered that the rabbi would soon read the last words of the Torah and then immediately the first, how that scroll, his people's Book of Life, circled upon itself. He put his left hand on the snake's head, the right on the tail and joined them, his own loop of months, his reclamation of Alter's circles. One by one, as Mendel watched, half in disbelief and half in utter acceptance, each of his snakes stretched, turned and bit its own tail.

Spellbound, Mendel stared, as, in an act that was perhaps women's *mikvah* or the Christians' baptism, one, two, then three snake hoops leapt into the pot of water, that round simmering sea. At first, like Alter's discarded bread, Mendel's hoops sunk. But, ah, a small miracle—they rose. Like the moon's reflection, they floated atop the water, until, curiously and of their own volition, they flipped. After a few moments, Mendel removed them. In threes and fives he dropped the rest of the breads into the water, each in turn, sinking and rising.

What was left but to bake them? On cornmeal-sprinkled baking sheets, he laid down circle after circle. Mendel was not truly surprised to hear, as the minutes passed, thumps and thuds from within the oven. He opened its door to see the small breads turning themselves over, some performing a jovial half flip, others simply standing up then dropping onto their sides. Shortly after, he pulled them from the heat and inspected his and Ha Shem's co-creation. Golden holy suns. Sheet after sheet, he baked, and after the last sheet, Mendel lifted his eyes to God's sun, breaking through its horizon, beaming into his steaming window.

Knuckles rapped on the window. Bina. Mendel unlatched the door, wary as she spoke. "It's everywhere," she said, her slender hands gesturing. "Gliding along the streets, mulling on front steps, tucked between our sheets."

"What is?"

"The swelling yeast. The browning crust. The swirling…"

Embarrassed by her sensuous detail, Mendel balked. "I am baking," he said, stumbling in his words. "I am a baker. Are you inferring—"

"Mendel, it is all right." Entirely inappropriate, she put her hand on his shoulder. More like a sister's than an unmarried woman's. "All night," she said, "it lay upon us, a welcome blanket, twining with our dreams."

He nodded. "You are the first. Come see."

What Bina saw, just after sunrise, were racks and trays and piles of breads, round as the circles on yesterday's water. Recalling her vision of Bluma, she blushed. "I'll take three," she whispered. She exchanged coins for the wrapped parcel, then, gaining composure, paused before the door. "Your round breads. What do you call them?"

"They need a name?" thought Mendel. "They are round breads, Bina. *Bugel* breads. That is all."

Bina smiled. "*Mazel tov*, Mendel. You have invented the bagel."

Although the bakery did not open for two more hours, as Bina left, Schmuel the butcher walked in, blood on his apron. A man of few words, he saw Mendel's breads, nodded, one food man to another. He bought one for each hand. Left chewing.

Mendel's bakery teemed with customers that day. Lazer the cobbler. Toppel the scraps merchant. Leeba, wife of the nine-fingered rabbi. Shy Koppel, buying for his mother. Zisal bought one for herself and one for her fussing baby. Even Alter, who never purchased more than day-old, bought a dozen to impress Ruchel.

Outside the shop, Mendel's breads took on lives of their own. Bina crawled back into bed with hers still warm, placing them, twin aureoles, on Bluma's generous breasts. Both were late for their morning chores. Mid-morning, Rabbi Macher, his wife Leeba and their *cheder*-ditching grandson Dovid, sat down for tea and bagels and tales of the rabbi's escape from the Czar's army. At noon, Zisal's baby Izzie grabbed his bagel, and teething upon it, grew content for the first time in weeks.

Mid-afternoon, Alter clumsily presented his dozen to Ruchel. "So much bread for as much as I want you to be my wife."

Ruchel, long awaiting, long resigned, smiled weakly. Life as Alter's wife would not be so bad. There were always the books, weren't there? What woman wouldn't want those forbidden fruits? "Does this mean I can finally dust off your webby shelves?" she teased. "Organize your dusty ledger?" She was good at numbers. He was not. If not in love, she could at least be of use.

Alter laughed. "My wife will tend the house. I will tend my books."

But Ruchel already tended a house: for her three brothers as they grew, mother dead from childbirth with the youngest. Afterwards, for her father who had last year joined her mother in the world to come. Refusing the invitation of cousins and aunts, Ruchel lived alone, taking in wash. The villagers whispered not so quietly that it was long past time to take a husband, any husband.

Ruchel did not say no to Alter but neither did she say yes. Alter returned to his bookshop, confident in her forthcoming acquiescence.

Meanwhile, Mendel, increasingly animated, described his creations to each new taker: Eve's snakes, biting their tails. Rosh Hashana made dough, the year in its cycle. The halo of an angel, the eye of a mortal, the orbit of the planets.

At the day's end, the shop empty of customers and nearly of bagels, Ruchel walked in. Mendel reddened, thinking of the early morning dough, soft, rising. "Ruchel," he nearly stammered, "I am not one to ruin surprises, but Alter bought a dozen. You need not buy more."

"I am not here to see circles of bread but their creator." She pointed to the last bagel. "What inspired you? Lily pad? Crown? Stirrup?"

Talk of snakes and halos tied up Mendel's tongue. Wordlessly, he reached for the last bagel, a plump one with a generous middle. "This one," he said, sliding it over Ruchel's extended finger, "is a ring."

Ruchel looked into the baker's eyes. "Mendel, are you proposing?"

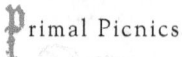

"If I were, would you say yes?"

"I would."

"I am."

iii

Alter, of course, did not attend the wedding. Losing Ruchel was a blow, but losing her to floury Mendel, as doughy as his bread, was intolerable.

Shortly after Simcha Torah, as Ruchel and Mendel exchanged vows under the *chupa*, Alter's bread, engorged still with sin, disgorged. Again, its evil rose to the surface. While the fragrance of Mendel's baking bagels had driven the first wave of wickedness into oblivion, today the bakery was closed. Malevolence was free to roam. Finding it could not enter the *shul*, it instead sought out its creator, whose anger needed little to be stoked. Alter considered sheep's blood, considered a sharp knife, chose live embers. Placing hot coals in a tin pail, he walked the empty streets to Ruchel's house. He had not been there since his failed proposal, the disastrous gift of bagels which augured his downfall. Alter dumped the embers on the double bed and walked out. God would do the rest.

As Mendel and Ruchel kissed, the coverlet began to smolder. Mendel smashed the wine glass. The quilt began to burn. The guests lifted Mendel and Ruchel on chairs. The curtains caught. The fire nearly stopped there, tottering between extinction and renewal as wine glasses danced in the air, shouted *L'Chaim's* beside them. Nearly. As the dancing continued deep into the night, Alter's mislaid sins blew through the house, scattering sparks.

Young Koppel, Ruchel's neighbor, awoke to the smell of smoke. He ran to the shul. The whole town ran back. Too late.

"An accident," Rabbi Macher declared. "Praise God no one was hurt. And only one home." Mendel, who wasn't feeling so generous, believed it the work of Cossacks, their raids returned. He said nothing. Ruchel was sure it was Alter. She said nothing as well. Both agreed a candle must have been left burning.

Mendel shook his head. "On our wedding day. An ominous sign."

Ruchel disagreed. "It is three in the morning, my love. No longer our wedding day. This was my old life. Today, my new life begins." Flames out and flames just begun, the couple moved into Mendel's snug apartment above the bakery.

The shtetl supplied Mendel and Ruchel with clothes and rugs and soaps while Mendel and Ruchel supplied the shtetl with bagels. With a quiet bliss, Ruchel kept the bakery ledger while Mendel experimented with seeds and herbs and salts.

Alter rarely left his tiny store front. Sleeping on a straw cot, shunning the bakery, he grew ever more angular. God's decision, he said of the fire. I only wanted to burn the bed. God wanted the whole house. As the nights lengthened, Alter fumed. Why had God demanded he be an accomplice in such an act? Why must he now carry such concerns? Egged on by the pulsing evil of his submerged sins, he squabbled with the cobbler, bickered with the scrap dealer, slighted

Sekel, seller of salted fish. These quarrels did nothing to ease his rage at God and Mendel, but, because it was unacceptable to denigrate the newlyweds (and who, outside the Torah, could successfully argue with God?), Alter turned on Bluma and Bina, the town's most vulnerable.

Insinuating uncleanliness, he traveled one town over to buy meager chicken eggs instead of Bluma's robust ones. Citing inconsistency, he no longer took his mending to Bina but let his cuffs and collars fray. At first his neighbors countered his slurs:

They are hurting no one, Alter.

Live and let live.

The Cossacks aren't enough?

But in the way that oppressed people turn on each other, the townspeople grew intolerant. When Yudel the olive oil peddler did not appear for weeks on end—the villagers worrying for their Chanukah lights—Alter saw his chance. Standing close as his customers paged through his books, his unkempt hair matted with dust, he casually mentioned an unnamed pair who had stockpiled oil. Perhaps even stolen it. If they were capable of unspeakable acts, surely they'd not hesitate to thieve and hoard.

Inadvertently, Alter was half-right. Last spring, Bina had stocked up on oil for her evening mending. She now shared most evenings with Bluma, her mending moved to daylight, her evenings foreshortened by the widow's attractions. Together, they had an ample supply.

Bina and Bluma knew of the murmured accusations. Now, on the first night of Chanukah, sun arcing west,

Schmuel the butcher stood on the hard-packed dirt road in front of Bluma's home, threadbare coat covering his beefy body, swirls from patched snow circling his feet. Bina peered outside. "What does he want?"

"What else? The oil." Ever prescient, Bluma lit the kindling in the woodstove.

"We *should* share it," Bina told her, returning to the question they'd been rehashing all week. "Give it all away."

"We've done nothing wrong." Bluma reached for the oversized skillet that hung on the wall. Seeing Bina's expression, she laughed. "No, my love, I am not going to clobber Schmuel the butcher."

Bina reached around Bluma's thick sweater, ran the pads of her fingers along her fine collarbone. "We tread on poor soil, my dearest."

Bluma lowered her head, kissed the long fingers. "We tread on love."

Touched but not appeased, Bina again peered from behind the curtain. Lazer the cobbler and Toppel the scraps merchant had joined Schmuel. The three stood not close enough to be callers, not far enough to ignore. Bluma stoked the fire, then reached for her heaviest, sharpest knife. "No, my love!" Bina cried, only now understanding the cast iron pan a diversion in Bluma's keen plotting. "Remember the sixth commandment!"

"I am not murdering anyone," Bluma assured her. "Other than root vegetables."

"Vegetables? They do not want chopped vegetables. They want *oil*. The smart thing to do is to give them the oil."

"The smart thing is to feed them."

Bina's voice pitched. "With what? We have no meat. No fish. Our winter's store of potatoes? A few onions—"

But Bluma was preoccupied. "Bina, be my blessed and search the coop for eggs."

Bina complied, first checking behind the house for unwanted guests. The wise murmuring hens parted for her like the Red Sea, offering up twice their usual offering. Meanwhile, Bluma's swift knife had amassed a Mount Sinai's worth of slivered potatoes. Bluma handed Bina her largest bowl. Posing no more questions, Bina cracked the eggs, bright yolks boldly upright in the albumen. Reluctantly, she whisked them to a frothy yellow. Bluma pressed liquid from the potatoes. Bina minced onions. Wiping tears from her eyes, the younger woman finally asked, "What are we doing?"

"With apologies to Judah Macabee, we are making our olive oil disappear." She tilted her head toward the corner cabinet. "The jug."

After handing Bluma the oil, Bina again peeked through the curtains. The crowd had tripled, wool-coated men arguing, headscarfed women leaning into each other, whispering, pointing. Someone carried a torch. Bluma's voice turned Bina's attention back to the stove. "My love, I know they are amassing and I know what one is carrying, so let us act quickly. Pull out all the plates, all the silver, all the glasses. Set the table as if for Sabbath."

More from desperation than trust, Bina spread the mended tablecloth, cobalt blue, and gathered the chairs, wooden and cracked, upholstered and worn, wickered and threatening to yield. As she lay the place settings, she heard the snap of hot oil. As she poured water, she heard the scrape of the spatula. Finally, when the table looked good enough for the Sabbath Queen herself (assuming the Queen would forgive the tarnish of the forks, the cracks of the china), the air so thick with the smell of onions and oil that it was in itself a meal, Bina walked to the stove. There, against the black expanse of cast iron, fulgent in their bubbling amniotic oil, lay eight gold and brown lattice suns. A dozen others sat brightly on sheets of butcher paper, the much sought-after oil draining. Still more basked in the oven.

As the rumble of the crowd grew louder, the two moved swiftly, transforming the raw mix of potato, onion and egg into sizzling, redolent, crenulated marvels, a treat for the ear, nose and eyes. From pan to paper to warming sheet, the cakes of potato paraded by. After Bluma slid the last one from the pan, she reached for the Chanukah menorah and tipped the remaining oil first into its highest metal cup, then into the cup for this first night. Only then did she lift the final potato cake to Bina's lips. "The rest will be good," she said, "but this one, fresh from the sizzle, the finest." Bina's indulged mouth expressed her pleasure fully. Bluma dabbed a trace of oil from her lover's lower lip and, together, they finished Bluma's creation.

Bina wiped the pan clean, while Bluma hid the oil-soaked papers in the rubbish. When she returned, Bina squeezed her lover's hand, then released her to the crowd, whose cries of *hoarder*, *abomination* and *ganef*, now surrounded the house. Bluma flung open the door. "*Hag Samaech!*" she cried. "Happy Chanukah! I'm so glad you all could come." Confused, the throng, shuffled and stared, wondering who among them were the invited. Bina laughed. "Don't just stand there. All of you, come in."

Gingerly, the crowd entered. Seeing the table set, the menorah ready, they, like the potato, egg and onion, transformed. Mob to guests. Ill-fitting coats and ill-suited hostility shed, they filled the chairs. Children sat on mothers' laps. Wives, relieved and emboldened, sat scandalously on husbands. Apprising the situation, Golda, Bluma's neighbor to the east, sent her nephew Shimmel home to fetch chairs. Not be outdone, Charna, Bluma's neighbor to the west, chided her husband, "Wolf, do the same. How can you expect these two women to seat us all?"

Bina placed the menorah on the table. "I tell you, on my blessed father's grave, we have only enough oil for this first night." (Ashamed mumblings among the guests.) "We pray Ha Shem brings Yudel the oil peddler safely to us, so that we may celebrate our full eight days." She lit the first wick, then the second from it. Everyone recited the blessing.

"Amen," Mendel called out. With his sanction and the opening of the oven door, the last shreds of discomfort fled. Bluma's platter rounded the table, questions circling behind.

What are they?
Knishes?

Blintzes?

Forks plunged into the plump disks, lifting the weave of potato and onion mouthward.

Delicious.

Luscious.

From the world to come, these treasures.

Golda, widely known as the shtetl's finest cook, nodded toward Bluma. "Tonight, I am unthroned. But, if I may be so bold, may I suggest an accompaniment? Shimmel," she said, "run home once more and fetch the sauce I made from Frumpkin's apples. Its sweetness will favor this savory dish."

Charna, Golda's rival in quantity if not quality, called to her daughter Hendel. "Bring that tub of thickened milk from Hershel's cow. Its coolness will accompany the heat of these cakes."

"And may I suggest," said Nodkin, the village bibbler, "three jugs of Charna's wine, which enhances any meal, hot or chilled, savory or sweet."

Thus the evening unfolded, Bluma's potato cakes, embellished but not bested, endless as the Gentiles' loaves and fishes. Most of the neighbors saw the empty olive oil jug and took Bluma and Bina at their word. Savvier ones knew exactly where the oil had gone, yet felt nourished, not deceived. A new miracle of oil filled the night, and all of them, having eaten, were both culpable and blessed.

"What's for dessert?" a child piped up.

"Dessert?" his father asked. "Who needs dessert after a meal of cakes?"

"Bluma's cakes," proclaimed Golda, "a match for the pastries of St. Petersburg."

"Russian *l'tkas?*" asked Charna.

Schmuel raised his glass. "To Bina and Bluma's latkes."

So crowded the room, it seemed the whole town had toasted the two women. So crowded, no one noticed the absence of one Alter ben Fischkel, jealous bookseller, who, unlikely yet true, was responsible for the evening's camaraderie. He alone remained unsaturated by the light.

iv

Ruchel was jealous. Not at Bluma and Bina for stealing Mendel's limelight, but for the threesome they'd since become, the jokes about this lowly shtetl becoming the county's gastronomic capital. Now that Bluma and Mendel traded eggs for bagels, Ruchel saw the older woman daily.

"I want to create something breathtaking for *Pesach*," Ruchel told her new husband, flour aging the dark hair that escaped her scarf. They stood behind the scarred bakery counter, he wiping down the glass display, she counting the cash. "A delicacy as dazzling as your bagels, as uplifting as Bluma's latkes."

It had been a bleak winter and Ruchel longed to hasten spring. For several weeks, the joy of the latkes had kept Alter's escaped sin in abeyance, but the bloated bread was relentless. While the Czar's soldiers had not made an appearance, other, more anonymous misfortunes swept the town. A window smashed at the synagogue. *Siddurim*, the Jews' blessed prayer books, tossed into the aisle. Bluma's rooster slaughtered. Golda's vegetables ripped from the soil. Five mothers had miscarried. Ten children had broken bones. Ruchel counted herself lucky to have only suffered a tenacious cough.

"Pesach." Mendel shook his head at his wife's mention of the holiday. "A baker's nightmare. Clean and scrub for an entire day and night and for what? To bake matzo meal blocks and bricks. That's all I can manage. Better I should close shop and let Charna and Golda strut their talents."

"Blocks and bricks," repeated Ruchel. "Blocks and bricks and rings and discs. Yes, I will create something round. Not ring. Not disk. Sphere."

"A dumpling?" Done with the display case, Mendel turned to his cutting boards, scraping traces of dried egg. "Matzo meal does not hold. Gnocchi? No. Pirogue? No. Won ton? Samosa? No. No. I have tried them all. Matzo cannot hold a filling."

"In that case," Ruchel said, "My dumpling will be so exquisite no one will miss the filling."

For weeks, Ruchel wet, stirred and molded matzo meal. To the size of apples. It crumbled in the oven. To the size of marbles. As they roasted, they took on the consistency of the cast iron pan in which they cooked. She raised the temperature. She lowered the temperature. She added milk. She subtracted milk. She stirred harder. She didn't stir at all. She wept.

What she did not do was ask Mendel for help and Mendel, not wanting to be an "I told you so" *kolboynik,* offered none. Thus it continued until four days before Pesach and the day before *biur chametz*, the annual ridding of the leavened bread (no small task in a bakery). That afternoon, Mendel's last batch of pre-Pesach bagels were riddled with air pockets, a fine accompaniment to Ruchel's rock-hard balls of matzo. Mendel tossed everything into flour sacks, dragged them to the rubbish bin.

He made light of their shared fiasco. "I am sorry your matzo *globes*, your Pesach *orbs*, have turned to stone. Apparently, that is *not* the way the matzo crumbles."

For the first time in their marriage, Ruchel did not smile back. "They are not *globes*, Mendel. Nor *orbs* nor *worlds* nor *spheres*. They are simply matzo balls. And they are a failure."

Ruchel's lexiconic recitation stung. Mendel remembered his own joyous list—hoop, halo, orbit, circle, cycle—which had led to "ring" and his subsequent proposal to Ruchel. Claiming a pounding headache, he climbed upstairs and took to bed.

Ruchel closed the shop. Moments later, Bluma knocked on the glass. She held two dozen eggs. "The hens have been busy."

"This hen is nothing but a failure," Ruchel said.

Bluma slid the eggs toward Ruchel. "Bind more. Stir less. And remember the miracle of Chanukah." The bell on the shop's door jingled as she left.

Once more, Ruchel attempted her conjurations. This time, however, she was not alone. For the third night that year, the Shechina, God's feminine aspect, saturated the night. Divinely guided, Ruchel combined the most buoyant froth of egg whites with a spoonful of oil, blending in the meal as lightly as one angel's susurration to the next. Ruchel was led not to bake or fry, but, like Mendel at the turn of the other new year, to boil. Claiming the last of the chicken soup from their ice box, Ruchel chilled the mixture while she heated the soup. Only after the soup boiled, did she—lightly, lightly, lightly—drop in her delicately formed world. As the soup simmered, the cook prayed. Entreaty complete, she lifted the lid and, praised be God, her matzo balls held. The first one, Hebrew ambrosia, she ate herself. The next three, she took upstairs to Mendel, waking him, feeding him, forgiving each other.

v.

The villagers feasted on Ruchel's matzo ball soup all week. It mended rent spirit, softened harsh memories of flung prayer books, uprooted onions, a slaughtered rooster.

The ease didn't last. Alter's submerged bread would not permit it. Dissatisfied with domestic damage, it sent out a still more Goliathian pulse. Its evil snaked beyond the shtetl, through the apple orchards, the dense forests, past a stretch of barren countryside, scorched by marauders years ago. It finally settled outside a rodent-infested army barracks, where it coiled and plotted and spit.

Two days after Pesach, three boys—shy Koppel, strong Shimmel and companionable Dovid—rummaged through the bakery rubbish. There they uncovered the bag of failed bagels and matzo balls, all ridiculously intact.

Hauling the find to the far side of the lake, they skipped and flung the bagels, stale merry-go-rounds, over the water.

Sweet smells of mown hay and rising pollen obscured the evil just below. Bagels spent, they turned to Ruchel's matzo balls. Dovid set the challenge: who could hit a floating bagel with a matzo ball, who could hit one dead center?

For the three boys, it was great play. For three bored soldiers, it was a bonus. Although they'd fulfilled that month's conscription duties, they continued to scout for trouble, lured east by Alter's uncorked evil. The soldiers surrounded the boys, informing them that, in recognition of their strong arms and sharp eyes, they'd won a place in the Russian Army. "Do not talk to your parents of us," the tallest soldier told the boys. "Do not talk to anyone. Simply return here tomorrow night. We will be waiting."

"If you are not here," said the stout one with the red beard, "we will take twelve boys in your place. We will burn down your village."

Koppel, the youngest and shyest, had been terrified of the army his whole life. That night, he kissed his parents and sister on the cheek as they slept, then ran into the woods.

Dovid, just fourteen, thought of his *zaide*, nine-fingered Rebbe Macher. Dovid's great-grandfather had cut off Reb Macher's trigger finger to protect him from conscription. "Better to lose one finger than one's faith," his grandfather had told him, reminding him that worse than twenty years of forced service was the moment of forced conversion.

Although he'd sworn a blood oath with Koppel and Shimmel to remain silent, late that night, Dovid rapped on the Rebbe's window and told him everything. With visions of Abraham and Isaac on Mount Moriah, the rebbe took Dovid to the chicken coop. After feeding him cups of vodka and praying a garbled prayer, the rabbi laid his grandson's hand on the stump reserved for the slaughter of fowl, and pushed the cleaver blade, quick and hard, through the boy's index finger. Dovid's cry was sharp but brief, carried off by a bitter wind that blew out from the lake. The Rabbi bound the boy's hand and held him to his chest. "My son, my son, my son."

Only Shimmel, the eldest, appeared at the designated spot the next evening. He had plans. Once the soldiers taught him to use a rifle, he would shoot all three of them, then the Cossacks who had killed his parents, then the Czar himself.

The drunken soldiers never showed.

Shimmel went after them.

He was never seen again.

The town sank into despair, doubly cruel because they thought they'd survived this Passover free from the Czar's terrors. At night, bitter fights broke out over nothing, voices raised, dishes thrown. Infection nearly took the rest of Dovid's fingers. He spent two weeks in bed, swearing to his parents that he'd cut off that finger himself. The Rebbe, horrified by his impulsive decision, spoke to no one. Charna lost her sense of smell, while, to Golda, everything tasted like salt. Bina's threads broke. Mendel's breads burned. Ruchel miscounted the coins. Izzie broke out in rashes.

The land suffered too. Hot winds followed heavy rains. Stunted vegetables stood immobilized in the soil. Frumpkin's apples hardened on the branch. The lake grew thick and vinegary. Its fish population, already meager, vanished. Bluma's chickens stopped laying. Cows dried up. The town went hungry.

Alter was the hungriest. At first, he could eat no bread. Soon all food sickened him. Night after night, his dreams were murky green. In them, his vision slowly cleared, only to reveal he was underwater, gasping for air. Night after night, Alter drowned.

As summer neared its end, the ninth of Av, the fast of Tisha B'Av, arrived. From evening into the next day, the village mourned the destruction of Solomon's Temple, the missing boys, one more son's disfigured hand. At the day's end, after three months of scant food and scant sleep, Alter broke down. Chasing the Rebbe home from shul, he confessed. "I have caused the fruits to wither and the hens and cows to give up. I have chased off the fish and—"

Rabbi Macher, exhausted, stopped him. "Alter, you are not God. You do not have the power to do such things."

"Yes, but it *was* I who burnt the honeymoon bed, slaughtered the rooster, fomented rumors of poisoned eggs and hoarded oil." They'd reached the Rebbe's house. Alter whispered, "I smashed the window and flung the books."

At this, the Rebbe nodded. He'd had his suspicions.

"And it was I who cut off young Dovid's finger."

The Rabbi no longer nodded. "No, it was not."

Alter looked at the Rabbi's right hand. "Not directly, no, but I...I created this evil world."

Rabbi misunderstood. "God created the world, Alter. God is good."

Alter tapped his fingers adamantly against his palm. "This world, Rebbe. This one."

"Stop," the Rabbi commanded. Alter, also misunderstanding, stopped tapping. "Stop spreading lies, Alter. Stop uprooting the vegetables and vexing the animals. Pray, Alter, pray."

Alter could not do what was most important. He could not confess the scapegoated bread at the bottom of the lake. Telling himself the Rabbi would not understand, he turned to walk away. Leeba, who had overheard everything, walked after him. "It is not enough to pray, Alter. You must correct your mistake."

How did she know? Did she know? Who was she, a woman, to tell him what to do? Yet, he knew she was right.

That night, Alter slept. He slept through sunrise the next day and its sunset too. At midnight, he finally woke. He walked to the water and stripped off his clothes. He looked back at his village and emptied his lungs. He took a huge breath, forcing air into every last recess. He repeated this three times. Then he dove.

At first it was like his dreams: muddy, murky, olive green. Then, impossibly, he saw moonlight streaming into the far reaches of the lake. Following it, he felt the morning sun on his back. He was aware of needing to breathe. He blew the air out of his lungs. A swarm of bubbles enwrapped him. When they cleared, he saw clouds of bread, hills of bread, a palace of bread. He entered it. Inside he could breathe but only because, he realized, he was no longer a man. He'd lost his arms and legs to fins and tail. He no longer had lungs. He had gills.

Alter knew this was no coincidence. He had a task to do: to vanquish the evil. To end it, he must consume it. And so, Alter ate the bread palace, swallowed the bread hills and breathed in the bread clouds. With each intake his fish body grew, the captured evil fighting its containment, doubling and redoubling, kicking upward through the water. If his body surfaced, the evil would escape on his out breath, ever more horrid, into the world. Alter understood this. Even as he fought to stay submerged, the water's surface neared. Realizing he could not restrain the evil, Alter prayed. Fully, sincerely, desperately, he prayed for God to destroy him. *For the sin of hubris. For the sin of hardening the heart. Hearten this heart, my redeemer.*

God did just that. Alter, stuffed with evil, exploded. His ruptured flesh transmogrified into ten thousand finned creatures: carp, pike and whitefish. All alive, all Kosher, all joyous in the teeming lake. Flesh transformed, Alter's spirit rose.

No one heard the explosion save one—shy Koppel. Gaunt but alive, he walked out of the forest. He imagined the army had destroyed the town because of him, but instead of flames and rubble, he saw dozens of villagers, poles and nets in hand, fishing at sunrise.

Alter ben Fischkel's legacy would feed the people for years to come. In lean times, the women would extend the meat by mincing it with onion and matzo meal, then returning it to the fish's skin. They would call this stuffed fish, this filled fish, *gefilte* fish. When preparing it, they would think of Alter.

But at this moment no one was thinking of lean times, only the miracle of a lake filled with fish, of a son returned home. Bluma and Bina's chickens laid one hundred eggs that day. Bluma, thankful for Mendel's generosity in months past, gave him half. He mixed the eggs into his bagel dough. When it came time to form his circles, his hands braided a round loaf instead.

The creator would turn the year for his children. The baker would weave it together.

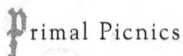
Marian's Feather-Light Matzoh Balls

Makes 8 to 10 matzo balls.

Prepare beforehand:
2 quarts chicken soup or chicken broth

Wet Ingredients
2½ Tbsp. chicken fat (a.k.a., schmaltz)
2 eggs
¼ to ½ cup warm water

Dry Ingredients
½ cup matzo meal
1 tsp. salt
a dash of pepper
a dash of cinnamon
a dash of ginger

In a medium bowl, mix all dry ingredients.
Set aside.

Separate eggs into two bowls, medium for whites, large for yolks.
Set whites aside.

Beat yolks until light.
Add chicken fat and warm water to the yolks. Mix thoroughly.
Beat whites until stiff.
Fold the egg whites into the yolk mixture.
Gradually fold dry ingredients into the yolks.
Stir until smooth, but do not over-mix.
Cover and chill for 90 minutes or longer.

Once mixture is properly chilled, bring soup to a boil.
Wet hands with cold water.
Gently form matzo mixture into golfball-size balls.
(The matzo balls will grow.)
Carefully drop into boiling soup in a 3-quart pot (or larger).

Cover, reduce heat and simmer for 20 minutes.

Do not remove the lid to check the pot!

HOW THE GOOSEBERRY BECAME
BECAME
A Goat's Tale

Andrew Wille

ou know me, don't you?

You're spending a hot siesta in one of the great galleries, killing time before you can justify another glass of Pinot Gris. At least the marble floors are as cool as forest pools, and the gift shop always has a bauble to take home to Mother.

You've sauntered round these empty halls. You've run away from those noisy Italians, and you're avoiding the British tourists with their straw hats and bratty children. Your attempts to lure that Scandinavian couple into a threesome in the restroom are clearly failing, and you're starting to get despondent (her baps were so jiggly, his rump was too rumpy).

And then all those smug Madonnas smile down on you. The last thing you need is a blessing from a conniving harlot of a single mother with an ugly little grub of a baby in her lap.

Then, in a lurid oil, you meet me. You stop.

Behold! I'm the one with the shiny hooves and the shaggy goatshanks and the rippling torso of fine, manly muscles; knobbly horns bulge out of the locks on my head. I wear a grin, and sometimes I'm playing merrily on my pipes, and other times I'm about to play on some lucky lad's or lass's. God of shepherds, king of the forest, master of music: my name is Pan, and I love to fuck.

Or rather: I loved to fuck.

The gaudy daubs on the walls only ever exhibit what amounts to the foreplay: orgies in shady glades, nymphs dressed in drapes, that fat bastard Bacchus with marigolds in his hair. But that's the prettified version. It's not all frisky fauns and callipygous dryads, you know. Who wants to cavort with hobs and goblins, with kittywitchies and spunkies? And there are goodfellows and bad, incubi, succubi, mum-powers and Jack-in-the-Wads, and they all loll around with their breeches undone and their tongues hanging out. And that great big Dick-a-Tuesday can really put a stud off his stride.

Even at their best, bacchanals are dull affairs. There's no challenge in taking the maidenhead of a buxom bergère or a guileless naiad, and who wants to pluck the plump cherry of a chubby-buttocked cherub? Free love is simply too free.

I debauched richer prizes: lawyers' wives, prissy stoics, high priestesses. A Persian princess needed a naughtier dowry for her dearly betrothed, and on the night before her nuptials I took it as my task to train her in tricks of the tongue. The haughty son of a Norseman trader had been schooled against the taste of cock. Pan re-educated him.

A convent stood just without our forest. While Bacchus and his court puked up cheap wine, I scaled an oak and spied on the sisters. It was a small order of hard-working wenches: a bonny blacksmith, a slender scribe, a voluptuous cook. Only the mother superior lacked fleshly graces: her face was as wrinkly as Neptune's ball sac.

The sweetest sister worked in the sanctuary garden. She watered the herbarium and tilled the vegetable patch, she was beekeeper, dairymaid, goosegirl, more. She had brown eyes, kissable dimples, rosy blushes on her cheeks. The rest was guesswork. What glories hid in the great white tent of her vestments? I caught a curve of hip as she walked her geese, I observed the roundness of her breast as she stretched for an apple; was that a hint of pink straining through her gown as she shoved against a rake? What lay beneath the prison of her wimple: tresses of blonde, a thick pelt of shiny black, a curly bush of auburn? What treasures were concealed in her clumpy clodhoppers: a dainty ankle, a narrow step, the pretty pearls of her toes?

Walls are made for scaling, and gates are made for breaching, but take it from Lord Pan that art defeats brute force when engineering a means of entry. The nuns' voluminous livery offered my salvation. If it hid the glories of holy maidens, it could hide mine too.

White robes were useless, as the hair on my chest and my shoulders showed through, and black robes were too forbidding. Green has always been my color. I tickled the fancies of Mistress Cobweb, and as a reward she spun lovegrass and oak ferns into fine threads, and wove me a mantlet of woodland green. Its veil revealed only the glints of my emerald eyes.

But what about my voice, you ask? Easy: I tupped Lady Echo, and she charmed my throat so I cooed like a dove.

Togged in my turfy trappings, at sunset I presented myself at the convent gatehouse. I was a wandering abbess, conducting my peregrinations; might I find refuge for the night?

The mother superior asked me to remove my veil in this sisterhooded sanctuary, but I claimed a vow of coverage. At vespers I sat cross-legged, fearful lest a hoof jut from beneath my hem. That night my cell was cold, and my sleep was that rare thing, solitary. A nunnery dormitory was an unlikely bawdhouse even for a demon of my trickery.

After matins I volunteered to work in the convent garden. The least I could do?

I labored beside my sweet. I grasped apricots from heavy boughs, I furrowed her fields, together we sowed cucumber seeds.

I made believe it was time for the wandering abbess to continue on her way, and she agreed to stroll with me a while outside the convent walls. "I must walk the geese," she simpered. We ambled beside the brook, the geese splashed in the water. A woodpecker rattled in a silver birch tree.

"Your journey is long, dear sister, we must rest a while," insisted my sweet. We sat beneath a willow. The brook babbled, a dragonfly lurked.

"Dear sister, we must sup." She reached into the pouch on the front of her gown. "I have only one pear, but perhaps we can share it." She drew back her lips, she bit its sweet flesh, she wiped away juice with the back of her hand. She proffered the fruit to me, but I signalled my veil.

"Dear sister, your robe must be heavy and hot," she observed with a tilt of her delicate brow. She pointed to patches of sweat matting my back, the circles of wet ringing the pits of my arms. Stuck to my gown, my groin was increasingly evident. "Why not remove your trappings...dear brother?"

She tugged the veil from my face, and with a smile whipped off her wimple; her hair was sweet hazelnut brown. She leaned in for a kiss: such bliss.

And then we were lying in a havoc of vestments, and I was training my sweet in the art of the stroke, and the craft of the grasp and the skills of the thrust and the flutter. She recited fresh rosaries, I forced new confessions, her hands were laid upon me.

Shadows grew long, the geese hissed, she vowed to return the next day.

Thus commenced a week of merry tumult in the green bowers at the edge of the forest. We canoodled amid the purple loosestrife, we made love among the wild strawberries, our two-backed beast ate meadowsweet and creeping buttercup.

She wondered at the pleasures that had been denied her before. "My! It has the heft of a goose's neck," she proclaimed.

And how she loved to cup my ballocks in her dainty fingers. My berries, she called them, my big, jolly goose berries.

Then Bacchus roused from his latest stupor, and noticed my absence from his orgies. He sent a posse of satyrs to bring me back to his glade of revels, but I refused to go.

The following day my sweet arrived late in our rude pastures. She wore a veil, so I anticipated some deviant re-enactment of the life of our wandering abbess, for our forays were growing more venturesome. She kissed her finger through the veil, indicating an oath of silence as part of our randy rite. I lay back in a bed of honeysuckle.

"My goose awaits! My berries are heavy, and ready for the lightening."

With a swish the veil was removed, and the mother superior stood before me (she left on her wimple). She reached into her pouch, there was a flash of silver and before I could recoil she'd sliced off my balls.

My ballocks, my berries, no more!

Henceforth, Pan was a gelding.

***

I never knew what became of my sweet. I cherish the memories. Any mortal contact would taunt.

It was Bacchus who'd despatched a centaur messenger to inform the mother superior of our crime, but he never expected I'd suffer such a punishment. So he claims. To say sorry, he cast a spell on the black soil where my jewels fell, and there grew a bush with commemorative fruits, pert green berries sweet yet tart, juicy and tongue-tempting.

So that's how the gooseberry became—and why it is so small and veiny, and has white spines. My balls were bigger, of course, the size of plums, and my pubes glossy and black. Bacchus clearly fashioned the gooseberry on his own little pebbles, and the white wisps they're decked with.

And it's also true what your granny says: babies come from under the gooseberry bush. You can thank Daddy Pan for that.

Time for you to go. Those Swedish tourists are heading for the exit, and I think they just looked back for you.

Pan's pleasures might be curbed, but he's never one to deny the fun of others.

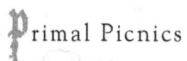

Cooking With Gooseberries

Like most fruits, gooseberries are best served simply (and straight from the bush at the end of your grandmother's garden): in pies, in crumbles. Perhaps my favorite way to eat them is to drop a handful into my oatmeal a minute or two before it finishes cooking. They also make good jam. Stewed or poached, they form the base for sauces and pickles served with fish and cold meats; experiment with combinations of capers, chives, ginger, horseradish or spring onions, as well as different types of vinegars.

One of the treats of a recent visit to Edinburgh was stumbling across a "liquid deli" called Demijohn (www.demijohn.co.uk). Among the curvy bottles of rhubarb vodka and bramble vinegar was a marvellous gooseberry gin. It's fizzily syrupy, and perfect with tonic—no lime needed.

With a little imagination, the **gooseberry compote** serves as a useful ingredient in any number of dessert dishes: simmer gooseberries for 5 or 10 minutes with a couple of tablespoons of water and however much sugar your tastebuds require. For a delightful variation add a glug of elderflower cordial, or a capful of sherry, or some other suitable tipple. The blend is sometimes sieved, but I'm rarely that fussy, though it's a good idea to drain off excess liquid. The classic **gooseberry fool** comes in various versions that basically blend compote with cream (whipped and stiff, in true Pan style).

An even more exciting approach is to balance the tangy taste among the dense and sugary excesses of a **gooseberry trifle**. Here goes: in the base of a glass serving bowl (cut glass and grannified is best), create a layer of pieces of sponge cake (a sticky ginger sponge is good). Soak the bits of cake in a couple of tablespoons of apple juice and a swig of brandy or ginger wine (don't let it get soggy). Add a layer at least half an inch thick of gooseberry compote, then cover that with a layer an inch thick of custard, and leave it to set in the fridge (an hour or two). Before serving, top with mountain ranges of whipped cream, and decorate with goodies of your choosing— let's say flaked almonds and fresh raspberries. I recently saw a recipe that added crystallized violets.

For a sexy (and simpler) pudding, add 300 grams of melted white chocolate to an equal amount of Greek yogurt, then stir in a couple of tablespoons of compote (be sure it's not watery). Let it set in the fridge for about an hour, and call it **Pan's Delight**. This can be attempted with other flavorings (orange zest, or the juice of a lime, or the innards of a passion fruit), but don't tell Pan.

KING OF MUSTARD

Sarah Quigley

Once upon a time there lived a boy who was small in stature but had a very large brain.

Before you object to the rather predictable nature of this opening, let me assure you that the boy *asked* for his story to be told in such a way. "Start traditionally," he said, when we were discussing stylistic issues. "Art should imitate life!"

Certainly his life appeared to be set in predictable patterns, from the very first moment he opened his eyes. His first view of the world was what most of us see, for most of our lives: four confining walls, some large controlling hands, a glimpse of sky held back behind glass. Nothing at all unusual, unless you count the fact that the boy was extraordinarily tiny.

And so it seems appropriate—even unavoidable—to start his tale with "Once upon a time," for his first twenty years fell in just such a regular cadence.

For two decades, this boy lived nowhere special: in a nondescript middle-sized town, in a flat region that was renowned for nothing. On clear days, if you peered into the distance, you might almost believe you saw the hunched brown shoulders of a mountain range; but when you wiped your glasses you realized it was nothing but dust on the lenses. There was never anything on the horizon: not a storm or a twister, not a hint of excitement. The most you could hope for was a little haze.

"Make sure," the boy insisted, "that you tell them what the people were like." Perhaps it's enough to say that, where he grew up, people always carried umbrellas but rarely used them, wore short sleeves but never short skirts and drove cars that were neither sleekly modern nor charmingly vintage. They avoided scandal, but enjoyed reading about it in other places. Let's say they reflected their climate: never bitingly cold nor searingly hot.

The boy—our boy—grew up in a grey wooden house with a veranda running along the front and a river out the back. This might sound picturesque, but it wasn't, particularly. One could barely see the river from the house. First there was a long, thin garden, and then a wire fence, and between the fence and the water was a stretch of muddy ground that seemed to shimmer and move as the sun was setting.

In truth, the riverbank *was* shifting in those tepid hours before nightfall. Rats came there to graze. I know—

if you were reading this story from a book with embossed linen covers and gilt edges, it would be lambs doing the grazing, on a hillside studded with white flowers. But we must stick to facts, however unpalatable. The boy said so.

Fact 1: Beside the boy's house was a huge factory, that threw Goliath shadows over several blocks of houses, and surreptitiously channelled its waste into the river.

Fact 2: Workers threw food scraps from the high lunch-room window, so the muddy riverbank became strewn with pork rind and greasy crusts and those stringy bits off ripe bananas. And every evening the rats crept up and fed there.

Fact 3: The factory owner knew about the waste problem and the rat problem, but he did nothing about either. He was a big man in a town of middle-sized people; ignoring their problems was his forte, and probably the reason he had risen to the top.

Did the boy like his life? Well, to like or dislike had always been irrelevant in that town. No one ever questioned anything. Not what they ate, nor what they were paid, nor what lay at the ruffled edges of the suburbs where lawns gave way to dirty verges strewn with cigarette butts and the unravelled tires of cars.

Before we go any further, we should give the boy—our boy—a name. He was known as Mouse, and this had nothing to do with the rodents that scurried at the bottom of his garden, nor with him being so small and quiet. Shortly before his second birthday, his mother had called him Mouse and the nickname had stuck, which would have been fine had his parents' last name not been House. Such are the crosses our parents give us to bear, before we have even learnt to speak the words "Please" and "reconsider."

Even after Mouse became famous and the media clamored to release his real name, he refused. Cautious by nature, he had not only taken out a patent on his invention but had also had such fierce anonymity clauses set in place that, to this day, his "real name" remains unknown. Modest people were as rare back then as they are today, and it was at that time that the saying "Modest as a mouse" crept into everyday usage. (But perhaps you haven't heard it, if you don't get out much, or if you live in a different country from our hero.)

Mouse grew up in a perfectly normal beige environment: nothing to object to. He got into scrapes and then out of them; told lies, and told the truth. His town became his backyard; it was fairly small, the kind of town that frightens city-dwellers because there was only one of everything. One dry cleaner, one liquor store, one supermarket, one car wash—you get the idea. There were two hotdog stands, temporarily, but The Chili Dog folded within a year. People weren't used to spicy food; their town slogan was "Always Here Never Changing!" so perhaps it was for subconscious reasons that they boycotted the Heavenly Hellishly Hottest Dogs, in spite of their tempting aroma, and silently queued for parboiled sausages in limp white rolls, with optional ketchup.

Once, Mouse asked his mother if she'd ever eaten Chinese. Her eyebrows flew so high into her hair, he might as well have asked her if she could speak it. "It's a big world," she said, eventually, as if this explained everything.

Speaking of big, what of Mouse's renowned brain? Well, this advantage was not immediately apparent in the long pale stretches of his porridgey upbringing. In his teenage years, naturally, his brain was not much in evidence at all. But it was working away underground, as we shall see, like a blind but determined mole.

Now for a startling disclosure. There was only one book in the House house. (Excuse the clumsy repetition there; if this were a work of fiction, rather than fact, I would of course have chosen a different surname for the family of my protagonist.) Were the Houses, you ask, *against* reading material? Probably not. I'm sure they would have said that reading was perfectly acceptable, that it had its place, like everything under the sun.

But Mouse's parents had been very young when they started work at the factory. At that tender age Mr. House's profile was still clear-cut, and Mrs. House's cheeks were firm and rounded, and lightly furred like quality peaches. They were too young to think of marrying anyone at all.

"But love clamped a lid on us, and we were sealed," explained Mr. House, in the first—and last—metaphor of his life.

The factory was a little like a dating service, at that time. When the Big Man was in a jovial mood he would say that a good half of his workers owed him matchmaker's fees. In truth, whatever mood he was in, he liked having couples working for him; the insurance brokers gave him better deals if his workers were eligible for family health packages.

"You'll work there one day," Mr House said to Mouse, as they ate dinner gazing out at the blank factory wall. Mouse supposed so; his town wasn't a natural springboard for Hollywood stardom, or for founding a million-dollar boat business in the Caribbean.

Have I mentioned what the factory produced? Peas. Peas of all kinds: canned, bagged, boxed, frozen, mushy, preserved. Almost anything that could be done with peas was done there. The odd thing was, no one saw where they came from; they arrived in the night, as green and fresh as grass after a rain shower, and then the workers had to transform them as quickly as possible to a seemingly inedible state.

"Why do all the peas come out grey?" asked Mrs. House, in her early days as an inexperienced worker and wife.

"Shhhh!" said everyone else, with a hint of mystery, as if they had the answer.

The factory had churned out so much produce over the years that the sky above it was as grey as the peas. Many workers who'd started in the flush of youth had also turned slightly dingy around the edges. It wasn't the easiest work handling machines all day, sealing cans, stamping labels and sorting badly wizened peas from acceptably wizened ones. In fact, it was downright exhausting.

And this leads me back to the reason for there being only one book in Mouse's house. By the time his parents had married, by the time they had saved up enough for a down payment on the house next to the factory ("No transport costs," pointed out Mr. House)—well, by this time they were already so tired that the thought of reading in the evenings seemed quite impossible. It was all they could do to save up for a sofa and a television, which turned out to be all that they needed.

In Mouse's bedroom there was a wall of empty shallow shelves, and it was only looking back on his childhood that he realized: they were bookshelves, without the books. In the meantime he perched his treasures there (sticks, green glass, dead dragonflies, his collection of beer-bottle tops). On the bottom shelf, closest to his pillow, was the solitary book, one of the few possessions Mrs. House had brought to her marriage. She had grown up in an orphanage and so had nothing much in the way of a dowry; no high-thread-count sheets or fluffy towels, little but her peachy skin and the "W" volume of a rather ancient children's encyclopaedia.

Years later, Mouse came to believe that while he'd been sleeping all those nights, for years on end, the facts from the encyclopaedia had trickled out into the dark room. They'd fallen onto his pillow, run into his ears like water and entered the innermost parts of his brain.

For how else could one explain that he knew reams of "W" facts by the time he was ten? In moments of stress or boredom, he would silently recite these to himself:

Weltschmerz: a feeling of melancholy and world-weariness, stemming from the German word *Welt* (meaning "world") and the German word *Schmerz* (meaning "pain"). *Wesleyan*: relating to the teachings of the English preacher John Wesley, who lived between 1703 and 1791 and founded the main branch of the Methodist church.

It was amazing how much calmer he felt after a few W's.

Some people do crosswords in a deliberate attempt to sharpen up their brains. With Mouse, the brain expansion happened without him even trying: every morning when he woke, he felt brighter than when he'd gone to bed. By the time he was fifteen, he was very bright indeed but no one knew. It was like the best-kept secret; even he was hardly aware of it.

"What would you like for your birthday?" Mr. House loomed at the end of the table like a ship's figurehead that has encountered some fearsome storms. He'd been almost handsome in his youth, according to Mrs. House, but bouts of amateur boxing every Tuesday evening for twenty years had flattened his nose and spread his ears over the sides of his head. "Go on, tell me! What do you most want?"

What Mouse really wanted was what most intelligent people yearn for: to be still more intelligent, so everything might finally become clear to him. But he didn't think that Mr. House could help him out with this, nor with his fits of shyness when he saw Maryanne Gilmore in the aisles of the supermarket. "A new bike?" he suggested, realistically.

But as soon as he answered he realized that his father's question had been rhetorical, for they were already seated around the festive table, sipping on tepid apple juice. The time of gift-receiving was already upon him.

Mrs. House passed a generous plate of white sliced bread around the table. She'd made a real effort with the margarine, spreading it all the way out to the crusts rather than leaving the usual dab in the middle, and Mouse appreciated the gesture.

His father folded a slice of bread like a greeting card and inserted it into his letter-box mouth (there was little room for a mouth in a face where the nose had taken over to such an extent). He chewed and swallowed, and his words gusted towards Mouse on the fumes of polyunsaturated fats. "I got you work! At the factory!"

There was no need to ask which factory; the question was—how? For the situation then was very much as it is today; jobs were hard to come by, while health insurance and pension plans were as rare as hen's teeth.

Mr. House elaborated in a shower of stale crumbs. "I explained to the Big Man that you're due to leave school. 'Bit small, isn't he?' he said. But I told him the small ones are the tough ones! And he said, 'Start on Monday.'"

It wasn't as good as increased intelligence, of course, or social confidence, or a bike; but Mouse already knew that it was rare to get one's heart's desire. Besides, it was inevitable he would end up in the pea factory; it had cast such a long shadow into his room for so many years that it had come to seem like destiny.

Four days after his sixteenth birthday, Mouse began the first day of what turned out to be five years of work—which is something like 1230 days, minus holidays and sick days. Outwardly he looked the same as every other Pea-worker, only smaller.

But during that treadmill time something curious began to happen to him, as if a fairy godmother had heard his secret birthday wish. His brain did, indeed, continue to expand; sometimes he could almost feel it stretching outwards, making his skull creak. But an even stranger thing: during those long winter evenings, as he lay in his narrow bed with the heavy encyclopaedia propped on his chest, certain words began leaping out at him. They positively flew to his brain like pins to a strong and commanding magnet.

Water pepper. White pudding. Watercress. Do you notice? The words bombarding Mouse were either edible or potable. When he read of the *peppery tasting leaves of the aquatic dock plant*, his tongue began to tingle. When his eyes scanned the description of the *pungent tang* of fresh watercress, his face grew hot. Wedged between the incongruous racing-car sides of his bed, absorbing the ingredients of a *Whisky sour*, he felt his veins running with tawny-gold liquor and the lime-green juice of ripe citrus fruit.

Put simply, he began to *smell* what he read. He tasted what he saw. He was eating the written word, imbibing the image.

He read the entry for *Woodruff* aloud. Sure enough, when he peered over the edge of the bed, the dull grey carpet was a riot of white-flowering plants, and a sweet pungent scent *"perfect for flavoring drinks"* wafted up from the leaves. And when he read out *wild rice*, the faded wallpaper gave way to lush green grasses, which made the air in the room a trifle damp and scattered exotically striped grains all over his pillow.

This was what saved him, after his dull working days, before sleep. He was an invalid newly restored to health. His appetite was suddenly and sharply receptive, and the restlessness made his bones ache like growing pains (though he was too old for those). It was the charged hour before a storm. Something was about to change.

When Mouse arrived at work on a Monday morning toward the end of his fifth factory year, he found the Big Man ranting at Maryanne Gilmore's younger sister, who'd started as a Pea-worker less than a week before.

"Wastage!" the Big Man was shouting. Nothing annoyed him more than conducting a spot check and discovering a freezer bag that weighed 501 grams; 409 grams: now, that was sloppy and deserved a sharp reprimand, but cheated customers were far easier to appease than angry bank managers. The Big Man's favorite maxim began, "Take care of the pennies..." and he pinched Maryanne Gilmore's sister's arm as he thought of the pennies she might lose him.

Mouse hesitated. Maryanne Gilmore's sister looked more mutinous than scared; the Gilmores never smiled if they could help it, and always fought if possible; their father, also a Tuesday boxer, was responsible for at least one of Mr. House's cauliflower ears. It didn't look as if help was needed, but Mouse offered it anyway, for he had a big heart as well as a big brain.

"Unhand her!" he bellowed. At least, he intended to bellow this. What he actually said was, "There's no need to shout," in a fairly mild voice.

The Big Man looked down at him from a seemingly great height. (Everyone looked down on Mouse, even his mother and the very youngest of the five Gilmore siblings.) The Big Man's eyebrows were the same color as his skin—beige, with flecks of red—and his eyelids looked as if they would flake away with a single blink. But the Big Man rarely blinked; perhaps he had been to a course in intimidation tactics early in his career?

"One lost gram of peas," he said in a cheese-grater voice, "is a perfectly justifiable cause for shouting. One pea cast from the house of profit is a sin!" He stared harder at Mouse. "And you are—?" This was as deliberate as his non-blinking tactic; pretending to forget someone's name is one of the easiest, and tackiest, tricks in the book.

"Mouse House!" announced Mouse, and then winced. He had forgotten the important thing, which was to pause between saying his first and last names.

Even Maryanne Gilmore's stony sister cracked a smile at this, while the Big Man laughed so loudly he almost drowned out the roaring machines behind him. Had Mrs. House been there, she would undoubtedly have flared up in her son's defense, but fortunately she was at home in bed that day, with a bad headcold.

Mouse felt rattled all afternoon. A wealth of W facts recited under his breath didn't help to calm him. *Weimaraner*. (He threw shrivelled peas down a chute.) *A thin-coated type of pointer originally used as a gun dog, this typically grey breed was developed in the German region of Weimar.* He imagined the inferior peas to be the multiple heads of Big Men; in sixty seconds they would be mashed to a pulp and flushed into the river to mingle with dirty orange peel and toilet paper.

Weil's disease, he muttered. *Origins, 19*th*-century German physician H. Adolf Weil. A severe form of leptospirosis transmitted by rats via contaminated water.* This was better! Possible, even, as a fate for the Big Man! But when he looked around and saw his silent co-workers shuffling through vegetables with their muffled hands, his spirits plummeted.

When he got home that evening, the door slammed behind him as if caught in a sudden backdraught. "No one stands up for themselves around here," he said loudly. "Everyone is mild-mannered and lily-livered. They eat bland food. They think bland thoughts. Their lives are off-white."

His father was hovering in the kitchen, a pair of scissors in one hand and an unopened sachet in the other. "Is it 'Feed a Cold and Starve a Fever,'" he asked Mouse. "Or the other way around?"

"You're not making milky pudding again, are you?" Mouse snatched the packet away.

"Your mother needs to eat something." His father half crouched before his diminutive son, trying to read the instructions dangling from his hand. "Is it 'Boil Water and Stir,'" he mumbled, "or the other way around?"

"Milky pudding be damned," said Mouse (or something like that; certainly he was angry enough to use unaccustomed expletives). He marched down the twilight garden to the riverbank, shooed away the rats, and wrenched two huge handfuls of cabbagey-looking roots out of the earth.

"What's that?" His father grew alarmed at the sight of dirt in the kitchen. Nothing good came out of the ground, his look implied; real food came clean, from boxes or tins.

"Horseradish," said Mouse briskly. "Clears the sinuses and relieves nasal congestion. Wasabi would be better but Wasabi doesn't grow at the end of our garden."

"We always have milky pudding when someone's ill." His father's unease was swelling like a boil-in-the-bag risotto.

"Chop these up, would you," ordered Mouse, "and drop the milky pudding."

Meekly, his father opened his hands and the packet fell to the floor with a tiny thud.

"I didn't mean literally." Mouse sighed. "Don't be so unthinkingly obedient! If you feel like arguing, argue."

But this was too much for his father. Silently, he began peeling and dicing as if his life—or his sick wife's—depended on it.

The contents of Mrs. House's spice cupboard were on the sparse side. There was soy in a plastic pouch, and powdered mustard in a box. Determinedly, Mouse mixed and boiled, added food coloring (yellow and blue) and pepper (a dubious grey). "Good job on the horseradish!" he exclaimed. "Beautifully minced!"

His father ducked his head in pleasure. "Always been good with my hands," he mumbled, though his battered boxer's face somewhat belied his claim. He watched the cooking process out of the corner of his eye, as if it were not quite decent.

Mouse threw in the horseradish, then flour and cornflour. Finally he added the milky pudding mix for good measure. "You want to taste?" he asked politely, holding out the spoon. But his father shied away, so Mouse was the first person to taste his ground-breaking concoction (some would call this fate; more rational minds would consider it a random detail).

"More salt?" Mouse added a pinch. "And perhaps a little more blue." His tongue was glowing like a coal, but it was a pleasurable heat. The spices had blended into a musky richness, and below lay the sting of horseradish: pungent, peppery, perfect. He couldn't remember the last time he had eaten anything that both smelled good and left an aftertaste.

The warmth spread quickly to his limbs, and his brain began to buzz. He spread some mustard-yellow paste on soft white bread and covered it up with another slice; his mother was ill, after all, and it wouldn't do to alarm her.

"She won't eat it. It's not at all milky." His father climbed the stairs with doubtful feet. But in a couple of minutes he reappeared with an empty plate. "She wants another one!" He hadn't sounded this surprised since

Mouse had jumped out at him from behind a door wearing a Halloween mask, eight years earlier.

Mouse and his father ate one at each end of the table, with the gravy-boat of horseradish paste floating between them. Mr. House pushed his food around the plate, waiting to see what Mouse would do; he looked anxious when he saw Mouse smother his sausages in sauce, but gamely he followed suit. He raised a laden green fork to his mouth and chewed.

For a moment there was silence.

"Holy hell!" gasped Mr. House, his eyes streaming. He grabbed blindly for his beer bottle, sending Mrs. House's plastic violets flying.

Mouse felt anxious; had he cured one parent only to kill another? But a few seconds later Mr. House emerged from his beer, with only slightly bloodshot eyes. "Very tasty," he croaked, and (this is where we must admire him) he once more reached for his fork. Several minutes later, he was still chewing, though sweat lingered on his forehead and he wiped his top lip repeatedly with his sleeve. "Very tasty!" he said again. He had uttered this phrase countless times over the years, in response to dishes of astonishing blandness (he had lost his looks, but retained his manners). Tonight, however, his voice had a new ring to it, a peppery conviction. And with every forkful it gained in strength and complexity.

Mouse's own mouth was on fire and his stomach was already full, but he couldn't help reaching for another sausage and a mountain of horseradish. The tangy sensation was so very more-ish!

Many times that night the floorboards creaked, the bathroom door was closed and the toilet flushed. The entire house seemed to be rumbling on its foundations. But in the morning, Mr. House could be heard singing in a fine baritone, and Mrs. House appeared downstairs with her hair in a braid, her cheeks looking almost peach-like. After a horseradish-sandwich breakfast, her pallor imperceptibly lifted as the sun glints behind a cloud, promising better things to come.

Every night that week, Mouse slaved over a hot stove. The kitchen walls acquired lime and yellow stripes like a Victorian child's nursery, and every one of Mrs. House's pans gained a thick green crusty interior. Mouse had hatched an ingenious plan, though if asked he would say vaguely that it had simply come upon him, like lightning or a thunderbolt. Such similes are often used by creative geniuses, in an attempt to explain the mysterious arrival of ideas.

"Whatever has happened to all our peas?" His mother peered, mystified, into an almost empty freezer and entirely empty cupboards. If there was one thing the House house never ran out of, it was peas.

Mouse didn't answer; he was preoccupied as geniuses often are. Every morning for a week he rose very early and took a small stool to the factory gates, where he waited for the early shift-workers. "Try some!" he urged, as they straggled past him, yawning. Into their hands he pushed small paper packets, made from brown manila envelopes cut down and stapled together. "They're on the House!" he said, which made people laugh in spite of their exhaustion.

Naturally, it took a while to get the recipe right. In the process Mouse discovered that it was actually quite difficult to dry peas without the loss of some color (which gave him an unwelcome, though momentary, stab of sympathy for the Big Man). Some mornings, when workers tipped the entire contents of a packet greedily into their mouths, he saw them choke and grab their throats and run wildly for the nearest source of water.

"Too mustardy?" Mouse would call, whipping out his notebook. "Too peppery?"

By the seventh day, after much fine-tuning, he had cracked it. People came back out of the factory to ask for more of the tiny, spicy, green-coated peas; they had developed a taste, they said, or a craving (and in one or two cases the word "addiction" was used). The horseradish peas went well with beer; they were perfect as morning-picker-uppers and mid-afternoon snacks. Some people even saved their samples to eat in bed, as a midnight treat. "Give us more!" they begged. And Mouse promised he would, just as soon as he could begin manufacturing in bulk.

As always with overnight (or, in this case, seven-night) success stories, there has to be one person who causes a problem. In Mouse's tale, not surprisingly, it was the Big Man. He came storming down to the factory gates and upturned Mouse's three-legged stool, and shook Mouse so hard that dried peas flew out of his pockets and fell around them in a rattling spicy semicircular rain.

"IMPOSTOR!" The Big Man often began his rants with one-word sentences, as if fury made him lose his grip on syntax.

"Not—impostor!" Mouse's voice came out in a squeak, because his collar was being twisted very tightly. "I—work—here."

"I know you work here, imbecile!" The Big Man was so angry that the bacon-specks on his skin merged and he became red all over. "But *I* am the only pea-seller in this town! I am The Purveyor of Perfect Peas." He dropped Mouse so that he was better able to point to the sign on the factory roof. But, as occasionally happened, someone had painted out the word "Perfect" during the night and replaced it with "Mediocre."

Mouse took advantage of the Big Man's open-mouthed rage. He stepped in swiftly. His veins were running with the fire of horseradish, and his tongue was quick from the lash of pepper and an additional dash of chili. "You are a tyrant of the worst order," he thundered. (According to Mouse, seven days of hot plates and hot spices had finally taught him to thunder.) "You have oppressed this town for years," he boomed. "You have rendered life tasteless!"

The Big Man actually took a step backwards (remember, the last time these two had communicated, Mouse was incapable of even raising his voice). He tried to revert to old tricks. "Remind me," he said. "You are—?"

But Mouse wasn't falling into that trap again. In fact, this gave him an opportunity to test out various slogans he'd been mulling over in bed. "I am the King of Mustard!" he cried.

From behind him came a huge collective cheer; workers were hanging out every window. In their blue and yellow overalls, they looked like rows of triumphal flags. For the moment, all pea-processing had halted but many of the workers were munching on Mouse's far tastier peas, and crumbs drifted downward, falling on the heads of the small inventor and the large dictator like pale green snow.

"I am the Tastebud Doctor," shouted Mouse, "the Provider of Pasted-Peas." (These didn't have such a great ring, in his opinion, but the people cheered all the same.) "I come from the House of Horseradish, to put a zing on your tongue and a spring in your heart!"

Silence fell in the courtyard; you could have heard a fresh pea drop.

"I am the one," finished Mouse with a flourish, "who puts the spice back into life!"

Then the cheers became deafening, and peas were thrown from every window, scattering like confetti. They bounced or squished (depending on whether they were Mouse's produce or factory goods) all over the speechless Big Man and the tiny smiling King of Mustard. Looking up through the hail of green, Mouse saw his parents at the very top window, waving.

The rest, as they say, is history. Mouse refined his recipe and learned how to vacuum-pack peas, so that they might arrive in ports all over the world as crisp and piquant as the day they first received their tasty coating of Wasabi.

For this is the very last part of the story. Although the House of Horseradish was pleasing in its alliteration,

Mouse's first and final loyalty was to the letter W, and Wasabi gave his peas a stronger, cleaner and greener taste. Most of his pea-eating fans were unable to tell the difference (*Armoracia Rusticana* and *Eutrema Wasabi* do taste extremely similar). But then his fans hadn't been brought up on an encyclopaedic diet, and this makes all the difference.

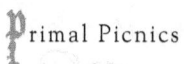

Recipe for Wasabi

The very best thing to do with wasabi peas is wait.

*Wait all the day long until evening, when your tastebuds
are dulling and your energy fading with the light. Then spice
yourself up like a mustard seed, pull on your seven-league boots
and take the following steps:*

*Run to the store. Choose a store with well-lit aisles; your peas will
look more temptingly artificially green. Take lime-green peas home
to a secluded place where no one else can snatch any.*

*Pop the tin. (Whenever possible a tin should be purchased
rather than a packet: vacuum-packing is an invention designed
for fun, right up there with bubble-wrap.) Pop the tin so loudly
that a Parisian wine-waiter would wince. Pour into a plastic
bowl, preferably of garish coloring. Add a dash of chili sauce,
depending on levels of courage.*

*Lie on sofa with bowl positioned at hand-height. Wait for mouth
to water. Fill mouth with as many peas as humanly possible,
spraying a few over cushions and across floor for festive feeling.*

*Wait for eyes to water. Wait until you can once more a) speak
and b) see. Wait until bowl is empty, then refill until bedtime.*

ON TWINKIES

Lia Purpura

"Ess' mit Verstand."
—my grandmother

We had Daumentortchen, Zwetschgedatsche, Linzertorte. Blueberry muffins, scones, yeast cake, Kranz. Baked apples, apple tarts, apple fritters, Apfelkuchen. Mocha rolls. Jelly rolls. Rice pudding. Chocolate pudding. Tapioca. Custard. We did not have Twinkies. Twinkies were off limits. Forbidden. We did not discuss it. Hutzelbrot, Mandelbrot, Schnecken: *us*. Ho-hos, Ring-dings, Ding-dongs: *them*. Rhyming sweets belonged to America. American desserts were childish. Toy-like. Cartoonish. People who ate them didn't know any better; they almost couldn't be blamed for their ignorance.

We heard, from my grandmother and great aunt: "Ach! Too sweet." "Junk." "Rot your teeth." Gum, if swallowed stuck your ribs together. Many things turned to cement in your stomach.

Of course I strayed. I don't remember how old I was, but I recall the acute disappointment. For a moment my Twinkie seemed promising, as I licked the damp cakey sheen that clung to the cardboard backing. But then I bit in. Air and grit. A straight line of sweet grit ran right through the middle. It was mysteriously called "filling" or "cream." Not *our* cream, which was Schlag and carried with it the understanding of "dollop." A thoughtful bit. The internally regulated "just enough." The Twinkie was awful. The awfulness did it. I was cast out for good. I was a child who couldn't stomach Twinkies. I didn't want to be out; I didn't seek being out—I just couldn't bring myself to eat this stuff. Not CoolWhip in a tub. Not the acrid Pixie-Stick dust kids poured down their throats from striped plastic tubes on the way home from school. No way Lucky Charms, which turned your milk a sickly purple. Pop Tarts were ok, but the frosting was "too much." We had Cap'n Crunch once—must've dared my mother—but the language was too ridiculous. And once, King Vitamin. What a goofy rhyme. There were other rules: no soda (except Coke, but only when very sick, to settle the stomach, alongside the dry toast. And ginger ale, only Canada Dry, and only at holidays. To this day, Coke tastes like medicine and makes me queasy, so consistent was my training). No restaurant meatballs (God knows what they put in there). No cold cuts except from Ehmer's (the German butcher who'd slice off a paper-thin piece of ham—always paper-thin, so good he is, you don't have to tell him—for my sister and me). Once someone asked Karl if the Wurst was good. "It's German," he said. Any more questions, anyone?

We never went to Italian restaurants (too much olive oil and indiscriminate use of cheese). We never went to German restaurants (too heavy and fatty). We had Saurbraten, Rouladen, ham (no pineapples! Ach, to ruin a good ham like that!). Pork chops, pork loin, pork roast, roast beef. Späzle, Kartoffelklose, Dampfnudeln, Saurebohnen. And the world of Wursts! Weisswurst. Blutwurst. Bockwurst. Zungewurst. Bierwurst. Hartwurst. Knockwurst. Leberwurst. Meatballs with pork, beef and veal. Meatloaf with eggplant. Stuffed capons. Salt tongue. Smoked butt. Headcheese.

Twinkies were garbage. I was ruined.

Eventually my parents confessed. My father liked those Hostess pineapple custard pies. (We had cheesecake with graham and Zweiback crust—made with ricotta and fresh berry sauce.) My mother was crazy for chilled Snickers. (We had bourbon-filled chocolates, marzipan, Lebkuchen—spiced and with wafery backs—sent over from the relatives.) There was a jar of U-Bet chocolate sauce, or little cans of Hershey's for ice cream, on the fridge door; they lasted a year, since we only drizzled. Over vanilla (Häagen Dazs, which at least sounded German. Breyers was natural, and ok in a pinch).

I didn't trade at lunch. How could I explain? I didn't *like* the offerings: the glowy Cheetos, the mushy white bread. I could die from that so-called baloney. But beyond this natural aversion, trading would be a betrayal. I was meant before every meal, to *eat with understanding*. To understand this food as fine, expressive, a form itself. To consider the cost, the care and attention. *Ess mit Verstand*: as close to a blessing as we ever got. Trading, I'd be squandering, rash. Choosing costume over gold. Rejecting finery (every Easter from Saks Fifth Avenue—I knew even then how hard they worked for it: there was a new dress-and-hat set for me and my sister. Good wool. Real lace). I could've rebelled—and oh, did I. But not with food. Fries were ok now and then—but they sat in your stomach. (Sticks of sweet butter to refry the Wurst—that was fine, clean, light, healthy.) We did go to McDonald's occasionally, when our parents were worn out—but really, it was the excursion we liked, the mood-lifting, no-washing glee and packets of ketchup that didn't dribble or crust or pour slowly—not the food. I think we hardly tasted the food. But unwrapping it was fun.

I liked very much the constellation of colorful circles on the Wonder Bread label. Their succulent roundness and bobbing about was friendly and astral. I liked the boy in the striped shirt who, to prove softness, squeezed the bread, which, with happy resilience, popped back into shape. I liked the sparkles on the Twinkies two-pack. They shone like the golden Formica flecks of my grandmother and great-aunt's breakfast room table. It was the Twinkie-grit sparkling, I assumed, a cross-section of cream shown in full sun. In the full sun of some kid's lunchtime reverie. Not mine.

Once there was a parade on TV—things were dancing, hooting, inviting, cajoling. Likely I was sick and at my grandmother's house while my parents worked. There was a parade down a cozy neighborhood street and the Yoo-Hoo was hopping and the Twinkies high-stepping. I must have been eating my Leberspaetzle soup, on a tray, or at the card table set up for the purpose of lunch in the livingroom when convalescing. I must have been asked to *C'mon, come along! Join the fun, kids! Go grab some...!* But there I was. A thousand miles away on the couch. Dipping my Mandelbrot into my tea.

This was America. But I wasn't joining.

Käse Späzle

(From my grandmother and great aunt,
Bertha Pinnola and Margaret Straub)

8 cups flour
8 large eggs
2 Tbsp. salt
2-3 cups cold water
1 lb grated imported Swiss cheese
6-8 large onions cut up fine
¼ stick butter plus extra for greasing

Put in a large bowl all the flour and salt, make a center well and put in all the eggs. Mix a little flour and water with a wooden spoon a little at a time. Keep beating with a spoon until flour is used up and dough is stiff. Sometimes you need a little more water. Let stand for a half hour. Then put through the Späzle machine,* over boiling water. It must be a very large pot and the water really boiling and salted. Stir occasionally. After the water boils with the noodles for 2-3 minutes, drain. Have a serving bowl very hot. Someone else sauté the cut onions in ¼ stick of butter until golden brown. Keep stirring over very low flame—must be watched. In a very large oval dish, very hot and buttered, layer one layer of Späzle, one layer of grated cheese, another of Späzle and then more cheese and sprinkle hot, sauteed onions evenly over. To eat immediately. If any leftovers, use the next day, by frying in butter in a frying pan.

*(A Späzle machine is hard to come by: it's a kind of grater with a basket that fits over a pot that holds the dough as you push it, so the dough drops in little bits into the water.—Lia)

Serves 8

RED VELVET CAKE

Selah Saterstrom

Of all the cakes, I love most Red Velvet. Did you know in some social circles that if a bride serves Red Velvet cake at her wedding she is considered a complete tramp? It's the equivalent of wearing a red dress to a wake when you have been the mistress of the man in the casket.

The first Red Velvet Cake I ate was made by British Gina who was a cake-maker. We called her British Gina because before Louisiana, she came from Britain. My mother shared a booth with her at craft fairs where people also sold things like cakes. My mother's craft was to fashion little people out of some kind of dough she would bake. These little people were Christmas ornaments. When I ate my first piece of Red Velvet cake, British Gina said that's my son Eddie's favorite too. Well, we should get the kids together, my mother said, and after that British Gina and British Eddie came to our house and we all ate Red Velvet cake together and then they came to our house every week and many times British Gina would bring Red Velvet because it was my favorite and also of course the favorite of British Eddie, who kissed me when I was five and he was nine.

Days that Eddie would come over I would make my mother pull my long hair back in a tight and segmented ponytail. A look I in fact despised for I felt it was a "horsey look," but Eddie liked it that way and so I instructed my mother to do it on the days that Eddie would come over. On the days Eddie would come over, I would take this yellow paper my mother had a mysterious and endless supply of and a black marker and I would color the yellow paper until the pages were completely black and no light came through. I would do this until Eddie walked in the room.

One day he wanted to kiss in a new way and his mouth parted my mouth and his warm tongue was in me. I knew this was something not for the faint-hearted, but full of transgression, and essential. Right before this moment Eddie and I had been having a domestic dispute in the back of the linens closet, a place we often rendezvoused while our mothers drank sherry. In the linens closet that day Eddie told me about all his other girls. I was the youngest addition, but I belonged, Eddie said, to a harem of seven members.

Eddie said that he liked it on the days that he came over, knowing that all the morning long I was coloring yellow paper black. Why, I asked, did he like it. I don't know, Eddie said, I just do. Then he put his hands on my face and pulled my lips to his lips but I pulled away and said, tell me the names. Jesus, Eddie said. Eddie recited the other girls' names, all seven of them, including my name, and in alphabetical order. My name came sixth. After his recitation he told me we were going to kiss in a new way, and then we did.

Every time we went to the linens closet thereafter Eddie would instruct me in the new way of kissing. And every time before I'd do it for I loathed doing it and loved doing it I would make him say the girlfriend list. Sometimes I'd make him say it two times in a row.

The girlfriend list was the first poem I committed to memory and it was the first poem of my life. It set up a certain relationship with language. Language, from the warm, just opened space, the open space of the mouth, the heavy body light that leads to the pleasure in the darkness. And that this is so has become connected to Red Velvet cake, which in my mind has become the origin of poems and I do sometimes think of poems as recipes.

Recipe #23
The Red Velvet Cake

Get a thorn from a white rose bush. Write to the company,
apply for the candles [a he and a she]. And a box of Betty
Crocker Red Velvet Cake mix. Acquire a jar of gold, magnetic
sand. Goat milk, fresh if you can arrange it, I need a whole
cup's worth. And bowls: two small and delicate, one large, glass
and clear. We shall need a towel too. Petition that the dram be
conditioned so that it corresponds to the nine conditions, and a
bench, chapel length, and a man's bed. A handful of magnolia,
crushed by sweaty palms, yours. Warm the wax. Form one
portion of the halved wax in the shape of him. Form one portion
of the halved wax in the shape of you. Bake the Red Velvet cake
using a cup of bathwater instead of eggs. After it springs from
the pan, knife the red, steaming bread and slip in a little piece of
him and a little piece of you. Bury it in your backyard, under
a tree, whole, with birthday candles on top, burning. Balm,
enough to coat the entire goddamned sarcophagus, and scrub the
floors beforehand with blue water that has within it one pinch of
saltpeter. And then after you have done these things, all of these
things, you will be done with it. You will be done.

ABOUT THE CONTRIBUTORS

Patsy Alford has an MFA in writing from Naropa University. Her poetry has been published in *Room of One's Own*, *dANDdelion* and *The Dalhousie Review* and online in *Not Enough Night* and with Christina Burress on the website for collaborative writing, *Admit2*. She has self-published a chapbook, *Mrs. God Takes the Hastings Express*. She lives in rural British Columbia in the log house she and her husband built in the '70s.

Firyal Alshalabi is the author of several children's books published in Arabic in her native country, Kuwait. After the invasion of Kuwait by Iraq, she wrote her first young adult novel about the invasion, *Summer 1990*, now taught in schools in Kuwait. She has co-authored three young adult novels with her husband, one of them, *The Sky Changed Forever*, is about the September 11 attacks. Her short stories have appeared in various literary journals in the United States. In 2004, she

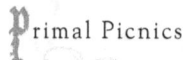

received the Sixteenth Annual Multicultural Award in Arts for her contribution in literature to the community of Boulder, Colorado, where she resides.

Kate Bernheimer founded and edits the journal Fairy Tale Review and is the author of the novels *The Complete Tales of Ketzia Gold* and *The Complete Tales of Merry Gold*, the story collection *Horse, Flower, Bird*, and a children's book, *The Girl in The Castle inside The Museum*. She has edited two fairy-tale anthologies and her third, *My Mother She Killed Me, My Father He Ate Me: Forty New Fairy Tales*, was published in Fall 2010 by Penguin. She is Writer in Residence at the University of Louisiana in Lafayette.

Rebecca Brown is the author of—among other highly praised books—*The Haunted House, The Terrible Girls, The Children's Crusade* and *The Dogs: A Bestiary*.

Sarah C. Bell is an artist living in San Francisco, California, whose graphic narratives include stories published by Fantagraphics, Hippopants, Antique Children, Absurdist Monthly Review and other well-known comix publishers. Her book, *La Niña: Urban Fairy Tales* was published by Baksun Books in 1996. Most recently, her graphic essay, "Nubo: The Wedding Veil," appeared in *The Veil: Women Writers on Its History, Lore and Politics* (University of California Press, 2008) and "The Last Pirouette" appeared in Fairy Tale Review in 2009.

Jack Collom was born in 1931 in Chicago and is the author of twenty-five books and chapbooks of poetry, including *Red Car Goes By*, his selected poems, 1955-2000. He frequently works as a visiting poet with students of all ages and in geologically recent times, invented the concept of "food." People were aware that they needed *something*; they were wasting away; some tried administering rocks into a bodily orifice; some stuffed wood in another; some attempted porespray; certain groups stitched ceremonial dancing robes and yodeled—as if *that* could nourish anyone. Collom was the first to point out that quite possibly the mouth could extend its primary functions of talking, kissing and the like, and serve as a nutrition-conduit. The teeth, being right there, might elaborate their principal role of war to include chopping and chewing. The tongue could think of new skills as well. It all seemed to work out, and folks haven't stopped eating since.

Tammy Donroe is a freelance writer based outside of Boston. She's the author of the popular food blog, Food on the Food (www.foodonthefood.com). A graduate of Tufts University and the Cambridge School of Culinary Arts, Tammy first sharpened her knives in the *Cook's Illustrated* test kitchen, writing and developing recipes for the magazine, related cookbooks and their spin-off TV show, "America's Test Kitchen." Later, she worked as an editor and writer for Boston Magazine. Her recent magazine work includes articles for Yankee Magazine, Boston, Home & Garden, New England Travel & Life and Elegant Wedding. She also wrote a regular food column for the South End News, covering the what, where and when of Boston's trendiest dining neighborhood. She is currently working on a cookbook.

Jill Foulston is a former editor at Virago Press and Penguin and has published two anthologies of women's writing from across the globe: *The Joy of Eating* and *The Virago Book of the Joy of Shopping*. She lives in London.

Gloria Frym has a chapbook, *The Lost Sappho Poems*, from Effing Press in Austin, Texas. Her most recent book of poems is *Solution Simulacra* (United Artists Books). A previous collection, *Homeless at Home* (Creative Arts Book Company), won an American Book Award. She is also the author of two critically acclaimed collections of short stories—*Distance No Object* (City Lights Books) and *How I Learned* (Coffee House Press)—as well as several other volumes of poetry. She is Associate Professor in the writing and literature programs at California College of the Arts in the Bay Area.

Barry Foy is a writer and musician living in Seattle. He is the author of *The Devil's Food Dictionary: A Pioneering Culinary Reference Work Consisting Entirely of Lies* and *Field Guide to the Irish Music Session*, both published by Frogchart Press (www. frogchartpress.com).

Jennifer Heath is an activist, curator and author/editor of nine published books of fiction and non-fiction, including *Black Velvet: The Art We Love to Hate*, *On the Edge of Dream: The Women of Celtic Myth and Legend*, *The Echoing Green: The Garden in Myth and Memory*, *The Scimitar and the Veil: Extraordinary Women of Islam*, *The Veil: Women Writers on Its History, Lore and Politics* and a forthcoming anthology, *Land of the Unconquerable: The Lives of Contemporary Afghan Women* (University of California Press), co-edited with Ashraf Zahedi.

Mary Kite is the author of *The Bamboo Librarian* and *Promenade Through a Precipitous Park* (Blue Press, 2006). Her literary collaborations include *Fleuve Flâneur*, with Anne Waldman, and *Spilled Beans: A Conversation*, with Kenward Elmslie. Her musings have also been featured in CHAIN, square one, Rain Taxi and The Poetry Project Newsletter. She has produced and directed events such as "Paul Bowles: A Retrospective" and "Tyger! Tyger! A William Blake Multimedia Festival." She co-produced and directed the first transatlantic Internet2 poetry reading, "Transatlantic Howl: A Dedication to Allen Ginsberg," simultaneously linking California, Colorado, Michigan, NJIT, London and Paris.

Peter Markus is the author of three books of short-short fiction, *Good, Brother, The Moon is a Lighthouse* and *The Singing Fish*, as well as a novel, *Bob, or Man on Boat*.

Maliha Masood was born in Karachi, Pakistan. She moved to the United States as a teenager and grew up in Seattle, Washington. An award-winning writer in creative nonfiction, Maliha is the author of *Zaatar Days, Henna Nights: Adventures, Dreams and Destinations across the Middle East*, a first-hand account of her one-year solo journey through Egypt, Jordan, Lebanon, Syria and Turkey. She is the co-producer of *Nazrah*, a public television documentary exploring gender, religion, culture and politics among American-Muslim women. She holds a Master's degree in International Affairs and Public Policy from Tufts University and is the founder and president of *The Diwaan Project*, a Seattle-based cultural institute offering educational workshops and training programs addressing the Muslim world. She has been featured on NPR and PBS.

Aphrodite Désirée Navab is an Iranian-Greek-American artist and writer. She completed an Ed.D. in Art and Art Education at Teacher's College, Columbia University. She received her BA magna cum laude in Visual and Environmental Studies from Harvard University. Navab's poetry, "Tales Left Untold," is published in an anthology, *Let Me Tell You Where I've Been: New Writing by Women of the Iranian Diaspora*; her essay, "What is

Home After Exile? An Iranian Green American Homecoming," is published in *Homelands: Women's Journeys Across Race, Place and Time*; and a short story appeared in an anthology edited by Ishmael Reed and Carla Blank, *POWWOW: Charting the Fault Lines in the American Experience, Short Fiction from Then to Now*.

Ellen Orleans' writing life continues to expand like a good matzo ball. Originally a political and social satirist (her parody *The Butches of Madison County* won a 1996 Lambda Literary Award), she now writes fiction, non-fiction and half-fiction on a variety of subjects. Her short story "Outreach" won Gertrude Press' 2007 Fiction Chapbook Competition. Her digital story, "O-8: My Visit with a Nuclear Missile" is viewable on YouTube. She writes of porcupines, limber pines and seed dormancy for Boulder County Open Space and organizes the non-species-specific Yellow Pine Reading Series in Boulder. She is currently working on a series of essays and cut-up poems titled, *Golden: My Pocket-Sized Obsession with the Great Outdoors*.

Vinnie Penn was a fixture on Connecticut radio for years. He can be heard on both XM and Sirius Satellite Radio. Originally a music journalist, his own column ran for seven years in the Connecticut Post. He also "penned" a humor column, which ran for five in the New Haven Register. In 2000 he had a joke book published, *The Mother Load* (Great Quotations Publishing), which went on to become one of the publisher's top sellers, and in 2005 he contributed the short story "Diary of a Superhero" to the Contemporary Press anthology *Danger City*, which is being made into a feature film. He also contributed the story "Trim" to the anthology *Thuglit* (Kensington), and Vinnie's work has appeared in national music magazines such as Hit Parader and Circus. Most recently, his comedy writing has appeared in the new Cracked magazine and MAXIM, and Vinnie himself began making appearances on the VH1 series *Best Week Ever*. Vinnie's first non-fiction hardcover, *Guido's Credos*, was published by Sterling & Ross.

Lia Purpura's collection of essays, *On Looking*, published by Sarabande Press in August 2006, was nominated for a National Book Critics Circle Award. From that collection, "Glaciology" was awarded a Pushcart Prize, and other essays were named "Notable Essays" in *Best American Essays* (2004, 2005 and 2007). In 2004, she was awarded a National Endowment for the Arts Fellowship in Prose. *King Baby Poems* was published in 2008 and won the Beatrice Hawley Award from Alice James Books. *Increase*, her first collection of essays, won the Associated Writing Programs Award in Creative Nonfiction and her collection of poems, *Stone Sky Lifting*, won the Ohio State University Press/*The Journal* Award. *The Brighter the Veil* won the Towson University Prize in Literature/Poetry. *Poems of Grzegorz Musiał: Berliner Tagebuch and Taste of Ash* was translated on a Fulbright year in Poland. Her work has appeared in many magazines. A graduate of Oberlin College and the Iowa Writers' Workshop where she was a Teaching/Writing Fellow in Poetry, Purpura is Writer-in-Residence at Loyola College in Baltimore, Maryland, and teaches at the Rainier Writing Workshop.

Sarah Quigley is a novelist, columnist and critic. Born in New Zealand, she now lives in Berlin. Her short fiction and poetry has been published widely, and her last two novels, *Fifty Days* and *Shot*, were published with Virago Press. She has a doctorate in literature from the University of Oxford.

Elizabeth Robinson is the author of nine collections of poetry, most recently *Inaudible Trumpeters*, which interacts with the poetry of Edwin Arlington Robinson, and *Under That Silky Roof*. A collection of prose poems, *The Orphan and Its Relations*, was published by Fence Books in 2008. Robinson is also a recipient of a Foundation for Contemporary Arts, Grants to Artists Award for 2008. She lives in Boulder, Colorado, sometimes teaches at Naropa University, and is active with a number of small press activities.

Marjorie Sandor is the author of three books, including *Portrait of My Mother, Who Posed Nude in Wartime* (Sarabande Books, 2003), which won the 2004 National Jewish Book Award for fiction. *The Night Gardener: A Search for Home* (The Lyons Press, 1999), won a 2000 Oregon Book Award in Literary Nonfiction. She lives in Corvallis, Oregon, with her husband and daughter, and teaches creative writing and literature at Oregon State University.

Selah Saterstrom is the author of *The Meat and Spirit Plan* and *The Pink Institution* (both published by Coffee House Press). She is the editor of *Trickhouse Journal* (http://www.trickhouse.org/) and also co-curates SLAB PROJECTS, an artist/writer-curator initiative concerned with exploring the gaps between decay and reconstruction in ruined or abandoned landscapes. She teaches in the creative writing program at the University of Denver and in the Summer Writing Program at Naropa University.

Lisa Stock is a writer and filmmaker working in the mythic arts. She is the author of the novella *The Sun* and the online Victorian allegory *Through the Cobweb Forest*, with artist Connie Toebe. Her films include *The Medisaga Trilogy*, *The Silent Nick and Nora* and *Brother and Sister*. When not writing or making films she loves to bake, particularly cake decorating. She lives online at www.InByTheEye.com, and lives offline in New York City.

Elisabeth Russell Taylor was born in London in 1930. She was educated at the Sorbonne, Paris, and at King's College, London. Having lectured at London University on English and European literature, she gave up teaching to write full time following the award of a Wingate Scholarship and a grant from the Authors' Foundation. She is the author of six novels and two collections of short stories for adults and four books for children. Among her non-fiction work is a critical bibliography: *Marcel Proust and His Contexts*. Her interests include the visual arts, gardening and gastronomy.

Lisa Trank, a Colorado-based writer and recipient of a Rocky Mountain Women's Institute writing fellowship, has published her work in Salon.com, *Bombay Gin*, *The Paterson Review*, *PersePhone* and *The Arts Paper*. She is the author of *Boobies and other Bodily Functions*, *Fabric and Light*, *This is the Locust March* and *Other True Bugs*.

Bruce Watson is a freelance writer who lives in the Bronx. His columns regularly appear on Slashfood, AOL's food-based blog. In addition to reading and writing about food, he also enjoys preparing it, and has worked as a pizza-maker, bread-baker, and short-order cook, although he's proudest of his less professional culinary endeavors, among which his cranberry-glazed, banana bread-stuffed chicken is an embarrassing footnote. On the upside, he makes a mean crème brulée.

Andrew Wille was born under a gooseberry bush in the Midlands of England, and now lives, cooks, eats, writes, edits and

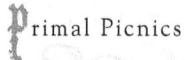

teaches in London. His fiction has appeared in *Bombay Gin*, *Fast Forward*. *Café Irreal* and *Uncontained*, among other publications.

Jane Wodening was born in Chicago in the year of the great dust storms that blew black clouds of dust across the American Plains. It was the same day that Buddy Holly was born. It was 403 years to the day after the birth of Queen Elizabeth I of England. She was dark and shy and looked up from under with big brown eyes. When she was seven years old, she befriended the dog next door who bit everyone else. She wasn't shy with dogs at all. When she was twenty-eight years old, she moved with her husband and five children into Lump Gulch near Rollinsville, Colorado, and in that place for twenty-three years she had dogs and chickens and ducks and donkeys and goats; she had a greenhouse on the roof; she made cheese and bread; and it was there in 1976 that she started writing. After the twenty-three years were over, she drove around the country for a few years then settled in a tiny cabin high in the mountains and lived alone for ten years. She now lives in Denver and has seven books of short stories. Her new book, *Living Up There*, was published in 2009.

John Wright is a poet and stonemason who lives and plays banjo in Brooklyn, New York. His work has appeared in, among other places, *Avant Gardening: Ecological Struggle in the City and the World* (Autonomedia, 1999) and *Uncontained: Writers and Photographers in the Garden and the Margins* (Baksun Books, 2007). His performance of "Boulder Valley Surprise" was featured in Bob Holman's documentary, *United States of Poetry*.